SUBMIT and SURRENDER

A Club Volare Novel

CHLOE COX

Copyright © 2014 Chloe Cox

All rights reserved.

ISBN: 1496168445
ISBN-13: 978-1496168443

DEDICATION

To anyone who ever gave me a book.

CONTENTS

Prologue 2

chapter 1 3

chapter 2 21

chapter 3 29

chapter 4 44

chapter 5 58

chapter 6 73

chapter 7 81

chapter 8 93

chapter 9 101

chapter 10 114

chapter 11	124
chapter 12	137
chapter 13	152
chapter 14	162
chapter 15	171
chapter 16	181
chapter 17	189
chapter 18	196
chapter 19	207
chapter 20	217
chapter 21	226
chapter 22	239
chapter 23	247
chapter 24	254
chapter 25	269
chapter 26	276
chapter 27	284
chapter 28	294
Epilogue	318

Those who fly…

PROLOGUE

Adra's skin grew hot as Ford approached. Slow. He was so slow. So deliberate. His eyes pinning her where she stood, the weight of him somehow overbearing even from a distance, making it difficult to breathe.

She felt like she was buzzing around the edges, like on the surface she was over-stimulated and on the verge of shorting out, but the core of her was…calm.

He'd made her admit it. He'd made her beg. And everything had fallen into place.

Just the way he was looking at her…

Like she was entirely his.

She shivered.

He saw. He smiled. Then he reached up and tore open her blouse.

chapter 1

Ford Colson cursed and slammed his hand against the dashboard. The Bluetooth in his truck had never worked right, and this was the only time he cared. The only thing he'd gotten from the garbled voicemail was something about Adra Davis, and how he needed to be back at Club Volare, and how it was very important.

He never gotten reception up in the canyons. Normally there wasn't anything he needed to be on call for, and there wasn't much that could get him to cut short a cross-country run—except Adra. And now that he and Adra were running Club Volare L.A. while the owner, Chance, was on a scouting trip for the next Volare location, he could add club business to that limited list.

He smoothed his hand over the dashboard, feeling kind of bad for taking it out on his truck, and took a deep breath. At least the PCH wasn't clogged up. He'd be there in a few minutes.

It was only Adra who could get him worked up like this. But he'd be damned if he let anyone see it.

Obviously that strategy hadn't worked as well as it should have. It wasn't an accident that Chance had left him and Adra in charge. The details of Ford's history with Adra weren't exactly common knowledge, but everyone damn sure knew that there *was* a history, and that something had gone wrong—and it was affecting the club. Chance wanted to force them to work it out by forcing them to work together.

The two of them could barely stand to be in a room together. Not because they hated each other, though what was that saying about a fine line between love and hate? Maybe she did hate him, who knew. But it wasn't that. It was because they *wanted* each other. And Ford knew Adra was someone he couldn't have. Not the way he'd wanted her.

She'd been very clear about that. Eventually.

But he missed her. Damn it, he missed her. Even though she'd turned out to be the kind of person Ford knew he couldn't have in his life, he missed her. He missed making her laugh, he missed her warmth, he missed her loyalty and her huge heart. He missed the way she smelled.

And now even the suggestion that something bad had happened involving her sent him speeding down the PCH like a mad man. It was like a bad dream he couldn't wake up from. Adra wouldn't let him. Not with the way she acted around him, like she was afraid of her own shadow, afraid of being seen, or of what Ford had seen of her. Afraid of what might have been.

Damn it.

It didn't matter. He would never do that again. He'd never again be with a woman who played games like that. That had been one expensive lesson to learn, but he'd learned it well. So well that sometimes he thought he should thank his ex-wife.

Ford laughed out loud, alone in his truck, imagining Claudia's face as he thanked her for the spectacular shit show that had been their divorce, and all the loss that had gone with it. Maybe he'd try it the next time she came to town.

Or maybe not. He was still going nearly a hundred miles an hour down the PCH, muscles twitching, wanting to find out what the hell had happened with Adra. Maybe some lessons you never really learn. He'd thought Adra was it. He'd thought…

Well, sometimes even a Dom could be wrong.

He didn't relax until he hit Venice and knew he was only minutes from the Club Volare compound. And then when traffic slowed to a crawl on Abbot Kinney, he was about to make an illegal turn onto a side street, just to cut through and get there a few minutes faster, when he saw the reason for the sudden standstill up ahead.

A silver BMW in an accident at the traffic light up ahead, the one that had been malfunctioning on and off all week. A silver Beamer that looked a whole hell of a lot like Adra's car. And a woman, standing on the side of the road, slim build, killer ass, brown hair, just like Adra, getting screamed at by some asshole with a comb over and a beer belly.

Ford was out of his truck and halfway down the block before he realized it *wasn't* Adra.

Relief surged through him, chasing the adrenaline threatening to pound out a hole in his chest where his heart was. It wasn't Adra.

But it was still a young woman who looked like she was about to cry from the abuse she was taking from that idiot with the comb over.

Ford didn't like the look of it. He liked it even less when he got close enough to hear was going on.

"How did you even get a license, you dumb bitch?" the man screamed, waving a reddened hand at his slightly dented door.

Not even dented. Dinged.

"You were too busy on the phone? Chatting with your girlfriends? Doing your fucking makeup?" the man sneered. "Jesus Christ, what is wrong with you?"

The guy wasn't even asking for her insurance information, wasn't trying to work out a solution to what was in reality a minor problem. He just wanted to humiliate her. It was working, too. Reading the woman's body language was like reading an open book for an experienced Dom like Ford—shoulders drawn in, back hunched, eyes down. Her whole body beaten down and trying to hide away. Whatever was making her feel like this went further than a fender bender with an abusive jackass, but the abusive jackass was definitely pushing all of her buttons.

And the jackass seemed to like it.

"Are you *listening* to me?" the man shouted, waving his arms around. The woman flinched.

"The light was—" she started to say.

"She speaks!" the man said. "Do you understand right of way, you idiot?"

"I do," Ford said. He walked up to the woman's side and took a moment to make eye contact—she looked bewildered. The man was a bully, larger than her, in her space, screaming. Spittle flying.

Ford took another step toward the man causing all this trouble, putting himself between that jackass and the young woman.

Ford pointed at him.

"You don't speak anymore," Ford said.

"Who the hell are you?"

"I said *be quiet*," Ford growled.

The man's lips fell open. There was sweat on his brow, his cheeks. He didn't seem to understand what had just happened or why he'd stopped talking.

The Dom voice was useful in the most unexpected situations.

"Has he threatened you?" Ford asked the young woman. Up close she was even younger than he'd thought, possibly still in college. Which might explain why she had no idea what to do in this situation.

She was staring at him. It took her a moment to speak.

"Not in so many words," she said. "But he seems totally crazy."

"I won't let him do anything to you," Ford said. "You should know this light has been malfunctioning for weeks. But even if it hadn't, this guy doesn't have the right to speak to you this way. If you want me to, I can help, but I understand perfectly well if you want me to mind my own business. It's up to you."

"What?" she said, looking up with suddenly alert eyes. "Oh God, no, I definitely want you to help. I mean...please."

Ford smiled. He probably shouldn't enjoy this, but hey. He was human.

"You," he said, turning on the now-confused jackass. The redness in the man's face had only intensified. He looked like an angry tomato. "You will back off, and you will apologize. You will pay for any damages to this young woman's car, and you will do it through me so that she doesn't have to put up with any more of your harassment or abuse. Am I clear?"

"What?" the man sputtered. "Who the hell do you—"

"My name is Ford Colson," Ford said, taking another step forward. "This light malfunctions frequently, as it's doing right now, and under the circumstances she had the right of way. You are a disgusting bully, and I have no goddamn patience for it. So I hope you have a good lawyer," Ford said, handing the man a copy of his card. "But you probably won't get one better than me."

The man stared back at him with his mouth open and the blood quickly draining from his face. Ford smiled again. Sometimes having a law degree was actually fun.

"You're a lawyer?"

Ford sighed. No one ever expected him to be a lawyer when he was in the truck. Hell, no one ever expected him to have the truck. For the most part, Ford was a slicked-down professional, driving something sleek and shiny to his places of business. The kind of man who could walk into an enemy boardroom and own it—which he liked to do as often as possible. But weekends were about the truck, trail runs, hikes, and the beach. California was a beautiful place.

Adra had shown him that.

He wasn't prepared for the pang of grief that sliced through him after that thought.

But now the man in front of him had found his voice, or most of it. "You don't have the right to just, just..." he stammered.

Ford took another step until his nose nearly touched the top of the fat man's head, and shrugged off his sweatshirt, exposing muscular, tanned arms that were still pumped from a set of push-ups and pull-ups at the beginning of his run.

"Tell me again what I can't do, you little prick," Ford said. "Because it looked to me like you were on the verge of assaulting that woman, and I know for damn sure that you're keeping me from getting to another woman who needs me right now. So tell me again what I can't do. Please."

The man said nothing.

"I'll give you hint," Ford said. "It's a short answer."

The man opened his mouth, closed it again. Then he said, very softly, "She had the right of way?"

Ford nodded. "She had the right of way."

"Mr. Colson?"

Ford turned. The young woman was smiling sheepishly at him—no, not sheepishly. Flirtatiously.

Shit.

"Yeah?" he said.

"Um, there isn't really any damage to my car," she said. "I don't need any money."

"You're sure?"

She smiled. "Yeah."

Ford shook his head at the man with the sweaty comb over, a man whose entire body language had changed in an instant. The asshole was now grateful. Unbelievable.

"You heard her?" Ford said.

"Yes I did," the man nodded vigorously.

"Then get the hell out of the intersection," Ford barked.

He hadn't forgotten about Adra. He could never forget about Adra. Which meant he had somewhere to be.

~ * ~ * ~

Adra Davis was in the process of delivering a box of donuts to Thea Benson, Volare's only honorary member, and the self-described "old lady across the street," when she got the call to come back to Volare. And she got the call just in time— Thea was in the process of calling her out.

"What's this?" Thea had said, narrowing her eyes. Somehow she managed to seem both suspicious and thrilled about the donuts.

"Well, I just thought..."

Adra wasn't actually used to needing an excuse to check up on people. Most people just took the donuts and ran.

"You thought I needed someone to look after me with Lena and John away?" Thea said.

Well, maybe. Lena, who was off with Chance looking for a new club location, was Thea's old tenant and current best friend, and John, Thea's new husband, was off on some kind of regatta sailing thing for a few weeks. And Thea had had a heart attack not too long ago.

Oh, damn. A heart attack.

"I'm definitely not supposed to be bringing you donuts, huh?" Adra said.

"Definitely not," Thea said. "But I am both benevolent and kind, so I promise not to tell Lena if you let me have at least one before you take them away."

Adra pulled the box away just in time to dodge Thea's hands. "One!" she said.

"Pfft, I'll eat donuts if I damn well feel like it," said Thea. She took a bite of a cream-filled concoction and moaned. "But really, take them away, because apparently there have been great advances in donut technology since I was your age. Jesus, that is good."

"Better than sex?" Adra smiled.

"Hell no, and you know it."

Adra's smile faltered. It was her own fault. Thea was right; nothing on this planet compared to the last time Adra had had sex.

It had been with Ford.

"What's wrong with you?" Thea asked. Adra tried to hide from that critical stare, but it was basically pointless. Thea didn't really believe in beating around the bush. "If you're over here taking care of me, you must really need to find a new lost soul to take under your wing the way that you do."

"Why's that?"

"Because I don't need taking care of, and you know it. You're just distracting yourself." Thea took another bite and closed her eyes. "You do buy a fantastic donut, though. Don't tell me where."

"I'm distracting myself?" Adra said. She almost demanded to know what she could possibly be distracting herself from when she caught Thea's look.

Ford.

God dammit, did the whole club know? Even Thea? It was that obvious?

"I'm *not* distracting myself," Adra said. "I'm just…"

And it was right then that her phone rang.

Funny. At the time, Adra was actually happy for a real distraction. And she was even happier when she realized who was calling.

"Lola?" she said, waving goodbye to Thea and starting back across the street to the Volare compound. "Why are you telling me to get back to the compound?"

"Because I'm at the compound," Lola said.

"Are you freaking kidding me?" Adra laughed. "How are you even allowed to fly?"

Lola ran the New York Club Volare with her husband, Roman, and she was also very, very pregnant. Adra had resigned herself to not seeing her friend for the next few months.

"I sneaked in just under the wire ages ago," Lola said. "Roman and I got a little private time up in Sonoma, and the New York winter was killing my pregnant lady joints, so I made an executive decision an escaped to L.A. while I still could. Now get your ass back here. We have to talk."

That sounded ominous, but Adra didn't care. Lola was in town.

***

Well, she didn't care right up until she realized what Lola was up to.

"So you're having the baby in L.A.?" Adra asked, leaning over to gingerly hug the very pregnant redhead.

"Roman researched all the best OBGYNs, and we're flying our New York guy out, and yada yada," Lola said, waving her hand. "He's running this show like he's planning an invasion or something. I'm just getting out of his way until showtime."

"You're a pregnancy diva," Adra said, grinning.

Lola sank slowly back into the comfiest couch in the Volare lounge and grinned back.

"Of course I am," she said.

It still didn't totally make sense to Adra, but who cared? She'd be lying if she said she wasn't thrilled to have Lola around, especially considering how difficult she was finding it to run the club with Ford. The club itself was fine, but working with Ford was…

Every moment with him stretched into an eternity. She noticed every gesture, every movement, every hint of an emotion. Anything that might indicate that maybe he was beginning to thaw, that maybe, just maybe, she hadn't screwed up the most important friendship in her life. And every time, he looked back at her with the cold, indifferent expression of a stranger, and every time she felt terrible.

Terrible, guilty, and somehow, *somehow*, still turned on. Because she couldn't be around him now without thinking about that night.

It was bad enough before they'd ever touched each other, when she just had to deal with the fact that he was this movie-star gorgeous blond Dom with the kind of body you usually only saw on television or in ads for Diet Coke. When she could only wonder what his touch felt like, or how he kissed, or how he moved. But now? Now she *knew*.

He'd ruined sex with anyone else, ever again. No one else could live up to that.

And she had screwed everything up.

"So you seeing anyone?" Lola asked.

Adra sighed. Of course. She supposed she should have seen that one coming. Maybe Lola decided to spend the rest of her pregnancy in L.A. for health reasons, or comfort reasons, or whatever, but she was clearly going to put the time out in L.A. to good use. Good, meddlesome use.

"No," Adra said truthfully.

"Uh-huh," Lola said, eyes glittering. "And who was your last relationship?"

Adra stifled a laugh. The answer to that was definitely not what Lola expected, but Adra could tell she wouldn't get away with evasive answers forever. Lola wanted to know about Ford. Volare was like a big family, and sometimes, like a family, everyone was up in everyone else's business. Adra also knew she had pretty much zero right to complain, considering she was usually the one poking her nose in where it didn't belong, setting people up, making sure people were happy.

Besides, Lola was kind of adorably bad at it.

"It was before I joined Volare," Adra said.

"Seriously? That long ago?" Lola said. "Would I know him?"

Now Adra really did laugh. The whole country knew him. It kind of sucked when your actor ex's career took off right after he'd dumped you for someone else and his picture ended up on every billboard in town, but it went with the business of being a talent agent. Adra had gotten used to it a long time ago, but other people usually freaked out when she told them, which is why she'd stopped divulging that little bit of her past.

"It's not important," Adra said. "We're not in touch."

"That bad?"

"That bad," Adra said, her tone clipped. Actually, she couldn't believe how much it still affected her. She'd learned a hard lesson with Derrick Duvall, and recently she'd spent a lot of time cursing the fact that she'd learned that lesson before she'd ever met Ford. It would have been…

No. It would have ended just as badly for her and Ford. And that would have been so, so much worse, because Ford was…well, Ford was Ford. There was no one else like him. And Adra already couldn't take the fact that Ford looked at her like she was a stranger, like he'd seen a side of her that he just didn't like. She couldn't blame him, but if she felt that bad now, she couldn't imagine what would have happened if she'd let it go on any further. She'd have been utterly destroyed when it ended badly, as it inevitably would have.

She shuddered.

"Yeah, well, you know that's not what I'm really asking about," Lola said.

"I know," Adra said. "Believe me, I know. But it's not my favorite subject at the moment. We're working together, it's not a big deal, it's not—"

"That's actually one of the reasons we came down from Sonoma," Lola said softly. "We have something we need to talk to you two about."

That shut Adra up for about a second. Then the words came tumbling out of her.

"Are you ok? Is the baby ok? Is Roman ok?"

Lola looked up, for once actually surprised. "What? We're fine, you crazy lady. My God, who does the worrying when you're not around?"

"I outsource."

Lola smiled. "Here, help me up."

"Where are we going?" Adra asked, pulling Lola out of the deep couch cushion. They managed to uncouch her on the second try.

"Remind me not to sit there," Lola said. "Not safe for my dignity."

"Please," Adra said. "You could command armies while wearing a pink bunny suit. You can handle this couch."

"Not if it swallows me whole," Lola laughed and pulled Adra toward the stairs.

The stairs that led to Ford's office.

Adra sighed. Well. They were supposed to work together.

"Lola, just give me a heads up," she whispered as they came in sight of the door. "Am I going to hate this, whatever it is? Like, how bad are we talking here? Soul-crushing—like having to work with the guy you maybe almost had a thing with and still haven't gotten over *and* his new girlfriend bad? Or just, you know, normal stressful for working with that guy you haven't totally gotten over?"

Oh God. Adra hadn't even thought about Ford getting a new girlfriend until she'd said the words out loud. The idea made her instantly nauseous.

Lola paused, her hand on the doorknob to Ford's office, the door already open an inch.

"Honestly?" she said, her eyes soft. "It could go either way."

"Fantastic," Adra muttered.

Lola took Adra's hand in her own and gave it a warm squeeze. "You'll be fine," she said.

Adra almost believed her. Until she heard Ford's voice on the other side of the door.

"Of course it was a goddamn mistake," Ford said to someone, presumably Roman. He sounded angry. Adra didn't need to hear the rest to know what he was talking about, and it broke her heart a little bit all over again.

Lola cursed, and banged on the already open door.

"Gentlemen?" she said.

Adra forced herself through the door and into Ford's office. There were three people already there: some guy in a Hollywood suit that Adra didn't immediately know, though he looked kind of familiar; Roman Casta, the owner of the New York club; and Ford.

Jesus, Ford.

He was standing on the opposite side of his desk, leaning forward on those ridiculous arms, muscles wrapping around like steel cables. He was wearing sweatpants that hung low on his hips and a tank top, a hoodie draped over the back of his chair—he must have been on a run. This was one of the rare times Adra got to see him like this now that they didn't spend weekends hanging out anymore. She had to remind herself not to drool. And for the first time in a long time, she saw an emotion on his face—surprise? Regret? Then frustration, and anger.

He was looking right at her.

She was the mistake.

It killed her to see what he thought of her now, but maybe that was good. Maybe it was good to kill all hope that they could recover their friendship. Maybe that's what she needed to move on.

Adra decided not to ask what they were talking about. She was only slightly masochistic, something Ford already knew.

"Hi Roman," she said, giving the big man a quick peck on the cheek. "You guys should have told me you were in California."

"We did," Roman smiled down at her. "Eventually."

Adra looked back at Lola to find the woman actually blushing, and couldn't help but laugh. Roman and Lola had been friends for years, but once they figured out they'd both been secretly in love with each other for nearly all of that time, they hadn't been able to keep their hands off of each other. And now that Adra had firsthand experience in how much time and energy it took to run a sex club, she figured they'd probably been dying to have one last getaway before the baby came.

Even now, Roman looked at Lola like everything else in the world was just a shadow. What would that be like? To have the man you loved look at you like that?

Adra couldn't help it. She looked at Ford.

He was still looking at her.

"Adra," Ford said.

She may have blinked. She definitely caught her breath.

"Roman wants us to consult on a film," Ford said. He was leaning on his fists, his knuckles white. He only did that when something was really bothering him.

Dazed, Adra said, "Wait, what?"

The man in the Hollywood suit stepped forward, his hand outstretched. "That's my cue. We met at the Golden Globes last year, Adra. Roger Corvis."

Oh God, Adra thought. She recognized the name. It had been everywhere lately.

"You're a producer," she said weakly. His hand felt cold.

"Yes, I am," Corvis grinned. "Working on a big one."

Oh please, no.

"They want to film it here. At the club. Starting this week." Ford was still looking directly at her. "I think it's a mistake."

Adra sat down heavily in one of Ford's plush chairs. "They want to film it here?"

"And we want you and Ford to consult on production," Roman added. "I'm sure you've heard of the film—*Submit and Surrender*?"

"Oh, yeah," Adra said. She was feeling light headed. "Can't miss it. Billboards everywhere."

"Then you understand why it's so important that we're involved in the process," Roman said, coolly confident. "We want to make sure the BDSM lifestyle is well represented. Roger's agreed that you and Ford will be invaluable assets to the actors while they're filming."

"I think you know the lead actor already," Corvis said. "Didn't you used to date Derrick Duvall?"

Adra watched Ford stiffen, visible even from across the room, and closed her eyes.

"Yup," she said. "Derrick's my ex."

Her last relationship. Her first and only D/s romance. The guy who'd proved to her that romance wasn't something she could have. And part of the reason she'd had to tell Ford she couldn't be with him.

"Shit," she heard Lola mutter. Apparently she was the only one, because Corvis was smiling like a lunatic when Adra finally opened her eyes.

"Great! That'll add some realism to the set," he said. "Listen, I have to run to a production meeting, but Roman's got all the details and the schedule and everything. I am so excited to work with you both. And Adra, you are just as lovely as I remember," he said, sliding on his sunglasses.

Leave it to a movie producer to be manically cheerful about something as insane as asking a submissive to consult on a movie in which her ex-Dom was starring.

Corvis clapped his hands together, pointed at Adra and Ford, and said, "I will see you two on Friday."

And then he was gone.

Ford hadn't moved.

Like, at all. He was like a statue. A beautiful, frozen statue. And Adra couldn't take her eyes off of him.

chapter 2

"Adra, I am so, so sorry," Lola said for about the millionth time. "If we had known that Derrick freaking Duvall was your *ex*, I just…"

"But you didn't," Adra said. "And even if you had, it wouldn't really have changed anything. Roman had a point. We do have an interest in making sure this movie is done right."

"The publicity is already insane."

"Tell me about it. I've been avoiding that giant wall of Derrick's face on Sunset for weeks. Thank God they're keeping the location secret."

Lola cringed. "Did I tell you how sorry I am?"

"Yes," Adra smiled. "But I will accept further apologies in chocolate form."

"Consider it done," Lola said, digging in her giant purse. In about a second she had several chocolate-containing goodies for Adra to choose from. "What? I'm pregnant, I have a supply."

Adra laughed and flopped down on the couch next to Lola. It was good to have her friend nearby again, even if it was under crazy circumstances. Recently her life had been kind of chaotic, as evidenced by the state of her apartment.

"What happened here, by the way?" Lola said, raising one eyebrow. "Natural disaster?"

"Hush," Adra said, tossing a pillow. She looked around at the open-plan living room and sighed. Somehow everything managed to be out of place. Plus she kept finding dirty dishes in hidden locations. "I know, I feel like I should just…burn it all to the ground and start over fresh."

"Was it a very specific earthquake?" Lola ventured. "An unfortunate misprint on a frat party flyer?"

"No, it was three boys under the age of eight," Adra said, throwing her only remaining pillow at Lola's head. "My nephews came to stay for a while, while my brother and his wife…worked through some stuff. I'm not totally clear on what's going on there, but Charlie seemed to need the space, so I offered."

Even thinking about her brother Charlie's situation made Adra uncomfortable and sad. Sometimes it felt like Adra was more invested in Charlie's marriage to Nicole than Charlie himself was, which Adra knew was spectacularly unfair to her brother, and was just old issues popping up. It was just that since Charlie had gotten married and had kids, he'd been like living proof that not all Davises had to ruin their shot at having a family. And considering how she and Charlie had grown up, that was maybe more important to Adra than it should have been.

Lola took another appraising look at the apartment.

"So this is what I have to look forward to, huh?" she said. "I can handle it. No kid can out-mess me. Roman, on the other hand..."

"Yeah, he doesn't strike me as a casual mess kinda guy."

"He is not," Lola said. Then she raised an eyebrow and gave a wicked smile. "And he is easily provoked into providing much needed discipline when I 'accidentally' mess up his stuff. Which I guess will have to be restricted to the bedroom once this little one arrives."

"Boy or girl, by the way?"

"Surprise." Lola smiled. "You know, I really enjoyed those accidental messes."

"I bet you did," Adra smiled. She hadn't seen Lola this happy in...well, ever, really. In fact, the last time she'd seen Lola, she was happily Domme-ing some guy back in New York as one of the few true switches that Adra knew.

"Hey, I've been meaning to ask you," Adra said, leaning forward. "You're a switch right? But I cannot imagine Roman as anything other than a Dom. Do you ever...?"

Lola popped a hazelnut chocolate in her mouth and smiled a mysterious smile. "We are not here to talk about *my* love life, lady," she said.

"Oh, come *on!*"

"Nope," Lola shook her head. "Why, you going to tell me all about Ford?"

That shut Adra right up.

"Yeah, I thought so," Lola said. "So what's the deal with Derrick? This going to be manageable?"

"I will handle it, Lola," Adra said. "You don't have to treat me with kid gloves."

"Who's got kid gloves? I don't know if I could handle it if I were in your shoes. And I know Roman couldn't handle it."

"Big, tough Roman?"

"He would lose his *mind*," Lola smiled. "He'd tough it out, but he'd suffer. It's not too late to change the plans, you know. We did kind of spring this on you."

"Thanks, but you know it is too late," Adra said. "And besides, I knew he was going to be in the movie, so this was kind of inevitable. At some point Club Volare was going to be pulled into the *Submit and Surrender* craziness. The first major film about a BDSM relationship? Please, it's going to be huge. I couldn't avoid it forever."

Lola winced. "One of those 'avoid forever if at all possible' situations, huh? I'd heard he was a Dom, I just didn't know anything else."

"I'm over it, really. It's just…"

Adra hesitated.

"Just what?"

"It was a terrible relationship, and he didn't treat me very well, and…he was still the one to end it."

"Ugh. So he thinks he has the upper hand."

"Yeah," Adra said. "And sometimes I do, too. He *doesn't*, I swear. I am…ugh, the idea of being anywhere near him gives me *hives*, but…"

"He got the last word?"

More than that, it felt like Derrick had defined everything about their relationship and their break up. He'd been a bad Dom—Adra knew that now. Controlling in a bad way, and selfish. But for a while Adra had thought he was different. He was the guy to convince her that not all relationships ended terribly, that not all men leave. She'd opened up to him completely. Derrick had known so much about her, about her family, about her fears, about everything, and then when he left her it was like he did it in the most destructive way possible.

He'd just thrown her away like so much refuse and shacked up with someone else. Adra still got mad when she thought about coming home and finding all of his stuff just gone. She'd cried for three days straight, and she'd never been more certain that love was a sucker's game as when she'd had to clean up that lonely house.

So Derrick was the first and last person she'd allowed herself to need since she was a kid. And she reminded herself every day what a stupid mistake that had been.

"Yeah," Adra said slowly. "He got the last word, and it bugs me. Is that petty of me?"

"Please. That would drive me crazy," Lola said.

Adra sighed. "Is there anything more annoying?"

"Not on this planet, no. Maybe, *maybe*, there's some undiscovered insomniac shrieking bat species deep in the Amazon rainforest or something, but barring a major scientific discovery, I'd say no, there is nothing more annoying than a bad ex who undeservedly thinks you're not over him," Lola said. She looked sidelong at Adra and grimaced. "Except possibly one you have to work with."

Adra started to giggle. The situation really did suck. "Except for that."

"Did I mention how sorry I was?"

"About a million times."

Lola got very quiet. She said, "So are you going to finally tell me about Ford?"

Adra fell back against the back of the couch, and exhaled loudly. "Yeah. Um. Ford. Can I get back to you on that?"

"Well, at least you'll have the intense awkwardness of coaching your ex-Dom on BDSM scenes to distract you from the awkwardness of working with Ford."

"I wish I had another pillow to throw at you."

"I deserve it," Lola said, leaning back against the other end of the couch and propping her feet up on Adra's legs. "Are you *ever* going to tell me about it?"

For once, Adra didn't quite know what to say. She didn't find it difficult to talk about her past, necessarily, but Ford…Ford felt so raw. She could barely think about it, let alone find the words to talk about it.

"Maybe when I finally stop wishing that things were different," she finally said.

"Don't wait too long, honey," Lola said.

Adra looked up. It didn't seem like Lola was just talking about opening up anymore.

Lola raised a sympathetic eyebrow. "You'll kick yourself for it later."

Adra looked down and fumbled with her phone for a distraction, suddenly uncomfortable under the glare of Lola's insights. There were a lot of things that Adra might regret, but that didn't always mean she had the power to change them. Case in point: the texts waiting for her on her phone.

They were from Derrick Duvall. A phone number she hadn't deleted just so she'd know to screen his calls if one ever came. It never had, until now.

"I hear we're going to be working together again," it said. "It will be good to see you, Adra."

How exactly was she supposed to react to that? She'd had no contact with Derrick since he'd literally disappeared from her life. Was she just supposed to pretend this was normal?

Adra hated doing that, which was ironic, given her job as an agent. But, she was a professional. She could do the job. She could *always* do the job. And she could remind herself that even though Derrick Duvall had confirmed what she'd always known—that trusting men was a losing proposition—he did it because he was an ass, not because of anything Adra had done. He'd probably left a dozen women high and dry in the intervening years. Perhaps not admirably, that made her feel better.

And then she read the next text.

"Just an FYI, Ellen's going to drop by the set the first day. Don't make it awkward."

Don't make it awkward.

Wow.

Ellen Rice was the woman Derrick had left her for. Another sub in the same club at the time, some awful place that had long since closed, but the only place Adra had known about at the time. Derrick was still with Ellen. He hadn't left because he was a serial abandoner; he really had left *her*.

"Well, if that's not a kick in the fork," Adra muttered.

"What's that?" Lola laughed.

"Nothing," Adra said, shaking her head. She plastered a smile on her face for Lola's sake.

"You ready for Friday?" Lola asked.

"Ready to kick ass, ma'am," Adra answered.

She even meant it, kind of. Didn't mean she was looking forward to spending all that time with the two men who had rejected her most profoundly, even if technically Ford had only rejected her after she'd kind of, sort of rejected him. Somehow it was worse to lose Ford's friendship than it had been to lose all of Derrick, but they both still stung. So no, she wasn't looking forward to having all that loss shoved in her face all day, every day.

Except that was a lie. She always looked forward to seeing Ford. Even when it hurt.

Maybe she was a *little* bit of a masochist.

chapter 3

Ford cursed and jumped up to do another round of pull-ups on the bar he'd had installed in his office. He had never needed to burn off excess energy like he had the past few days, thinking about this freaking movie situation. No, not the movie. Adra and the movie.

The meeting with that insane producer had been bad enough. Ford had arrived on edge already, worried that something was wrong with Adra only to find out that if there wasn't already something wrong there would be soon, because they'd have to work on this movie together.

He was pissed.

And then Adra had walked in just in time to hear Ford talk about what a mistake he'd made. Ford had been talking about the movie contract, but Adra didn't know that. The look on her face had told him everything he needed to know: she'd looked hurt. Sad. Heartbroken. She'd assumed he had been talking about her. The worst part was that he *could* have been talking about her — sleeping with Adra the way he had obviously had been a mistake, because look at them now.

The difference was that was a mistake he could never bring himself to regret making.

Jesus, just looking at her. Just *thinking* about her made him insane with lust.

And then he'd seen her hurt, and it had hurt him about ten times more than he'd thought possible. He'd spent the rest of the meeting trying to find some damn way to let her know that's not what he'd meant without embarrassing the hell out of her. Well, he'd managed to focus on that until the bomb was dropped.

Derrick Duvall was Adra's ex.

It had taken all the self-control Ford had not to lose it. In that moment he was pretty sure he could have literally killed Roman.

It wasn't until later, when he'd had time to calm down, that he thought about all the other implications of this little revelation. First and foremost, he hadn't known about any of Adra's exes, let alone one that was fucking *famous*. She'd been his best friend, and he hadn't known this basic fact about her past. Adra knew practically everything about everyone, because everyone inevitably confided in her, because she was always taking care of everyone. But no one knew about her, not even, apparently, Ford.

He'd just assumed that what Adra had told him had always been true — that she didn't do relationships. That she couldn't get "involved."

Ford had been straight up dumbfounded when Adra had told him that after they'd slept together, not least because they very obviously already were "involved," whatever she wanted to call it. He'd almost laughed—it was this weird role reversal, the kind of thing you'd expect a young guy to pull on some poor woman after a one-night stand. Except Ford was a grown man, and he knew what he had in front of him. He knew what they'd both felt. He knew what they were to each other.

And it wasn't nothing.

And then he'd been so goddamned wrong.

So why did he feel like he was the asshole here?

He'd trusted what he'd felt for the first time in years with Adra, and he'd been wrong. But then, the more Adra retreated, the more she tried to steal looks at him and then ran away when he looked back, he knew he hadn't been wrong about what she wanted, or about what she'd felt. Maybe he'd just been wrong about her. She played games.

And Ford couldn't do that, ever again. His ex-wife had seen to that. And he was too old to go chasing after women who gave him mixed signals. More than that, he was a goddamn Dom. His whole existence revolved around consent. If Adra told him she couldn't do something, he would respect it. So he had removed himself.

But he couldn't shake the memory of Adra's heartbroken face when she'd heard him say the word "mistake."

Where the hell was she?

Ford checked the time. He'd spent too long thinking about Adra and trying to work off all this aggravation—that producer's schedule had them meeting about five minutes ago. Cursing, Ford jogged down the stairs, descending into the madness that was a movie production crew.

Club Volare was overrun.

These people had brought power tools. There were construction workers and electricians and people with light meters running around. Ford had no idea what went into making a movie, but whatever it was, it wasn't magic—it was work. All those people were busy running wires and setting up giant lights and in general messing with his club. They'd wanted the entire compound, but Ford had put his foot down. They could have access to the public club, nothing more. The rest of Volare was still for the members.

He wouldn't know it to look around, though. Pure freaking chaos. And in the middle of it all, there was Adra.

She looked pale. Weak. Unhappy. And Ford recognized who she was talking to from the billboard on Sunset. It was Derrick Duvall.

"Dammit," he muttered.

That was the last time he'd drop this particular ball. He wasn't going to let Derrick Duvall add to Adra's stress. Just because Adra had messed with his own head and turned out to be someone he couldn't be with—and, he reminded himself, who didn't want to be with him—didn't negate all the other wonderful things he knew about her, and he'd be damned if he saw her hurt anymore.

~ * ~ * ~

Adra was drowning.

She'd thought she'd be able to handle it, sort of. But the truth was, this was the first time she'd seen Derrick since he dumped her, and this was the first time ever that she'd met the woman he left her for — Ellen Partridge — and she was having to do it all in front of the actress who was cast as the female lead in *Submit and Surrender*, Olivia Cress.

To make everything about a million times worse, Ellen Partridge was really, really nice.

Couldn't you just...be awful? Try being awful. Just try, Adra urged silently.

Nothing.

Adra actually kind of felt sorry for Ellen, because Derrick had not changed. Or, maybe he had. It was actually way more comforting to think that he had changed, and that he hadn't been this obviously lascivious and leering when she was with him. But Adra knew better.

She was pretty sure that Derrick had already undressed her with his eyes. Like as some sort of bullshit proprietary ex-Dom thing that made her feel vaguely dirty. So here she was, having to play nice, disgusted by Derrick and yet still overrun with insecurity. She had to admit, though: she kind of liked that Ellen apparently insisted on meeting Olivia. Adra would feel the same way if her Dom had been cast to star in the first major Hollywood movie about a BDSM relationship: she would want to meet that on-screen sub. And if a real-life ex-sub was the one consulting on the sex scenes? Ouch.

Yeah, Adra actually felt for Ellen. Even if Ellen was shooting dagger eyes at her the entire time.

So there was some tension when Ford arrived.

And then there was considerably more when Ford actually touched her.

It was just a little thing. Just a hand on her arm, pulling her gently back, putting space between her and Derrick. Adra hadn't even realized how much Derrick had encroached on her space until suddenly Ford was there, between them, like a human shield.

And she hadn't realized how much she had missed Ford's touch until it had set fire to her skin.

"Sorry I'm late," Ford said. "What'd I miss?"

God, his voice. Gruffer than usual. Rough, with that deep undertone. Like the palms of his hands—rough in some places, smooth in others.

Not a helpful thought, Adra.

She cleared her throat, fought to find words, and tried to ignore the very interested expressions on Olivia and Ellen's faces.

"Nothing," Adra said, perhaps more forcefully than she needed to. "We were just getting to know each other."

"Some of us already know each other," Derrick said and extended his hand. "I'm Derrick Duvall. This is Ellen, my girlfriend, and that's Olivia Cress."

There was a pause before Ford shook Derrick's hand.

"I'm Ford Colson," he said, nodding to both Ellen and Olivia. "I'll be working with Adra here to show you guys the ropes."

Olivia laughed and raised an eyebrow, but didn't manage to hide her nervousness. "Literal ropes?" she said.

Ford smiled politely. "Maybe. I don't know what the script calls for."

Adra felt vaguely ill. Which is possibly why she tried to change the subject, even if she changed it to, well, an even worse subject.

"We're supposed to give them a tour," she blurted out.

Which, of course, Adra was dreading. It meant giving a tour of all the rooms, the equipment, the whole shebang. That was specifically what the producers had asked for: "the whole shebang." They'd also said, "You know, like a kinky orientation," principally for the benefit, Adra guessed, of Olivia.

Because Derrick, of course, was already very familiar with all of it.

So now she got to go on a tour of kinkdom with both Derrick and Ford. Yeah, she wasn't looking forward to this at all. Which must have been obvious, because the next thing she knew, Ford was standing a little closer, his brow all furrowed, his eyes worried.

His hand on the small of her back.

"Don't worry," he said, smiling gently. "You give the world's best tours. As long as you don't make me dress up this time."

"That sounds like a story," Olivia laughed.

It was.

It just took a while for Adra's brain to realize there was anything else in the world going on except Ford's hand on the small of her back.

When she did? When she remembered what he meant? She almost wanted to cry. It was how they'd become friends, when Ford had first come out from New York to L.A. to help set up the new Club Volare location.

"It is," Adra said, trying to recover her voice. She looked up at Ford, afraid of what she might see there. He was smiling, his eyes dancing like he was remembering, too. "I told Ford I'd show him around L.A. when he first moved out here, but he was such a New York snob about it—"

"Hold on. I wasn't, and never have been, a snob," Ford objected. "A realist, maybe."

"A snob," Adra went on, smiling herself now. "So I thought I'd mess with him a little bit."

"Just a little," Ford said.

Adra finally let herself laugh. It felt unreasonably good. "I took him to see a midnight screening of *Clueless* and told him it was like those midnight screenings of *Rocky Horror* where everyone gets dressed up."

"You didn't," Olivia said, covering her mouth with her hand.

"Oh I did," Adra said. "He wore a mid-nineties stoner costume. For me."

"You did that, dude?" Derrick asked.

"You got the worst of it," Ford said to Adra. "I just had to dress up like a stoned skateboarder."

"You dressed up, too?" Even Ellen was smiling.

Adra laughed again. She'd grown up in the Valley around the time Clueless had come out; it hadn't been exactly hard to pull off something a little retro. But it had involved some truly regrettable clothing.

"Well, I had to sell it," she explained. "Besides, I make a great Cher."

"You made a fantastic Cher," Ford said.

There was a silence.

Or maybe she imagined it; Adra had no idea anymore. She just knew she couldn't stop looking at Ford. He was smiling at her. He was looking at her like he used to, like *Ford*, like…like not a stranger. Or not like he was trying to keep something from her, like he wasn't a million miles away anymore, but right here, back with her.

It was like coming in from the cold. Which a part of her rebelled against, because how screwed up was that? How much sway did this one person have over how she was feeling, over her happiness? How could that possibly be healthy?

And the rest of her was shouting, *Just shut up and take it*. Because he felt a whole lot like shelter in the middle of this shitstorm of a situation.

So of course it was Derrick who broke the silence.

"Yeah, well, how'd that turn out for you?" he said.

It took Adra more than a moment to realize he wasn't talking about her and Ford, but Ford and the movie masquerade prank of 2012. And that he was being a little bit of a dick.

"Actually pretty well," Ford replied. "Definitely broke the ice."

"Speaking of which, we've got a read-through in a bit, so we should probably get going?" They all looked at Olivia, who appeared to be the only one capable of staying professional at the moment, even though she was doing it with a kind sort of smile. Adra liked her already.

"Tour?" Adra said.

"Tour," Ford said. Ellen reluctantly said goodbye to Derrick, and the rest of them headed up to the play areas.

Adra, for her part, kind of checked out at first, and let Ford give the standard intro to Club Volare and BDSM. Safe, sane, consensual, etc. Some of it was definitely old hat for Derrick, but Olivia seemed to be soaking it up. Adra, on the other hand, was mostly reveling in the relief she felt around Ford.

It was…it was intoxicating, somehow. How easy it was with him. How much she'd missed it. And given how long she'd gone without this easy rapport, this certainty that she could give him a sidelong look and he'd just *get* it, this feeling of comfort that he was always at her back, it was disorienting as all hell. Out of nowhere, he'd gone from avoiding her, to…what? What was this?

It was like having her best friend back, and more. That "more" was maybe the problem.

And so was the fact that she had no idea if she could trust any of it.

"Adra?"

She was startled out of her own thoughts by the voice of her ex. Adra looked at Derrick, kind of dumbfounded—apparently he'd been talking for a while. And apparently he'd asked her a question or something.

She had *no* idea what.

But she could tell from the look on Derrick's face, as she just kind of shook her head and shrugged, that he did not appreciate being ignored. It was a look she recognized from years ago, when he'd screwed up a scene, or when some other Dom had disagreed with him and had the nerve to be right about it. She used to dread seeing it because it would mean he'd be all sullen and difficult until she'd managed to assuage his ego.

God, had she really done that? *Why?*

Now Adra just hid a smile.

Derrick glowered.

"That covers the basics," Ford was saying. He smiled. "Now to the fun stuff."

Olivia almost seemed to shiver, but she was smiling, her eyes searching the room, resting on various pieces of equipment. Adra couldn't help but follow her gaze, thinking back to how it had all looked when it was new to her.

It was a fun memory…until her eyes rested on the restraint table.

Oh God.

That was where she and Ford had…

They hadn't even used the restraints at first. There hadn't been *time*. It hadn't felt like there was time for anything at all, not for talking, not for thinking, not for freaking *breathing*. They'd just needed each other, right then, right there, as much as possible.

Adra felt his hands on her body all over again and shuddered.

When she refocused her eyes, Ford was looking at her. And so was everyone else.

Oh *shit*.

Adra cleared her throat. "Do you want to go over the stations we have out on the floor?" she said to Ford.

"I think most of them look pretty self-explanatory," Olivia said softly. "But you should definitely go over them." She looked pretty enthralled. Particularly by the spanking bench. Adra tried to quell the jealousy that flared up inside her, but to no avail.

Only Derrick looked annoyed.

"This is a waste of time," he said.

"Not to me it isn't," Olivia said, looking sideways at her costar. "If you're going to have me over one of those things, I damn sure want to know how it works."

Adra and Ford looked at each other. Olivia might actually be pretty great, so long as she stopped looking at Ford.

"I mean, not…*have* me," the actress said, suddenly flustered.

"We knew what you meant," Ford said. "And you're right."

Adra hadn't been able to take her eyes off Ford since she'd remembered their night on that table. In this room. All over the club. And finally, in his bed.

Then Olivia had talked about being had over pieces of equipment, and now Ford was looking back at Adra, too.

She could barely breathe.

"Then let's get on with it," Derrick said.

Ford broke his gaze from Adra's face, shaking his head, turning away slightly. He paused a moment, and then pointed up, toward the center of the room, where a suspension apparatus hung from the ceiling.

"That might not be quite as familiar as the spanking bench," Ford said.

Adra thought she heard Olivia catch her breath, unaware that anyone had noticed her reactions to all of this. But that wasn't what caught her attention. It was Derrick, staring right at her.

"I know Adra's familiar with it," he said.

It was like being slapped in the face. With something gross.

Adra was so shocked she honestly was sort of speechless. Never mind the level of unprofessionalism that Derrick had just sunk to; it was the fact that it was clearly some sort of weird power play that got to her. Yeah, they'd done bondage and suspension play. Years ago. They'd taken a class in rope bondage, for safety, and he'd tied her up and suspended her, and, well. It had been ok. Just ok.

But to bring it up? Now? When they hadn't seen each other in years, when this was supposed to be a professional setting, when Adra was supposed to be an authority, when all it would do would humiliate and demean her, when—

"Mr. Duvall," Ford said. His voice was different. It was *the* voice, only deeper. Threatening.

Ford had turned back around and was staring at Derrick, his eyes on fire, his face dark. He took two steps and put himself between Adra and Derrick, and then...he kept going.

Derrick stepped back.

Ford walked him back until he bumped into the wall. Adra could see Ford's fists opening and closing, opening and closing, his huge, hulking back obscuring Derrick's face entirely. Everything was very, very quiet.

"Every competent practitioner is somewhat familiar with suspension techniques, Mr. Duvall,"

Ford said. "We run a professional club here. I recommend that you behave professionally."

"Holy shit," Olivia whispered, looking sideways at Adra.

Adra couldn't speak.

Then came Derrick's thin voice. "Or what?" he said.

Ford was silent for a long, long time. Adra had never seen him like this. Only once had he been close—the night of Volare's Bacchanal party, when some jerk had gotten drunk and practically yanked Adra's arm out of its socket. That guy had left with a broken nose, and Adra had thought that was the most primitive, violent, and slightly frightening thing she'd ever seen from Ford.

Until now.

Ford was breathing deep, his shoulders heaving, his body coiled tight. He hadn't touched Derrick. He kept his hands to his sides. And he hadn't looked away. But there was something about the intensity of it all, about the impression of supreme control, that made you wonder what would happen if Ford decided he needed to let go.

He's protecting me, Adra realized. *He's protecting me from Derrick.*

The thought hit her like a hammer to the chest.

"Or what?" Derrick said again, his voice slightly higher.

Finally, Ford said, "Don't find out."

Oh God, she needed to stop this. She knew Derrick; he was an idiot. And she hadn't planned on Ford *caring* about Derrick being an idiot, and she definitely hadn't planned on this testosterone-filled display. The two of them beating the crap out of each other would be an absolute disaster for the club.

"Ford," Adra said. She didn't know what she planned to say next. But she didn't have to.

Like freaking magic, Ford walked away.

He turned around, looked at her, sweat beading on his forehead, and he walked over to Adra's side.

She could smell him. Oh God, she could smell him. She'd almost forgotten how badly she could want him, and now here it was again, that *want*, alive and clawing at her, climbing up her skin, her whole body aware of nothing more than his presence next to hers.

And then they were all saved from whatever was going to happen next by Roman.

"Am I interrupting?" Roman called, striding into the room. Adra knew Roman Casta well enough to know that with one glance he absolutely knew that he was interrupting something, and that it was something bad. The man could read a room. Thank God.

"Nope!" Adra said, way too enthusiastically. "We were just about to take a break. What's up?"

"Ford, you have a phone call in your office," Roman said.

"I'm busy," Ford said.

"I suggest you take it."

"Whatever it is, it's not more important than what I'm doing," Ford said through clenched teeth. "I'm busy."

Roman sighed. "Ford. It's your ex-wife."

Adra could actually feel the air go out of the room.

Or maybe it was just the air going out of her lungs.

Ford had an *ex-wife*?

chapter 4

"Claudia," Ford said into the phone.

It felt surreal to even say. They hadn't talked in over five years. Even now, he half-expected silence.

Would have preferred it, even. He couldn't think of a legitimate reason for Claudia to contact him that didn't involve tragedy.

"Hi, Ford," she said after far too long. "How are you?"

Ford clenched his teeth. Polite conversation took on a whole new meaning with his ex-wife. And she had no business knowing anything about him anymore.

"What's wrong, Claudia?"

"Nothing is wrong."

Roman had said it sounded urgent; otherwise Ford would have stayed with Adra. But then again, Roman wasn't familiar with the Claudia Bane — make that Gifford, now — definition of "urgent."

Ford took a deep breath, and tried not to think about where he'd left Adra, back in that room, with Derrick's words hanging in the goddamn air.

"Why are you calling me?" he said.

"Ford, don't you think we can be civil, after all this time?" she said.

"I'm honest," he said.

She was silent.

"Well," she finally said, "I thought you should know that Jesse and I are moving out to Los Angeles."

"That has nothing to do with me."

"Jesse has done some work for the studio on the *Submit and Surrender* movie," she went on. "They asked for him specifically because they'd heard he was in the lifestyle. It didn't seem relevant to me, considering he just worked on the contracts, but what do I know? Anyway, we're moving out to L.A."

"And?"

"And we'll be applying for membership at Club Volare L.A.," she said lightly. "I just thought you should know."

"Are you asking for my recommendation?"

"Of course not," she said, trying to sound as if she didn't think she needed it. "I just thought you should know, that's all."

And she was counting on this call to make Ford feel too proud to actually block their application. Clever, but he could see right through her. It had taken him a long time and a lot of bullshit to learn that skill, but now that he had it, it was like riding a bike.

Unfortunately, she was also right. Ford was over Claudia; that wasn't in doubt. But he hadn't forgiven her—or Jesse. So while he didn't want them walking around his goddamn club, his integrity wouldn't allow him to blackball them just because he didn't like them.

"You've told me, Claudia," he said. "Is there anything else?"

"You won't go all Neanderthal or anything?" she said.

That should not have pissed him off as much as it did. She was trying to joke around, to lighten an awkward conversation; even Claudia wasn't outright evil. But she had no way of knowing that Ford actually had just gone "all Neanderthal" on Derrick Duvall for daring to make Adra feel even the slightest bit uncomfortable.

God*dammit*.

He'd overreacted. He'd seen Adra hurt, and he'd just...

He'd felt *guilty* about it. And then he'd gone after Derrick.

"Ford?" Claudia said.

"I won't go all Neanderthal," Ford said. "Your life isn't any of my business anymore, Claudia. Good luck with your move."

And he hung up.

Only then did he realize there was some nervous looking kid with a clipboard hovering about his open office door. It took a moment for Ford to remember that there were a few dozen movie people wandering around the club, and that this poor kid wasn't actually an intruder.

The kid took a step back anyway.

"Mr. Colson?"

"Yeah?"

"Um, Mr. Corvis said he needs you in the conference room?"

"What?"

"Mr. Corvis? The executive producer?"

Ford tried to make his face as gentle as possible. The kid looked like he might actually be shaking.

"I meant, what conference room?'" Ford said. "We have a conference room now?"

"Um, I can take you to it?"

"Lead the way."

Ford shook his head as he followed the kid through the club, marveling again at how surreal the whole situation was. Within a week everything had been turned upside down. Within a week, he'd gone from...

What the hell had he been doing? Fucking up, that's what. As a Dom, he'd fucked up royally. Both he and Adra had screwed up by giving in and neglecting to talk about what they were doing before they slept together; Ford didn't realize until later that he'd been so certain that Adra had also wanted what he wanted: a life together. A relationship. All of it. He'd wanted all of it. And he'd been sure she did, too.

And he'd been wrong.

Well, shit happens. But he'd screwed up after that, too. Adra had told him, in her own limited way, what she could handle. She didn't tell him why she couldn't be with him, but she wasn't obligated to, and that didn't excuse his own lack of communication.

Because after that, he'd pulled away. He'd distanced himself from a friendship that was important to both of them, and he'd done it without explanation. He'd told himself it was because Adra had played games with him, was still playing games with him, and that was true—but it wasn't the whole truth. He'd also done it out of self-preservation, because he thought he'd been in love with her, or who he'd thought her to be, and he'd needed time to get over that.

And today he'd been confronted with just how much that had hurt Adra.

"Goddammit," he said under his breath.

"What?" the kid said.

"Nothing. Where are you taking me?"

"Right here, sir," the kid said, pointing at one of the playrooms. Ford laughed out loud—this was what they were calling a conference room? Well, he supposed that could work, in a way...

"Thanks," Ford said. The kid was staring at the floor. He still looked like a frightened fawn. "Hey, listen. Try to relax. You're doing a good job."

The kid looked up, his eyes bright. "Yeah?"

Ford smiled. "Yeah. Any idea what I'm supposed to be doing in there?"

"It's a script read," the kid said, proud to know something useful. "The production is under high security because of all the fan interest, so they don't let anyone go home with a script. You have to read it in there, and the script can't leave the room. I'm supposed to stand out here until you're done."

Ford shook his head again. Hollywood.

"I'll try to be quick," he said.

"Take your time, sir," the kid said. "The other consulting producer is already in there."

The other 'consulting producer'?

But even as he opened the door, Ford knew. It was Adra. Lounging on a divan, long legs spread out in front of her, hair falling over her face, eyes on the script she held in her soft hands, her brow furrowed in that look of concentration that got him every damn time. She was beautiful.

Then she looked up and saw Ford. And the look of confusion and pain that spread across her face was unmistakable.

Sometimes there wasn't a way to fix things. Ford would respect whatever wishes Adra had, even if he thought she was wrong, even if he'd learned that she wasn't the woman for him, even if he wanted her more than he wanted his next breath. But he'd be damned if he could continue to stand by and watch Adra be hurt because it might be easier on him.

That he could fix.

~ * ~ * ~

Adra had read the same page about a dozen times and she still had no idea what it said. That poor production assistant who was supposed to stand guard outside while she read the *Submit and Surrender* script was going to be there for a long, long time.

Ford had an *ex-wife*?

How was she supposed to think about anything else? Literally, anything else in the world? The Big One could turn L.A. into a floating island in the middle Pacific in the next two minutes, and Adra would still be wondering about Ford and his freaking *ex-wife*.

How could she not have known that? That Ford had been *married*? Thinking about it now, the man was in his thirties; it was ridiculous to imagine he hadn't had important relationships. It's just that Adra didn't know about any of them. The idea that there'd once been a woman important enough to Ford that he'd declared his love, that he'd promised himself to her forever, that he'd...

Adra's head was spinning. Which, that she could handle; she was used to her head spinning around Ford. But her heart felt empty, too. There was this huge part of Ford's life, of his past, that he'd never shared with her. That she wasn't a part of, even indirectly, even as just a friend who could show support.

She wasn't used to being kept in the dark. She was used to people confiding in her, and she was used to being able to take care of them when they did. Somehow knowing that Ford hadn't trusted her with this made the hurt of losing him seem fresh all over again.

Which was stupid, and selfish, because in the end, hadn't he been right not to confide in her? Would she really have done anything differently if she'd known about the ex-wife? If she'd known about whatever emotional land mines Ford had in his past? Adra had felt them getting too close, and she hadn't stopped it, and then she'd slept with him anyway, because she couldn't stop herself. And then she'd had to tell him that she couldn't be with him.

She didn't tell him that she couldn't be with anyone at all. Who'd understand? Hell, Adra herself didn't always understand. She just knew that when she got too close to needing anybody, that was when she needed to get the hell out, because otherwise it would end in heartbreak in tears.

Well, *more* heartbreak and tears, anyway.

And so she'd been on the verge of crying all over again when Ford walked in.

And oh God, just the sight of him.

He was still wearing a white button down shirt, but he'd rolled up the sleeves, showing those powerful forearms, those big hands. First button undone, the crispness gone from the material. His hair kind of tussled. His eyes taking in the room in that commanding way he had, like he was surveying his territory.

Jesus. He didn't even have to look at her to make her wet.

And then she remembered that she'd lost this man entirely, this man who had been her friend and who was even more beautiful inside than he was outside, and it crushed her.

They stared at each other.

Ford closed the door.

And Adra couldn't take it anymore.

"I know you must hate this," she blurted out. "I'm so sorry, Ford, I—"

He looked at her. "I don't hate this."

"I'll just…I'll do my best to stay out of your way."

Ford cocked his head, and almost seemed to smile. "How the hell do you think you're going to do that?"

Adra had nothing. He was right; it was impossible.

"Adra, look at me," he said.

Jesus. He could have been a movie star during the Golden Age, with that bone structure, the sheer size of him. If he were all she had to look at for the rest of her life, she'd be fine with that. His eyes held her in place.

"I don't hate this," he said. "And I don't want you to stay out of my way."

Looking at Ford now, Adra couldn't help but think about what his face had looked like when she'd told him that she didn't want to be with him. And she felt absolutely miserable.

"Maybe you should hate this," she said. "Maybe you should hate me."

Ford's Dom voice cracked the air between them.

"Don't talk about yourself that way," he said. "That's an order."

Adra blinked.

She couldn't move. Couldn't look away. Couldn't think about anything other than Ford. They'd never gotten to do a proper scene during their one night together. There were hints of what he'd be like as Dom, and he'd dominated her without question, but it had been…very animal. Feral. Wild. What would he be like cool and calm and controlled? What would he be like with complete, deliberate control over her?

She could *feel* his eyes on her skin as sure as she could feel the wetness spreading between her thighs.

Breathe, Adra. You have to breathe.

She tried. It didn't work. His eyes were on her lips.

Say something!

"You have an ex-wife?" she said.

Ford finally smiled. "You have an ex-Dom who's a movie star?"

Adra laughed.

She'd been obsessing about how these secrets had revealed the gulf between them, but here, in the room, laughing about it with him, knowing in that moment that he understood what she'd been thinking because he'd been thinking it, too…she felt closer to him than she had since it all happened. Since maybe before that. It was the weirdest thing.

And it was, of course, terrifying. Because no one had ever gotten to her like Ford. No one had ever gotten so close to making her feel like she needed him. And the last time that had happened, she'd tried to quench that rising panic by sleeping with him.

Get it together, Adra.

"Ford, what happened with Derrick…"

Ford crossed the room quickly, looming over her in a way that nearly pushed all thoughts out of her mind.

"He can't talk to you like that," Ford said.

"I agree," Adra said. Derrick really was an asshole. "But it's not like we can kick him off the movie. And I don't want you going to jail."

"I'm not worried about that."

"Well, I am," Adra said. "What *was* that, Ford? I thought you were going to kill him."

Ford stood there, silent, looking down at her. She felt like there was something important happening, something churning around them, and she almost didn't want it to end. She wanted him to look at her like that all the time.

Finally he sat down on the end of her divan, lifting her legs up and putting them on his lap. He was so close. His hand burned into the outside of her thigh.

"That was guilt," he said.

It took her a while to process that one.

"Wait, what?" she said.

Ford leaned on one arm, an arm Adra knew was strong and hard and felt amazing wrapped around her waist.

"Adra, what happened between us," Ford said. "We screwed up."

It was like being punched in the stomach.

Why did it hurt so much to hear something she already knew to be true?

"We should have talked first," Ford went on. "We were friends, and we both know better. That's on both of us. But I should have talked to you afterwards. After you told me that you didn't want to be with me."

"Ford..." she said softly.

"Quiet," he said. His voice was soft and strong, and his eyes didn't leave hers. She had no chance. "I pulled away from you, because I thought that's what you wanted, because I thought..."

He shook his head, frowning. Adra thought he was going to say more, but he swallowed the words, whatever they were.

"I pulled away from our friendship, but I didn't explain it," he said. "And that hurt you. I saw, today, for the first time, how much that hurt you, and Adra, it made me fucking crazy."

She didn't know what to say. She hadn't thought she'd deserved an explanation, since it had made perfect sense to her, but of course it didn't make perfect sense. Ford was not the kind of man to throw a temper tantrum because he didn't get what he wanted. He wasn't the type of man to throw away a friendship because of a bad decision.

So she'd just thought he'd changed his opinion of her. Like, he'd seen through her, he'd gotten close to her, and then the way she'd behaved afterwards had made him...

Adra blinked again. She really didn't want to cry.

"Adra, it made me crazy with guilt, and then Derrick stepped out of line to hurt you on *purpose*, and I just snapped. I took it out on him."

"You took it out on him?"

"I'm not sorry about it, but yeah," Ford said. "That's what happened."

He was so freaking earnest, looking at her like that. She felt terrible.

"Ford, you don't have anything to feel guilty about," she said. "I..."

But she couldn't bring herself to say it.

She couldn't say that it was her fault, that this perfect thing between them was just something she knew she couldn't have because she was screwed up, or because the world was screwed up, or both, and she couldn't bear to one day see Ford screwed up, too. That things always ended, that they ended badly, that people inevitably walked out. That if that were to happen with him, it would destroy her. That she couldn't even bring herself to tell him about it, because that would make her need him even more...

And he was the one who felt guilty.

"I let you think I no longer cared about you," he said bluntly. "I let you think we weren't friends. That was wrong. Adra, look at me."

Adra couldn't make herself look up. He was so freaking *good*, looking at her with all that concern, that sense that whatever it was, he would take care of it. It was enough to make anyone feel weak.

"I avoided you, too," she said quietly. "I didn't know how to—"

"Look at me."

Shit.

Slowly, she raised her eyes. He was just like she remembered. She almost couldn't bear it.

"I've missed you, Adra," he said.

She opened her mouth to speak, but nothing came out. She felt stunned, breathless, incredulous, even.

He was relentless.

"You were the best friend I've ever had," he said. "I don't want to lose that."

He leaned forward, his eyes bright and his jaw clenched.

"I *won't* lose that," he said.

The word "friend" kept bouncing around inside Adra's head, making her feel happy and sad at the same time, but in the end she couldn't tear herself away from Ford.

When she spoke, her voice was small.

"Ok," she said.

Neither of them looked at each other like a friend. It didn't feel like a friend's hand on her thigh. It didn't feel like a finished conversation, like there was so much unsaid, so much hidden behind those blue eyes. It made her want to reach out and touch him, to just…

No. That's what happened last time. That was how they'd gotten into this mess.

"Ok?" he said finally.

"Ok," she said, nodding. "We should be friends again."

Ford smiled at her.

"I never wanted to stop."

Adra smiled back. "Me, neither."

And as soon as she said it, she knew it was a lie. She didn't want to be his friend. She wanted to just be his.

Which was the one thing she couldn't be.

chapter 5

"So you're friends," Lola said flatly.

"That's what I said," Adra said, handing the menu back to a very patient waiter. "Friends."

"Friends."

"Yes, friends. Why are you saying it like that?"

Lola gave her a classic "are you shitting me?" face.

"Because there's friends, and then there's *friends*, and you know the difference," Lola finally said, turning on the waiter. The very pregnant redhead had more than the usual glow about her; somehow pregnancy had amplified both Lola's Domme and sub characteristics. The waiter couldn't take his eyes off of her, and it was funny to watch him try to figure out why.

Adra figured Roman had his hands full.

"What can I get you, madame?" the poor man said.

"Everything on this page," Lola said.

The waiter rocked back on his feet.

"Madame?"

Adra stifled a laugh.

"The appetizers," Lola explained gently. "I want them all. I can't decide, so I won't. I know it's weird, but I am hungry and pregnant and I don't care. Bring me all of them. Trust me, I'll eat them."

Adra decided to help the poor guy out.

"I'll just pick off of her plates," she said.

"My appetites are *insane*," Lola sighed as soon as the waiter was out of earshot. "It's absolutely killing me."

"Appetites, plural?"

"Yeah, you wouldn't believe what these hormones do to you," Lola said. "I'm seriously pissed off at Ford for taking up any of Roman's time tonight. Getting back to bed is practically all I can think about. No offense," she added.

"None taken," Adra said, trying to act nonchalant. "So Ford is taking up Roman's time?"

Lola groaned. "Oh God, please don't make me be tactful," she said. "They had to talk about something, I don't even know what." Lola arched an eyebrow. "Possibly friendships."

"Smooth," Adra laughed.

"Are you going to tell me?"

"No," Adra said. "Ok, maybe a little. We are…we did say we'd be friends."

"You know that's not the good part."

"There isn't a good part."

"Bullshit!"

Adra sighed. She knew she wouldn't get away with this forever. Maybe it was better to get it over with. "We had one night."

"Oh my God, one? All of this from one night?"

"You knew?"

Lola laughed. "Of course I knew," she said. "Adra, you know I love you, but near-sighted strangers who see you two from across the street know. There has never been anything more obvious than the sexual tension between you and Ford."

"Don't tease me," Adra begged. "It's a fresh wound."

"Then tell me about it!" Lola said. "You keep so much bottled up, Adra. I worry about you, you know?"

Adra shook her head to keep from showing how much that affected her. It shouldn't affect her, right? The idea of Lola worrying about her? That there might be reason to worry shouldn't make her want to cry?

"I don't even know what to say," Adra said, and realized it was the complete truth. "He is perfect. Everything is perfect. Except that nothing is really perfect, you know? And I just…I know I'm not built for it, Lola. I know how it would end. And I just can't do that again."

"Adra…" Lola said.

Adra looked away. Just Lola's tone of voice told her what she needed to know. Lola thought Adra was being foolish, running away from love or emotion or whatever, but Lola didn't know. She didn't know Adra's past, she didn't know Adra's family, and she didn't know what Adra knew. And it was impossible to explain.

And luckily Adra's phone rang—with her sister-in-law's ringtone.

Adra had never been so glad to answer a phone call in her life.

"Sorry, Lola, family stuff. One sec," she said. "Nicole? What's up?"

There was a far too lengthy pause. And a sniffle.

"Is he with you?" Nicole finally asked.

Adra's heart plummeted to somewhere well beneath the earth's crust. Her brother Charlie had…

No, better not to say that he'd run off yet. She didn't know anything. It might not be that.

"No, honey, he isn't," Adra said. "What happened?"

"Has he called you? Do you know where he is?"

"I haven't heard from him yet, Nic," Adra said, trying to quell her own panic. This brought up every fear Adra had, but it was nothing compared to what Nicole must be feeling. "What happened?"

"I'm probably just overreacting," Nicole said. "He's probably just out late bowling or something. It's just he's been distant again, and he isn't answering his phone, and…"

"I thought things were getting better," Adra said, pulling her chair back as the hapless waiter rolled an entire cart of appetizers up to their table. Lola couldn't hide her excitement.

"They were, for a little while," Nicole said. "But he won't talk to me. He gets so stressed out, and then he just shuts down, and then…"

Adra didn't need her to finish that sentence. It sounded sickeningly familiar. She steeled herself for the next question.

"Is he drinking?" Adra asked.

"Oh God, no, he wouldn't do that," Nicole said. "I know he wouldn't do that. He's not your dad. It's so important to him."

It was important to Adra, too.

"Adra," Nicole said, her voice catching. "I'm sorry to call like this, it's just I don't know what to do, and I just…"

"I know," Adra said. "I know, Nic."

And she really, really did. She remembered it very well. And maybe that's why this was the one time when she had no idea what to say. Everyone always came to Adra with their problems, and she always knew how to help, whatever it was. She would listen, and she would comfort them, and she'd be able to see, somehow, what the unspoken issue was. And maybe it wouldn't fix the problem, but it would help them feel better.

Except for this. This was the one thing that left Adra speechless. All she could think about was all the times she'd felt the same way, needing someone who wasn't there and might not be coming back and powerless to do anything about it. She'd never figured out how to make that better. If she had, her life would be a whole lot different.

Lola offered her a plate of something delicious looking covered in cheese, and Adra looked up to see her friend's worried face.

"I'll call him, Nic," Adra said into the phone. "I'm so sorry."

"I'm worried about him," Nicole said softly. "I know it's totally screwed up to be calling you about our marriage problems, but it's not…I mean, you know it's that I'm worried about him."

"I know," Adra said. "Me, too."

"Thank you," Nicole said. "You'll call me?"

"Of course," Adra said. "And you let me know when he comes home, ok? Give the boys my love."

"Thank you, Adra," Nicole said again, and hung up.

That was it—that final thank you. That was what broke Adra's heart. That gratitude for something that shouldn't have to happen in the first place. Because Adra wasn't even worried about her brother's physical well being, as screwed up as that was—Charlie was always fine. Instead, Adra knew what this felt like. This was Charlie freaking out. This was Charlie acting like their father.

Adra sent a simple text to her brother: "Call me so I know you're not dead."

It was what they used to ask their dad to do years ago. If that didn't get a response, then there was a problem.

Goddammit.

"Adra," Lola said.

Adra forced herself to smile. "Yeah? You gonna hog all that calamari or what?"

Lola passed another plate, disturbing the precarious balance of the mountain of appetizers between them. But she didn't lose her focus. Lola never did.

"Adra, I really do love you," Lola said softly. "So I'm saying this from a place of love. You don't have to talk to me, but you've gotta talk to someone eventually. You can't keep carrying the weight of the world on your shoulders like this. You have to let someone help every once in a while."

"I know," Adra said, nodding slowly. "I know."

Except that she didn't, really. It was one of those things that made perfect rational sense, and yet whenever she thought about it, her entire body revolted against the idea in a fit of panic.

And Lola was watching her try not to freak out.

"Well," Lola said, popping a bacon-wrapped scallop in her mouth. "If you want something else to freak out about besides your reluctance to rely on your friends, I can help with that."

Adra laughed out loud, her hand to her chest. "Please."

Lola smiled evilly.

"I hear tomorrow you begin coaching the actual scenes? Like, *scene* scenes? With Ford? And your ex? In the same room?"

"Oh my God," Adra said, laughing helplessly until a tear rolled down her cheek. "What is my life."

~ * ~ * ~

Ford and Roman's pool game had been ruined by a single phone call from Roger Corvis, executive producer of *Submit and Surrender*. It had started off badly. Ford could hear Corvis's tone from across the pool table, and laughed when he thought about how Roman would handle the guy.

But when Roman came back, he wasn't laughing it off. He looked serious.

"Something happen?" Ford said.

He hated the idea of the film taking over Volare, but it did give him back his friendship with Adra. He cared now. Damn it.

"Someone leaked the filming location," Roman said, setting up another shot. "Security is going to be an issue. Corvis seemed to think it was someone at Volare."

"Bullshit."

"That's what I said, in so many words," Roman smiled. "That said, we need to cut this short."

"Of course."

Roman looked at his friend carefully.

"What did Claudia have to say?"

"Nothing important. She's moving to L.A. They'll want memberships."

Roman raised an eyebrow but said nothing. Roman had known Ford when he'd found out that his wife had been having an affair with his best friend and colleague, Jesse Gifford, and that that had been the real root of the problems in their marriage. The games that Claudia had been playing with Ford for months while their marriage deteriorated were just about her guilt, nothing more, and that had been one last mindfuck to add to the list. It wasn't something Ford talked about much, but Roman knew, and that mattered. Still, there were some things even Roman didn't know.

Like about the child. No one knew about the child.

"Ford," Roman said, setting his pool cue down. "You know that Adra is nothing like Claudia."

"Of course she isn't," Ford said. The idea pissed him off, and what Roman was getting at pissed him off even more. It wasn't about simple parallels; Adra didn't have to be just like his ex-wife to be incompatible with him. And Adra was the one who'd called it off. "Don't compare them."

Roman put his hands up. "Of course. I shouldn't have offended Adra with the comparison."

"No, you shouldn't."

"Do you know what you're doing, Ford?" Roman asked seriously.

Ford met his gaze. It was obvious what Roman was talking about: Adra.

"About as much as you knew what you were doing with Lola," Ford said. "She's my best friend, Roman. I won't let anything or anyone hurt her, including me."

"Your best friend?" Roman said.

"Stop smiling."

Roman only smiled again, this time ruefully. "Neither of us should be smiling. Someone leaked the location, and that might hurt all of us. We have a long night of security preparations ahead of us. That, and finding out who the leak is."

"You got a guy for that?"

"Not in Los Angeles. Do you?"

"Yeah. Private investigator I've used for legal work," Ford said. "He'll get it done."

Ford made the call, and then spent the rest of the night trying to figure out how to secure an entire compound from a ravenous press and a rabid fan base. By the time he drove by the Volare compound, the photographers had already staked the place out, and there was another accident at that damn stoplight involving a news van and a food truck that had shown up to feed the gathering fans.

It had taken just a few hours for the circus to start. People were going completely crazy over this movie.

And Adra was going to have to get through this sea of security risks the next morning. The studio would take care of the movie people, but Ford didn't trust them to take care of Volare people. Which was how he ended up knocking on a neighbor's door at about six in the morning.

***

The neighbor—Volare's neighbor to the south, to be precise—was actually surprisingly accommodating. An older guy named Dan had owned his Venice property since the seventies, and he still surfed every day. He was friends with Thea, and was perfectly willing to let Ford hang out until Adra was due to arrive.

Just as he knew Adra would be about to get up, Ford texted her directions. "Avoid Abbot-Kinney, and don't go directly to Volare. Meet me at 28 Altair."

"What happened?" she asked.

"Secret's out," Ford wrote back.

It wasn't until he saw her face as she stood on Dan's front porch, waiting for him, that he realized he could have chosen his words better. She looked confused and way too anxious for this early in the morning.

Ah. She thought he meant *that* secret. Which now meant he was thinking about that night.

Who was he kidding, he'd be thinking about that no matter what. Just looking at her was enough to stir up those memories. He just had to deal with it.

"The press knows they're filming the movie at Volare," he said, trying not to smile at her nervousness.

"Right, of course," Adra said. She bit her lip and looked down at her feet. Damn, did he want to kiss her. "So what am I doing here?"

"You're getting sneaked in the back way," Ford said. "No way you're going through that goddamn gauntlet out front."

"The back way?" she asked, eyebrow raised. "And what about Derrick and Olivia?"

"They're the studio's responsibility," Ford said, leaving it unsaid what he knew to be true: Adra was his responsibility. "Follow me."

He took her hand, and ignored the nearly overwhelming desire to take the rest of her.

Neighbor Dan's house had a sizable backyard with plenty of pretty looking trees with decent climbing branches. Ford had no idea what kind they were, but he would have been all over them as a little boy. Volare had been careful not to screw with the Zen appeal of Dan's garden when they'd constructed the tall wall that bounded the compound, and Dan had remained grateful. And now Ford was grateful for those trees.

"That's our wall," Adra said, pointing.

"Yup," Ford said.

"And that's a tree right next to it," she said.

"Yup," Ford said.

"You have got to be kidding me."

"Nope," Ford said, grinning.

Adra crossed her arms. "Do I look like the tree-climbing type?" she said.

"You used to jump the wall every day in high school," Ford laughed. "You told me yourself."

"That was in different shoes."

"Well," Ford said, lifting himself up onto the lowest branch and then jumping lightly onto the top of the wall, "You don't have to worry about that."

He knelt down on the top of the wall and extended his hands.

"Just grab on and I'll do the rest."

Adra smiled and bit her lip again, this time with a decidedly different expression.

"What?" he asked.

"My high school boyfriend tried this once," she said. "It didn't work very well. He fell and broke his arm."

"I am not your high school boyfriend," Ford said.

Adra looked up at him.

"You most certainly are not," she said.

Then she put her hands in his.

It was almost cheating, considering how light she was. He'd forgotten about that. He could have thrown her up in the air and caught her, just for fun, but settled for lifting her up and into his arms, balancing them both on the top of the wall.

Adra clung to him, unsure of herself in her heels. God bless women's shoes.

That was not a friendly thought. But Ford decided to give himself some leeway when she was actually in his arms. He was only freaking human, after all.

And it's not like they'd stopped wanting each other. He could tell, from the way she was breathing…

Damn.

"Sit down," he said to her, holding her hand. "Put your legs over the edge."

Adra kept hold of his hand as she lowered herself into a seated position, her movements somewhat constrained by the skirt she was wearing.

"Oh, screw it," she said when she was seated, her legs hanging over the edge. "You are in charge of finding my shoes," she said, kicking them off.

"Yes, ma'am," Ford said, jumping down to the ground easily. Trail running over boulders had served him well.

When he looked up, shoes in hand, Adra was watching him.

"You ready?" Ford said.

"You know I hate heights," she said.

"But you're not a wimp," he said.

"You're going to catch me?" she asked.

"Always," he said, grinning. "Wouldn't have it any other way."

She smiled.

"You didn't just engineer this whole thing to get a look up my skirt, did you?"

"You know I wouldn't have to go to this much trouble to get a look up your skirt."

Adra's mouth dropped open in mock outrage.

"If I still had my shoes, I would throw them at you."

"Yeah, that was a tactical error on your part," Ford said. "Now jump before I come up there and get you."

She bit her lip again. It was damn distracting.

And then she jumped.

And if she'd asked, Ford would have to admit how good it felt to hold her in his arms again. But she didn't have to ask. He held on to her for just a little longer than he had to, feeling the softness of her body against his, the warmth of her hands on his chest, the little whisper of her rapid, ragged breaths.

Neither of them said anything as he helped her into her shoes. If they'd said something, that would have meant they would have to deal with it all over again. Ford remembered how much that conversation had upset Adra the last time around and so he kept his mouth shut.

Besides, they could only be friends.

He let her go.

It wasn't until they were already inside Volare, mounting the stairs to the second floor, that Adra found her voice.

"So was all that really necessary?" she said, trying to sound light. Teasing.

"Look out the window," Ford said.

It was pandemonium.

The police had only just arrived to try to clear the street for traffic, but it was taking forever, given the sheer volume of people who had shown up. And that wasn't even including the press. The entrance to the compound was completely overrun.

"Oh my God," Adra said.

"Someone leaked the location of the shoot," Ford said. He was still pissed off about it.

"Who?"

"I have someone on it."

"Do we need, like, security guards? What the hell are we going to do? We have the members' privacy to think about. Oh God, and the safety issues. This is nuts."

Ford held open the door to the main playroom and watched Adra walk through it, reminding himself that he would have to keep an eye out for Derrick's antics. They were coaching the first scene today.

"Roman's looking to get security set up by tomorrow," Ford said. "Today, unfortunately, we rely on the studio."

Adra stopped suddenly and turned around.

"You really didn't want me running through a gauntlet," she said.

"Of course not."

A beat.

"How early did you get up to talk to Dan?" she asked.

Ford wasn't even surprised that Adra knew their neighbor already. She'd probably brought around a plate of cookies or something when Volare first set up shop.

"Does it matter?" he asked.

"No," she said, her eyes soft. "I guess it doesn't."

"They're all here already," Ford said, looking over her shoulder. Olivia and Derrick were each reading from their scripts, while the director, a man who went only by Santos, paced erratically between the various play stations. It was kind of a weird sight.

Adra smiled at the floor, nodding her head. "Then we'd better get going," she said.

Ford grabbed her arm at the last minute.

"You don't have to take any crap from Derrick, you know," he said.

Adra gave a grim laugh. "Let him try to give me any." She took a step then looked briefly over her shoulder. "As if you'd let him."

chapter 6

Ford looked over the pages that had been thrust into his hand by the harried director and frowned. It was apparently the first BDSM scene they were shooting, but one that occurred somewhere in the middle of the movie, at least in the script he'd read. He would never understand why they filmed things out of order, but he did have a grudging respect for the ability of actors to jump in and out of their character's heads like that.

Still, for the life of him, he couldn't remember what this scene was actually about. All he saw was some light discipline. That wasn't nearly enough to go on.

"What do you want from us?" Ford asked.

"Anything you can give us," Olivia said, laughing nervously. "I have so many questions."

"Ask away," Adra said.

"I just…I don't understand what's going through her head, here, you know?" Olivia said.

"Like, I get the motivation—she's just defied one of his orders, but it's because she realizes that she's actually in love with him, even though it's supposed to be 'no strings attached,'" Olivia said, rolling her eyes slightly at the phrase 'no strings attached.' "And so she has to like...pull away, or rebel or something. And he's not having it."

"You seem to get it pretty well," Derrick said from where he was lounging on a couch. Ford wondered if his smile was leering, and then decided to let it go. For now.

Besides, Olivia did seem to have a pretty good grasp on the material.

"Yeah, I get the emotional aspect," Olivia said, picking at some non-existent lint on her jeans. "I just don't know what she's supposed to be actually feeling, physically and mentally, as this is going on. As a submissive. Or how it relates, I guess. Like, I have no idea, even the gestures... I don't know."

Santos, who had been on the phone, whispering frantically, finally looked over.

"You can help with this?" he demanded, looking at Adra and Ford.

Adra looked up from the script. "Yeah," she said quietly. "I can definitely help with this."

Ford did not like how that got Derrick's attention.

"Good," Santos said. "You coach, I'll be back in ten. This fucking shitshow outside has thrown everything off."

And with that, the director actually walked off.

Ford frowned. This entire production was a disorganized mess, from the lax security to the lack of planning and preparation for the actors. Ford and Adra had no experience with coaching a scene, Olivia had no idea what she was doing, and Derrick was focused on Adra. The disorganization showed.

Olivia looked at Adra, her expression shy.

"Can you show me?" she asked. "I don't even know where to begin."

"Um, yeah," Adra said. She smiled nervously. "I guess I'm not sure what I'm doing either? I've never acted or anything, so…"

And Derrick made his move.

"Let's show her," Derrick said, getting up off his couch. Looking directly at Adra. "Let's do the scene together."

That was it.

"Sit *down*," Ford ordered.

Derrick sat, slightly stunned. Everyone else froze.

Ford had read the scene. He knew the words—what few there were. But more than that, he *knew* the scene, in his bones. Now that Olivia had given an emotional context it made sense. He knew what it was, what to do. He was a Dom. And he was damned if he was going to let Derrick use Adra to demonstrate anything.

He pinned Adra with his eyes and said, "Pay attention, Olivia."

Then he walked over to Adra, threaded his hand through her hair, pulled her head back, and started the scene.

"You knew the rules, and you broke them," Ford said, his eyes taking in all of Adra—her big brown eyes, her parted lips, her delicate neck. Her undeniable reaction to him. "Now there are consequences."

~ * ~ * ~

Adra's mind went blank.

For an eternal second, her mind actually went blank.

There was just Ford's hand in her hair, his lips so close to hers, his body controlling her own…

And then she remembered. The scene. This was the scene. He was speaking lines.

She barely remembered to breathe.

"This," Ford said, tightening his grip on Adra's hair, "shocks her into a submissive mindset. It bypasses thought and goes directly for the body. You see her eyes, the pupils dilated? Her lips parted, her breathing shallow and fast?"

He was speaking to Olivia. But his eyes never left Adra's.

"Yes," she heard Olivia say.

"This is where he would kiss her," Ford said.

He pulled Adra's head back just a little more.

"Softly, at first, but thoroughly," he said, his eyes on Adra's lips. "Then harder. Firmer. Establishing dominance."

Adra licked her lips and felt her breath hitch. His mouth was so close, hovering over hers while he described what he could do to her. What she was feeling. How it would work.

And damn him, he was right.

"This is where she would begin to yield," he said. "Where she'd begin to feel powerless."

He was *right*. The warm, wet feeling started to spread from her core, her skin dancing with a million little tingles. She was enthralled.

"Adra, tell them what you feel," Ford said.

It was an order.

"Warm," she said, before she could stop herself. "Warmth. Light. I need—"

"She's starting to lose words," Ford said softly. "This is the first reason he reminds her of the safeword."

He leaned his head down, his mouth by Adra's ear.

"Tell me the safeword, Adra," he said.

"Red," she whispered. "It's red."

"What's the second reason?" Olivia said. Adra could barely hear her.

"To make sure she knows she's making the choice," Ford said. "That she's choosing to submit. That his dominance is so complete that she doesn't even have control over her own desires."

There was a pause.

"Oh," Olivia said quietly.

"That's when he leads her over to the bench," Ford said, walking Adra the short distance to one of Volare's own spanking benches.

When he let her go, she missed him. Felt adrift. Staring at the bench, thinking about what it meant. About who was behind her.

About how he had taken control of this situation without consulting her, without asking. About how she had no idea what this meant, if it meant anything at all. And about how she wanted it to go on so much that she didn't even care.

She had her safeword, after all.

"He would make her look at the bench," Ford went on. "He'd make sure she knew what it meant, what it was for. This is when she's confronted with that choice — submit, or safeword out."

Adra felt Ford's hand on her shoulder, pushing her one step forward, just in front of the bench. She couldn't do this. If she did this, she'd be betraying their friendship. They both would. But Adra would fall so much harder. If she did this, she didn't know if she could stop. She didn't know if she could come back from it. She didn't know if she'd want to.

"Her mind would be in conflict," Ford said behind her. "The tension between every social convention, every emotional defense mechanism, telling her not to do this, to run away from what she feels, versus the overwhelming urge to obey. To let go, give in, and be free."

Adra closed her eyes. How far would he take this?

"And then he would give the order," Ford said.

His hand pushed on her shoulder.

"Bend over," he commanded.

Adra obeyed.

She did it reflexively, automatically. She bent at the waist, her ass up in the air, her hands reaching out for the handles, fingers spread wide as she savored the way it felt to wrap her hands around the contoured rubber. She turned her head, resting her cheek on the bench. And she gave in.

"She surrenders," Ford said.

His voice beat with a rhythm she could feel between her legs. Her body hummed with the timbre of his voice.

"Her entire body is like a primed instrument," Ford said, his hand moving to her hip. "She can feel everything. She can feel me breathe. She is pulled tight, waiting for it. The slightest touch, the slightest impact…"

Would he do it?

Jesus, would he do it?

She'd let him.

"Do you know anything about impact play?" Ford said.

Olivia didn't answer him.

No one answered him.

Adra waited.

And then she heard the door and Santos's hurried steps, and the spell was broken. Ford's hand slid off her hip, and his other hand came up under her arm, lifting her up gently, his fingers soft. His voice murmuring something in her ear, something calm. Something caring.

Santos pulling at his hair, yelling. Derrick staring angrily, Olivia just staring.

"What's going on?" Adra finally asked.

"I need you two downstairs to shoot scene 3A right fucking now," Santos was shouting. "Now, now, now! We can't secure the grounds, so we have to set up inside, and we can't lose a damn day to this leak!"

Adra watched this renowned creative genius pull at his hair while Derrick and Olivia scrambled to get ready for a different scene, and couldn't feel anything but detached. It was like everybody else was shouting underwater. The only person she was aware of was Ford.

Ford, standing next to her, watching her.

They stood like that until they were alone, watching each other. Adra could feel her mind begin to churn, begin to wake up, to scream at her about what the hell had just happened. What about him? Did he feel that? Did he have that uncertainty, that doubt, fringed by this dark desire that threatened to overrun everything? Or was he just calm, and collected, and so goddamn Dom-y it was infuriating. Unperturbed, unbothered. Certain.

He knew what he was. He knew what she was. He knew what he'd just done.

"Goddammit, Ford," Adra whispered.

"Talk to me," he said.

She shook her head. Now that reality was rushing in felt like she was drowning. You can't talk about drowning until you're safe. Until you're on dry land.

"I need time," she said. "Go deal with the security issue. Go make it safe here."

Ford frowned, his eyes sad, but he didn't move. "Adra," he said.

"Please," she said. "Please, Ford? This isn't my first time."

Ford smiled a kind of haunted smile.

"No, it isn't."

"I know what I need," Adra said. "I need you to go make the club safe. I need…"

"You'll need to talk to me," Ford said. "Eventually. But I'll deal with this now. I'll do you anything you want."

He had walked half way to the door before he turned around.

"You know that, right?" he said.

"You'll do anything I want," Adra said.

Ford grinned. "Within the rules."
And then he was gone.

chapter 7

Adra spent the rest of the morning into the afternoon by herself. She didn't know if she truly wasn't needed on set or if Ford had told everybody to leave her alone, but she was grateful for the respite either way. She needed it.

After Ford and that scene, she *really* needed it. A lifetime might not be long enough to calm down from that. Adra was grateful for whatever she could get.

Besides, the Volare gardens were somehow peaceful, even if all hell was breaking loose outside. The police still hadn't managed to get the crowds totally under control, the photographers kept trying to climb trees or whatever else they could find, and that stupid stoplight still wasn't working, adding traffic to all the confusion.

Too bad Adra felt anything but peaceful.

He had absolutely *wrecked* her. She spent the first hour at least just dipping her toes in the koi pond, playing chicken with those huge, hungry fish, waiting for her heart rate to go down. Part of her was angry with him, though she knew he wasn't at fault—he'd checked the safeword; she'd consented. She wasn't angry with him for what he'd done; she was angry with him for what he'd revealed.

What he'd revealed about her.

About them.

She wasn't going to be able to run from this. From what she felt. The physical need she felt for Ford Colson was so strong it had become a deafening chorus, drowning out all other rational thoughts, making it impossible to tell what she actual wanted, thought, felt. It all got subsumed to this *want*. It reduced her to nothing more than a physical need she knew she couldn't meet.

Oh God, if she let it go... if she let herself want him... *need* him...

That would be the end. She was so, so scared that that would be the end of her. It felt like letting herself fall into the gravitational pull into the sun: inevitable, and ending in fiery death. Everyone would get burned.

Hours of lying out in the sun, breathing, meditating, stretching—nothing worked. She was a goddamn mess no matter what she did. So she was more than just relieved when her brother Charlie finally called her back. She was grateful.

"You're a jerk, Charlie, but I am so glad to hear from you," she said.

"Well, I love you, too," he said.

Adra sighed, and dipped her toe back in the koi pond. There was one fish that seemed really, really hungry for some toe, and she just could not leave well enough alone.

"Charlie, what are you doing?" she asked.

He was silent until he sighed.

"I don't know, exactly."

"I don't need to tell you what it does to Nicole."

"No."

"So what… Charlie, just why?"

"I wasn't actually gone that long, you know. I was just out late. I came back right after she talked to you."

"Yeah, I know, she texted me," Adra said, getting annoyed. "And you know that's not the goddamn point."

"I just needed some time to think, Adra," Charlie said. "I know how shitty that sounds, but you don't know what it's like. I get so overwhelmed, with the kids and everything, and I just need like…I need to get it out of my system. Like a safety valve, you know?"

Adra could feel herself starting to freak out, could feel the tears welling up inside her, and willed it away. That was her own reaction, not Charlie's, and she wasn't going to put it on him.

She would, however, tell him the truth.

"You sound like Dad, Charlie."

"I'm not like Dad," he said vehemently. "I'm sober, Adra. And I come home. I've always come home. You know, you have no idea what it's like, having a family that depends on you for everything. You have *no* idea."

"No, I don't," she admitted.

"Everyone needs a safety valve," Charlie went on. "It's not just me. I'm just... I just suck at it, that's all."

Adra thought about her own situation, and how wonderful it would be to have a freaking safety valve. And then she laughed. "You really, really do suck at it, big brother."

"I know."

"I mean, disappearing like that?"

"I know."

"Is this sustainable, Charlie?" Adra asked softly. She didn't really want to hear the answer. She already knew the answer. Of course it wasn't sustainable; the only question was how it would end, and whether Charlie could find a way to make it work before he flamed out.

They both knew how it had ended for their father.

"I don't just mean for Nicole, Charlie. I mean for the boys, you know? They know something's up. You know what it does to them."

"I don't know what to do," he said finally.

"You know I'll help however I can," Adra said. "I can pay for a nanny, or—"

"I'm not taking any more money from my little sister," Charlie said.

Adra cursed.

"Of all the stupid, macho—"

"That's not it, Adra. It's just..." Charlie sounded tired, all of a sudden. Very tired. "That's not sustainable, either. You can't fix my problems."

Adra felt little tears pricking at her eyes. She hated it whenever anyone said that, because there was nothing she could say back. No matter how hard she worked, no matter how much of herself she gave, it remained true: she couldn't fix their problems. It always put another crack in her heart.

"So what are you going to do?" she said softly.

She knew she didn't quite hide the sound of those tears fighting to come to the surface, and she cursed again, this time silently, knowing it would kill Charlie.

"I don't know, Adra," Charlie said. "But I promise you I'm going to figure it out. Ok? I promise you."

"Just find a safety valve, will you?" Adra said.

"I will," Charlie said. "I have to. Don't stress, ok? Please?"

"Ok," Adra lied.

"Maybe find your own safety valve in the meantime," Charlie said, only half-joking. "Love you."

Adra laughed it off.

But when she got off the phone, she was somehow even more of a mess than she had been before. Charlie turning into their father, or some milder incarnation of him, running away from his family over and over again, was one of Adra's worst nightmares. She knew that wasn't fair, and she knew it was kind of screwed up, how invested she was in Charlie's family, but, well, it was all she had. Charlie had managed to make a go of it, even after their disastrous childhood, watching both parents blow in and out of their lives. Adra hadn't even made it that far. And she couldn't. She knew she couldn't. She'd learned that the hard way.

But she so badly wanted Charlie to make it.

And yet it was something else he said that kept rattling around inside her brain while she sat back down by the koi pond. Something else that wouldn't let her go.

Find your own safety valve.

Yeah, that would be freaking fantastic. A safety valve. That was exactly what she needed, before she did something irreversibly stupid.

Well, it was possible she already had done something stupid.

Adra leaned back in the sun and took her jacket off. Thinking about Ford made her feel too feverish, too restless.

And powerless. Absolutely powerless to prevent the worst from happening.

And maybe that was because she was fighting it.

Adra sat bolt upright. She almost laughed out loud. She'd run from Ford after the one night they had because she didn't think she could handle a physical relationship with him without falling hopelessly in love, and then it had turned out *he'd* wanted more anyway, and so she'd had to stay away. But things were different now, now that they'd talked about it. Now that they both knew the score.

Weren't they?

At least for Ford?

And for Adra…who the hell knew. But maybe if they gave in, if they had rules, maybe it would all be manageable. Maybe it would make sense. Maybe she wouldn't feel constantly on the edge of delirium, one touch, one thought away from losing herself in this need for someone else.

That gnawing terror crept in to her thoughts then, that sense that needing someone would be the worst possible thing she could do, and that she might not be able to prevent it from happening. Which turned out to be a good thing, because Adra did what she always did when she felt frightened: she held her head high.

And saw a goddamned photographer.

The man was in the bushes. The actual, real life, bushes. Pointing a camera at her while she lay out half clothed in the sun.

For a second, they stared at each other.

And then Adra shouted, "Are you fucking *kidding* me?"

She surprised herself with her reflexes. She'd always been kind of quick when she was pissed off, and the idea that this scumbag had just been taking photos of her while she contemplated the most intimate, important facts of her life enraged the hell out of her. Which must have surprised the photographer, because she actually blocked his exit out.

"Where the hell do you think you're going?" Adra demanded. "Give me that camera!"

"What? No!" he shouted back as Adra grabbed at it. It was huge, an easy target.

"Give me the freaking camera!"

Adra might have had the element of surprise and general shock, considering the photographer probably never expected to be tackled by a female featherweight, but that didn't last. There was a definite moment, when they were both struggling for the camera, when it became obvious that no, this was a fully grown man, and this was not a fair fight.

"This is private property, you bitch!" the photographer screamed and yanked at the equipment with his full strength, sending Adra sprawling backwards.

And right into Ford.

She didn't need to turn around to know who it was. She recognized the feel of him. The size of him. The planes and angles of his muscled torso, the strength of his arms, the roughness of his callused fingers.

He'd caught her, the way he had before, and this time she couldn't fight it.

She forgot about the photographer.

She forgot about her brother.

And she forgot about the looming dread she felt whenever she thought about letting herself give in to it.

She looked up at him, dazed and dizzy, as he spun her around. She felt her fingers on his chest, and couldn't help but press into his hard flesh, couldn't help but feel the warmth start to spread, the beat start to throb between her legs, and she thought, *Oh God, this is happening.*

"Are you ok?" he asked.

"Yeah," she said. "Yes. I just…"

She shook her head.

"He was taking pictures. From the bushes. We got into an argument about it."

Adra looked over at the photographer who was busily checking his camera for damage, muttering to himself.

When she looked back, Ford was still looking at her with an intensity that left her breathless.

"But you're ok?" he asked again.

"Yeah, I'm fine," she said.

"Excuse me," Ford said.

He stepped around Adra and walked toward the photographer.

Adra couldn't see Ford's face, but she recognized that body language. He'd looked like that when he'd confronted Derrick for being rude on the very first day, only this time he looked much, much more dangerous. He looked like the Terminator, walking toward his target with that inexorable sense of destruction.

Whatever the photographer saw on Ford's face, it scared the crap out of him.

"You called her a bitch," Ford said. "And you took pictures of her without her consent. Is that correct?"

"I'm just doing my job, man," the photographer said. He raised the camera again, like it was a means of self-defense. "Maybe she shouldn't be out where anybody can—"

Ford knocked the camera out the man's hands, sending it flying into the koi pond.

"*This* is private property," Ford said. "You are trespassing. And the only reason I'm not grinding you into the dirt is because she wouldn't like it. Adra, do you want me to hold him for the police?"

Adra knew she shouldn't be smiling. She really shouldn't. But that scumbag had made her feel somewhat violated, and now it felt like she had the world's biggest, baddest pit bull on a leash.

Sometimes you just had to take a win where you found it.

"No, thank you," she said. "The camera was enough. Now I just want him gone."

"Are you going to let me throw you over the wall," Ford asked the photographer. "Or are you going to climb?"

He climbed.

And then, suddenly, they were alone.

And as soon as that photographer had cleared the wall, Ford was back at Adra's side, in front of her, running his hands down her arms, her cheek, her neck, as though he were checking for cracks in fine china, his eyes burning and his body seemingly oblivious to the effect he was having on her. She was dizzy, drunk with it all over again, her mouth refusing to form words lest they get him to stop what he was doing.

"You're ok?"

She nodded.

"I am so sorry, Adra," he said, his voice rough. "That was completely unacceptable. That will never, never happen again, I promise you. Look at me," he said.

He tilted her chin up toward his, and his blue eyes locked on hers.

"I promise you," he said.

"It wasn't your fault," she said, legitimately confused.

"I said I'd keep these people out," Ford said. "And I said I'd make sure you had time after this morning."

This morning.

Adra shuddered. Just the mention of it, and the sensations poured over her again. The memory of the complete control he had over her *mind*...she'd had no idea he was such a good Dom.

No, she had. She just hadn't let herself think about too much. No point in driving yourself crazy with what you can't have.

Except now it was all she could think about.

"You gave me time," she said quietly. "Plenty of time."

"Do you need more?"

Adra swallowed. His hands were still on her shoulders, his thumbs resting on her collarbone.

"No," she said. "No, I'm ok. It was...it was ok, Ford."

Adra studied his face, looking for a sign, any sign at all, about what he was thinking. He hadn't needed time to collect himself, to recover, to process. Had it really not affected him the way it had affected her? Oh God, what if it hadn't? What if it was just routine for him, just a scene, not something that grabbed him from the inside and wouldn't let go?

"Adra, are you all right?" he asked.

"I'm fine," she said, and forced herself to look away. "I'm totally fine."

She stepped away, and Ford released her. The sudden absence of his hands felt cold.

"Santos wanted to know if you were available to coach the second scene this afternoon," Ford said. "I offered to do it alone, but he thinks he needs a sub's perspective."

Adra licked her lips. Her mouth was dry. Could she do it again? With Ford? It was like entering the

Thunderdome or something. She was still wrecked from this morning.

"I can tell them no," Ford said. "I can tell them to fuck off, right now, if you want me to. I'll get them all out of here."

Adra smiled. That was insane.

"No," she said. "I said I was fine. Let's go do our jobs."

"Our stupid, stupid jobs," Ford said. "Remember when you were only an agent?"

"And you were only a lawyer?"

"We had no idea how good we had it."

No, Adra thought. *No, we didn't.*

"Any idea what Santos wants from me?" Adra asked.

Ford held open the door to Volare, his face darkening slightly.

"I can't wait to find out," he said.

chapter 8

As he walked Adra back inside, Ford kept thinking about this old television show he used to watch as a kid. It was the first version of the Hulk that he'd ever seen, the mild mannered doctor who, when provoked, would turn into this crazy green giant and violently save the day. Only Ford's inner hulk was his dominant nature. And he felt like he was on the verge of Dom-ing out every time he touched Adra's skin. Every time he saw her brush the hair out of her face. Every time he saw an emotion, any emotion, pass across her beautiful face, and that was all the damn time, because he didn't know anyone who felt as much as Adra.

He was doing everything he could to rein in his inner Dom until he was sure. And she was making it damn hard.

And more than that—definitely more than that—he wanted to protect her. *Needed* to protect her. He couldn't believe he'd allowed a goddamn photographer to get that close to her, but he knew his anger over that had as much to do with what had happened between them this morning as it did anything else.

After all, the damn photographer hadn't messed with her head by spontaneously dominating her. Ford had.

That morning, with the scene, there had just been...something. Some moment. One of those crystalline moments when it was suddenly clear what was what, what needed to be done, and who needed to do it. One of those few moments that happened in a lifetime, and Ford had seized it. And it led him to the inescapable conclusion that Adra was the perfect sub for him.

No. Not just perfect for him. Adra *was* his sub. He was her Dom. They both knew it. And there was no escaping it.

There was only dealing with it.

He didn't understand what had made her run away from him after they slept together, but now he was damn sure going to do his best to try. One thing he was sure of: it was more complicated than 'she played games.' He'd been an idiot on that front. He'd been a selfish, proud idiot. He should have given her more credit. And whatever was going on with Adra, whatever she hid away from everyone, whatever led her to believe that they couldn't be together, it wasn't just hers anymore.

It was theirs, together.

He'd walk away if that was what she needed. He would always, always do whatever she needed. And if whatever was going on with her meant that they couldn't be together, well, then that's what it meant. But he was damn sure going to find out why.

"Ford?"

Her voice shook him out of his thoughts. His whole world had narrowed to where Adra was, and now, all of a sudden, he was in the middle of a freaking film set.

It was insanity.

There were stand-ins being positioned about while tech guys shown lights at them, figuring out how to light the shot, there were sound guys yelling at the lighting guys, there were production assistants running around everywhere, and Santos, in the middle of it, was sitting in his director's chair looking morose. And staring at Adra.

To be fair, so were Olivia and Derrick. And those two had had a rough day already.

"We have had to change the shooting schedule again," Santos said.

Jesus. This production was just one clown parade after another.

"So what do you need our help with?" Ford asked, keeping his eye on Adra. She still looked a little shaky.

Without thinking, he put his hand on the small of her back.

Shocks.

Immediate shocks, shooting up his arm, through his body, making his cock come alive. He saw Adra's body go rigid, knew it had hit her just as hard. He removed his hand like he'd been burned.

Fuck.

"We need to do the *shibari* scene," Santos said. He looked at Adra. "She will help."

For a long second, Adra didn't say anything.

"I can certainly tell you about rope bondage," Adra began, "but I don't know if—"

"No, you'll do it first, to show her," Santos said, pointing at Olivia. "We have only one shot."

Ford knew there were important things going on, but he was fucking mesmerized. He put his hand full flat on her back, let it slide down over to her hip. Watched her breathing change. Watched her back straighten.

Knew exactly what she was feeling.

Knew exactly what she would say.

"No," she said to Santos.

Santos opened his mouth, but Ford cut him off.

"She said no," Ford said.

She was his, and nothing else mattered.

"Um, I can do it myself without Adra," Olivia said into the silence. "I mean, I think I would like to know what it's like, if there's someone who can show me. I can practice, and that...I think that will be fine."

Under different circumstances, Ford would be noting all the details of Olivia's emerging interest in submission, of her curiosity and openness. He'd be thinking of the appropriate Dom to set her up with, of the right way to introduce her to the club, the lifestyle. But there wasn't much room for anything or anyone besides Adra at the moment.

As it was, he had to tear himself away to make sure someone was looking out for Olivia.

"You'll do it with expert supervision," he said shortly. "I will send two masters down, one male, one female. Your choice, but you will be monitored, and they may safeword you out. They will answer any questions you might have. You will be taken care of. Is that something you can do, Olivia?"

"Yes," the actress said.

"Good," Ford said. He hadn't moved his hand from Adra's hip. The contact made the thing between them seem alive. "We have some club business to attend to. You'll deal with Master Roman and Mistress Lola for the rest of the day, and we will see you tomorrow."

"But—"

"Non-negotiable," Ford said, waving a trainee over who'd heard everything. Then he bent his head toward Adra. He let his eyes rove over the delicate line of her jaw, the soft curve of her earlobe, the smoothness of her skin.

"Adra," he said. "Upstairs. Now."

She turned toward him then, gently, gracefully. She looked up, let her brown eyes meet his. And then she smiled.

He followed her up the stairs.

Holy fuck did he want her in an animal way.

He had to mentally scramble to keep up with his body, to assemble his thoughts before everything else took over. This was too damn important. He had to do this right.

"My office," he said.

She paused, briefly. It was a meaningful choice. It meant she'd think about it every time she went into that office. It meant that this wasn't just a one off game, wasn't something to do once in secret and then forget about.

Adra paused. And then she walked into his office, and waited for him.

Jesus, just that act—standing in front of his desk, eyes ahead, waiting.

Fuck.

Ford followed her in, closed the door, and took his seat. Then he took a moment to admire the view.

Adra was the most beautiful woman he'd ever seen. That he would ever see. Not one of her features was perfect, but she was. The way she almost lifted a hand to brush the tendril of hair that had fallen in her face, then thought better of it. The way she let every emotion, every thought, play across her face as though she were unafraid of the world, and yet still kept so much of herself hidden. The way she licked her lips when she was nervous. The way he could tell she was thinking of the last time they'd been in a situation like this, and because of that, she was afraid—for him.

That last thing just about killed him.

"Adra," he said. "Do you believe that I know you?"

She looked at him, cocking her head like it was a silly question.

"Yes," she said.

"So you know I can tell you're worrying right now," Ford said. "About our friendship. Possibly about me."

She licked her lips.

"Yes," she said.

"Don't," Ford said. "From now on, you never worry about that again, because there is nothing to worry about. Nothing can change it. Nothing can damage it. I am not going anywhere. I will not encroach upon the limits you've already set. Is that understood?"

She blinked back tears.

"Yes," she said.

"What are you not going to do?"

"Worry about you or our friendship," she said.

"That's an order, Adra," he said.

He watched her chest rise and fall a little faster. Goddamn if he didn't just want to rip that shirt off. He took a deep breath himself.

"That's going to be hard for you," Ford said, "because it means you'll have nothing to worry about but yourself."

Her intake of breath was sudden, sharp.

"But I'm going to take care of that, too," Ford went on. "Do you know why?"

She didn't say anything. She had started pulling at the material of her skirt with her fingers, her nervous, nervous fingers.

"I know what you are, Adra," Ford said. "And you know what I am."

"Yes," she whispered.

Ford studied her. He would commit this to memory. This sight, this moment. He needed her, and he knew she needed him, probably more than she knew. But she had been the one to walk away, and she had drawn the boundaries of their relationship, for reasons he still didn't understand. She needed to be the one to admit that things had changed. She needed to consent to the fucking whirlwind that was about to engulf them both.

"You have to ask me," Ford said, leaning back in his chair.

Adra closed her eyes.

"That's an order, Adra," Ford said. "You have to ask me. Politely."

He added that last bit just for fun.

A slight smile played across Adra's lips, and then she opened her eyes, and held him with her gaze.

And said, "Please fuck me, sir."

Ford almost lost his mind.

He had meant that she ask him to be her Dom. She knew that. He was *positive* she knew that. And with four words, she'd short-circuited his brain.

"More," he said hoarsely.

Adra took a deep breath, and shuddered.

"Please be my Dom, sir."

"With no reservations, obligations, or implications, save exclusivity," Ford said. "I don't share. Otherwise this is no strings, just as you said. No romantic obligations. Except, Adra, that you *are* my sub."

He rose slowly from his desk chair, keeping his eyes on her beautiful face, his whole body telling him to take her right then and there.

"And you always have been," he said.

Adra swayed slightly where she stood, her eyes never leaving Ford's.

"Then show me," she said. "Sir."

chapter 9

Adra's skin grew hot as Ford approached. Slow. He was so slow. So deliberate. His eyes pinning her where she stood, the weight of him somehow overbearing even from a distance, making it difficult to breathe.

She felt like she was buzzing around the edges, like on the surface she was over-stimulated and on the verge of shorting out, but the core of her was…calm.

No, not calm. Just certain. It was like the whole world had shifted slightly and everything had clicked into place.

He'd made her admit it. He'd made her beg. And everything had fallen into place.

How was it possible? They hadn't played together. How could he know how to dominate her most effectively? How could he know what she was like as a sub?

But, oh God, somehow he did. Just the way he was looking at her...

Like she was entirely his.

She shivered.

He saw. He smiled. Then he reached up and tore open her blouse.

Adra gasped as she heard the buttons skitter across the floor. The air felt cool on the tops of her breasts and she knew without looking that her nipples were already hard. Ford held her eyes and slipped his hand into her open shirt, his hand big and warm and kind of rough, smoothing his thumb along her ribs, taking his damn time.

Making her crazy.

Unhurried, he moved his hand over her breast, and Adra's breath hitched. Ford smiled slightly. Then he squeezed, hard.

Adra's knees buckled.

Ford caught her, held her up. Popped her breasts out of the top of her bra just so he could play with her nipples, all the while watching her, that calm expression of cool superiority on his face.

It suddenly dawned her what she was in for, and she was instantly wet. Well, wetter.

Oh holy shit.

Ford stripped off her shirt, unhooked her bra, left her bare above the waist, and pinched her nipples until she stifled a moan.

The corner of his mouth quirked up.

"Go bend over the desk," he said. "Arms flat, cheek down."

Adra did her best to keep herself steady. Four-inch heels were normally second nature for her, but now her ankles wobbled all over the place. Still, she kept her head high.

He'd make her bow it soon. That was part of the fun.

Slowly she bent over at the waist, lowering her torso onto the polished wood. It was cold, and a small thrill raced through her as her naked breasts pressed into the coolness. It was also the perfect height—in her heels, she was bent just past a ninety-degree angle, her head a bit lower than her waist so that her ass was angled up for him.

He must have known.

And he must have known that morning, when he just...dominated her, re-enacting that scene. Must know now that she'd think about that. About what it had felt like, about what she'd been thinking, about what she'd wanted...

The rush of embarrassment was totally unexpected. Adra felt her cheeks grow warm and her fingers dig into the unyielding wooden desk at the memory of that morning's scene coaching. Ford had so quickly and effortlessly turned her into a pile of jelly, it was almost obscene. Had everyone else known? Had it been completely obvious that she'd been in his thrall, halfway to subspace, willing and eager to do whatever he wanted?

Had they all watched and *known*?

Adra felt Ford's hand on her leg, her thigh, pushing her skirt up over her ass. She tried to regulate her breathing while he pushed the material up to her waist, but it was no use. She couldn't stop thinking about how he'd had her like this before, how he'd dominated her so thoroughly that he'd controlled her very *desires*...

Then he ran two fingers the length of her sex, teasing her outside of her underwear, and she moaned.

"You were wet this morning," Ford said behind her.

Adra closed her eyes.

"Yes," she said.

"Just like you are now," he said.

"Yes," she said.

"You wanted me to spank you," he said. "Right then and there."

"Yes," she panted.

His hand cupped her sex from behind, the touch making her arc upwards toward his hand, breasts pressed further into the desk, balanced on her toes in freaking four-inch heels, just wanting him to…

She moaned again. Ford chuckled.

"Tell me why," he said.

"Oh fuck," she said. She couldn't keep her ass from wiggling, trying to get anything from him, having trouble thinking of anything other than the need to have him inside her right that fucking second.

"Tell me why, Adra, or I won't let you come," he said, squeezing her briefly, making her groan, and then releasing the pressure. God, she just wanted more pressure, and he already knew the damn answer.

"Adra," he said, his voice a warning.

He took his hand away and pulled her panties down to her thighs.

"You know why!" she said.

Ford laughed, and then came the *smack* of his open palm on her left cheek, the sting blossoming into pleasure almost immediately.

"You know that's not good enough," he said.

She managed a groan.

Smack. This time the right cheek, hard enough to jostle her into the desk, to make her flesh shake. She knew she wasn't going to be coherent enough to answer for very long.

"Because," she said, "I wanted…"

Smack.

"What I couldn't…"

Smack.

"Have."

"Almost right," Ford said, smoothing his hand over her now tender flesh. All she could think about was how she was bare, exposed, so close, and he still wasn't inside her. Her pussy ached.

Damn Dom.

And then she heard the unmistakable sound of a buckle. He was taking off his belt.

"Oh God," she murmured.

"Hands," he said.

It took her a second. Already her brain wasn't working so well. But then he took her wrists and brought them behind her back and she understood—he was binding her with his belt. He was binding her wrists to the skirt he'd hiked up to her waist, looping the belt through the bunched up material.

He knew what bondage did to her.

Just the knowledge that, being bound, she couldn't do anything, couldn't move, couldn't resist—that alone could nearly send her over the edge. She felt a low, constant moan rise in her throat, almost a wail, and tried to hide it.

Then her underwear fell around her ankles, and he told her to step out of them, his hands on her hips for balance while she did so.

Oh God, she was about to lose her mind.

"Spread," he ordered, his foot pushing between her own. "A warning, Adra. Do *not* come until I tell you to or I will redden that perfect ass—do you understand?"

Adra closed her eyes and smiled into the desk. That did *not* make it easier for her to resist an orgasm. Just as he knew it wouldn't.

"Yes, sir," she breathed.

There was a beat. She almost had herself under control. Years of subbing hadn't been for nothing.

And then he spanked her bare pussy.

She yelped.

Strained against the belt at her wrists.

Tried to remember desperately: Do *not* come.

Do *not*.

"Now tell me why," he said.

Adra knew perfectly well what he wanted her to admit, knew he'd given her the answer already, knew that he'd done it on purpose. Worse, she knew that it was true. She had been fighting it for so, so long, and this, right here, right in this moment, was the last vestige of that resistance, and for the life of her she couldn't find a reason to hold on. She'd been so afraid that if she gave in it would mean everything, but he'd just told her it wouldn't, it didn't have to. And he'd let her get away with fighting the inevitable for so long, but now he wasn't having it anymore.

He spanked her again, this time dipping a finger into her, making her cry out.

"Adra," he barked. "Tell me."

"Because I'm yours," she panted.

He thrust another finger into her.

"You're my what?"

He pulled out, and she groaned.

"I'm your sub, sir," she said.

He grabbed her again, this time with enough force to lift her on to her toes, spreading her legs further on the way down. His big hands rested on either side of her ass, his thumbs brushing close to her sex.

"And?" he said.

When Adra spoke, she could barely hear herself.

"And I always have been," she said.

And then she felt his thumbs part her and his cock enter her in one sure stroke, his girth stretching her almost to he point of pain, her eyes and mouth flying open in surprise until he was fully seated inside her. Her body adjusted around him and her eyes lost focus, her pulse starting a heavy beat in her core, her every nerve begging him to *move*.

"Don't come, Adra," he warned as he pulled out of her slowly, the head of his cock dragging along her g-spot. "Don't you fucking come."

"Fuck," she groaned, trying to dig her fingers into the hard, polished wood. Nothing would give, not the desk, not Ford.

She heard him chuckle again.

And then he grabbed hold of the belt binding her wrists to the skirt around her waist and pulled her back as he thrust forward, impaling her to the hilt. She screamed, felt her legs shake, her back arch. He kept ahold of her as he drove into her again and again, riding her, bringing her so close, too close, too close for her to…

"You can come now," he growled. "Once."

She did immediately.

She came so violently that her legs spasmed and he caught her by the hips, not stopping at all, still fucking her until her body stopped convulsing and she stopped crying out his name. And then only stopping long enough to pull out, pull her up, turn her around, and push her back on the desk, her arms behind her supporting her back and butt, propping her up to him.

She looked at him wildly, not entirely able to focus, and saw that animal look on his face, that feral ferocity as he lifted her legs where he wanted them.

"I want to see your face while I fuck you," he growled and plunged into her again, sending her head back in a silent scream.

She couldn't move, couldn't speak, couldn't do anything but take him. He owned her so completely, so thoroughly, it was like her body didn't even belong to her anymore. It only responded to his commands, coming whenever he demanded, until she lost track, lost all sense of time and place, any sense of impossibility. She hadn't really believed her body could actually *do* that. Having that many orgasms was like some kind of athletic feat; she might have been in training her whole life, but she never expected to get to the freaking Olympics.

By the time Ford was done she was a complete mess. She couldn't speak properly, couldn't stand, couldn't do much of anything. It was Ford who wiped her down, Ford who carefully unbound her wrists, gently massaging the skin as he did so, Ford who took off the rest of her wrecked clothing—just a skirt and heels at this point—and then carried her, naked, to the couch he had in the back of his office, a tiny little snug alcove, where he sat with Adra in his lap and covered her with a blanket.

She was enveloped in him. In warmth. She found herself wishing he was naked, too, but it didn't take away from the feeling of utter safety. Of comfort.

She came down from her subspace high onto a cloud, in his arms. She came to with his fingertips stroking her hair and the bare skin of her arms, his heartbeat in her ears, his lips leaving light kisses on her forehead.

And then, when her brain was in full working order, she got nervous.

No, not just nervous. Freaked the hell out.

Because this? This was bliss. This was tender. This was...

This was everything she couldn't want.

Adra shot out of Ford's arms, taking the blanket with her, and took several safe steps away.

Ford watched her.

"What happened?" Ford said.

"We didn't set ground rules," Adra said, wrapping the blanket around her with as much dignity as she could muster. "I think, given last time, we should set ground rules."

Ford leaned back, his long arms resting on the back of the couch. "Agreed," he said.

"So, like, this…" Adra began. She paused. Screw it—she had to say it. "I mean, this was really nice, afterwards, but I worry that it shouldn't get too nice, you know?"

"I'm not compromising on aftercare," Ford said, leaning forward. The intensity in his blue eyes was startling. "You're going to get the aftercare you need, and so am I."

"No, of course," Adra said, wishing she could tear her eyes away and look somewhere, anywhere else. "I mean, yes, that makes sense. But *after* that."

Ford smiled.

"You mean cuddling?"

"Maybe there should just be, like, a time limit?" she said.

"You're putting a time limit on cuddling," Ford said. Now he was smiling.

"Yes, I am rationing cuddling," Adra said, trying to keep from smiling too. This was serious. "There should be a cuddle quota."

Ford stood and tucked his shirt back into his slacks, his eyes dancing while Adra thought again about how well she'd just been fucked by this god of a Dom. She was surprised she could even form sentences.

"So what's a friendly amount of cuddling?" he said.

Adra tried to look stern. He was making fun of her. "Five minutes?" she said.

Ford just looked at her.

"Ten?" she said.

"Ten," he said, shaking his head. "It is well known that after ten minutes cuddles turn from friendly to sinister."

"Take this seriously!" Adra said. She wished she were wearing more than a blanket as she said it.

Ford looked her up and down, not bothering to hide his amusement. But when he got to Adra's face, his expression changed—he was serious. Solemn, even.

"I've never taken anything more seriously, Adra," he said. "If you think I'm going to risk losing you again, you've lost your damn mind."

For a moment, Adra couldn't breathe, all over again.

"But if you think I'm going to let something like the cuddle quota go by without teasing you mercilessly for it," he said, striding toward her. He paused standing over her, then smiled. "Well, then you've also lost your damn mind. Stop losing your mind, Adra. It brings up worrisome issues of consent."

When she could breathe again, Adra stuck her tongue out. That was the only possible response.

Ford raised an eyebrow. "You keep sticking that tongue out, I'll put it to work."

Something in her belly lurched, and her body came alive again as if she hadn't just been fucked into a total stupor. She actually really wouldn't mind giving her tongue a work out…

Someone walked by Ford's office, footsteps heavy on the wooden floor, and Adra flinched.

"What?" he said.

"We're in your *office*," Adra said, suddenly feeling naked despite the blanket. It was ridiculous.

She'd been naked in many places, and this was the room it felt suddenly weird in? It was Volare, for crying out loud.

But...Ford's *office*.

Ford held her steady. "And we'll stay here until it's sorted out," he said.

The implication was clear. This was real. They were both going to have to navigate it.

Somehow Ford's insistence was comforting. His hand on her arm, steadying, guiding. At least she wasn't going to be figuring this emotional quagmire out on her own. There was some solace in that.

Then he touched her face. He was looking at her with such heat and such tenderness, it was stunning.

And then she realized: They hadn't even kissed yet. Not since that night.

"Oh God, Ford," she said, her eyes searching his. "What about... I mean, I'm not making a big deal about it, and it's ok if you don't want it, I understand, because maybe it is weird? It's just...I haven't even kissed you since—"

Suddenly Ford's arm swept around her waist and pulled her in close so he could shut her up with a kiss. He kissed her hard, he kissed her thoroughly, and he kissed her well, until she was melting into him all over again, supple and willing to bend whatever way he wanted. It was a claiming kind of kiss. The kind that showed utter dominance. Even ownership.

"I won't compromise on that, either," Ford said gruffly when he was done. Adra looked up at him through half-lidded eyes and tried to nod.

"Ok," she said.

"There's a shower through there," he said. "And I'll send someone for your clothes. We have dinner in an hour."

"What?" she said, still not thinking clearly. Was he asking her out?

Ford smiled. "We have dinner plans. Roman, Lola, Olivia, Derrick. Roman set it up."

Adra stared at him, horrified. She was supposed to sit through dinner after what they'd just done? She could barely remember her own name, let alone small talk. Oh God, small talk with *her ex*. And she wouldn't be able to think about anything else; they'd all know!

Ford only laughed and grabbed hold of one end of the blanket. "You better get moving," he said. "Because the blanket is coming with me."

chapter 10

Ford barely tasted his food. He was thinking about what Adra tasted like. He couldn't believe he hadn't taken the opportunity to try her again.

He'd fix that later.

She sat across from him at this weird dinner that Roman had set up, her brown eyes big and soft, barely able to conceal what she was thinking about. She kept looking at him. It was hard not to just pick her up and take her to the nearest room.

Christ, it was like he'd been starving all this time and now he could have whatever he wanted, whenever he wanted. It was tough not to be a barbarian about it.

Hell, maybe he would be a barbarian about it.

She was still looking at him. Her lips were parted. He knew her well enough to know she was about to lick them, and he knew his cock would jump when she did.

And he was interrupted.

"I hear you let a photographer get on the grounds," Derrick said pointedly.

Ford turned his head. While Adra had spent most of the meal locking eyes with Ford, Ford had noticed that Derrick had spent most of his time watching Adra. Something that also did not escape the notice of his girlfriend, Ellen.

"A photographer made it onto the grounds, yes," Ford said. "Whoever leaked the location of the shoot made that inevitable."

"You know what? We were promised security, and this is bullshit. You can't understand what it's like. I can't go anywhere without getting mobbed," Derrick said.

He seemed kind of satisfied with that fact. Like he was complaining in order to brag. Out of the corner of his eye, Ford saw Olivia roll her eyes.

"The studio is responsible for security," Ford said. "They're actually in breach of contract right now, though they are working on it. But if you're feeling frightened, Derrick, I can accompany you on set."

Derrick's face reddened.

"I don't need you as a bodyguard," he said.

"Glad to hear it," Ford said.

Adra smiled at that. Derrick saw. And Derrick got even angrier.

Derrick Duvall was the worst kind of Dom, because he wasn't really a Dom at all. He was all about ego. That alone wasn't necessarily a problem; domination was often about ego. But with Derrick it came from a place of insecurity, of needing validation, and that made him fucking dangerous.

Ford hated the idea that a man like that had ever come anywhere near Adra.

And Derrick seemed to know it.

"Adra, how's Charlie doing?" Derrick said, looking at Ford for a reaction.

Subtle.

Still, Ford wracked his brain to remember everything he knew about Charlie. He was Adra's brother. But still not someone she had talked about enough that Ford felt the need to check in on his well-being.

Worse, Adra seemed distracted by the question. Upset, even. She was looking down at her plate, denying Ford those brown eyes.

What the hell did Derrick Duvall know about Adra's brother?

"He's fine," Adra said, staring at her food. "Doing well. Everyone's doing well."

So not fine, actually. Ford wanted to curse. There had been something wrong with her family for long enough for this jackass in a Dom costume to know about it, and Ford had not only been largely ignorant of it all, he hadn't done anything to help.

That was another thing he was going to fix.

It looked like Derrick was going to launch another attack when his long suffering girlfriend stepped in, demanding, in that friendly, dinner party kind of way, that Olivia and Derrick walk her through the drama of the day's shoot. The relief emanating from Adra was palpable. She'd been stuck interacting with the movie people while Roman and Lola, on the other side of the table, had been in their own little world.

But now she was staring at Ford again.

And for the life of him, Ford could not look away. Why would he want to? Every second he took in her beautiful face, he thought of another thing he wanted to do to her. Wondered what that pale skin would look like properly bound, wondered how red her ass could get, wondered how many times he could make her come when he took his time. Wondered how big he could make those brown eyes.

She licked her lips, and Ford gripped the side of the table.

"Ford," Roman said.

"What?" Ford asked. He was actually annoyed to have to look anywhere else but at Adra's face.

"I asked if this Olivia woman knows yet," Roman said, his voice lowered.

"That she's a sub?" Ford said. "I don't know, I didn't spend the day with her."

"She doesn't, but she's finding out," Lola said with a broad smile. "I always love watching that process. It's like my favorite thing."

Adra smiled at Ford, her eyes shining, and he thought, *Yeah, that's a pretty fun activity.*

Too late, Ford realized that Lola was watching them. That woman had an eagle eye, and he and Adra hadn't discussed whether their new arrangement should be public.

Damn.

"So what's up with you guys?" Lola asked, leaning her head on her hand. Looking devious.

"Working together is going well, I trust?" Roman added.

Adra started to blush.

"We've worked out a pretty good system," Ford said.

"No news?"

"None," Adra said quickly. "I mean, just that everything is good. The movie is challenging and everything, but Ford is really good at taking charge, so...everything is good. It's good."

"So it looks like everything is good," Lola said with a smile.

"Great, even," said Ford.

"Definitely great," Adra said.

Her voice had dropped to this throaty, velvety pitch. Ford's cock was ready to punch through steel. The tension between them was unbearable.

He'd show her great.

"Glad it's working out," Roman said, pouring himself—and Ford—another glass of wine. "Because Claudia and Jesse have applied for membership."

"Roman!" Lola said.

"It has to come up some time," Roman said, shrugging. "And it's not like Ford objects."

"Of course not," Ford said. There wasn't a bone left in his body that cared about what Claudia and Jesse chose to do. They were like strangers to him now. In fact, they'd proven themselves to be strangers to him.

Adra, on the other hand, seemed to care.

"Who?" she said.

Then it dawned on her.

"Oh, your ex-wife," she said softly.

"I'm fine with it," Ford said gently.

"They asked if we had a nursery at the club," Roman said darkly. "A *nursery*."

For the first time in years, Ford felt a pang of loss. A stabbing, icy pain piercing his chest, reminding him of what it had felt like when Claudia first told him the truth. He had not counted on the kid being around. He had not counted on having to face that particular loss all over again. Already he could feel that hardened cynicism begin to takeover, to calcify over his heart, to…

Fuck.

He didn't want to be that guy. He wanted to be able to trust people. He wanted to believe that people were worthy of trust.

"Well, if *I* can't get a nursery in this place, Ford's cheating ex-wife and former best friend aren't getting a goddamn nursery for their kid," Lola said, stabbing at the last piece of her chicken.

For a second, Lola seemed just genuinely annoyed at the idea of Claudia's presumption. Then she realized what she'd said.

"Oh God, I'm so sorry," she said.

But Ford wasn't looking at her. He was looking at Adra. Adra, who's face had fallen, who'd looked more hurt than he had at that particular revelation. Adra, whose heart was just too big to fit into the world on most days of the week.

"Ford, I have no idea what I was thinking," Lola was saying. "Hormones make me a crazy person half the time. I am so, so sorry."

Roman was smiling, knowing Ford didn't give a crap. "You can't blame everything on pregnancy, sweetheart."

"Yes I can. Shut up," Lola whispered.

"It's ancient history," Ford said. "Don't worry about it, Lola." Then he looked directly at Adra, who still looked like she might be about to cry sympathy tears. "I don't talk much about it because it's not relevant to my life anymore. That's all. That's why I'm not blackballing their membership. It's just not important."

Slowly, Adra smiled at him, a soft smile. Gentle. Then she turned to look at Roman, her face just as sweet as ever, and said in a voice like steel, "Can I blackball them if Ford is too good to do it?"

Ford stared at her.

Then he burst out laughing. He wasn't used to a woman getting protective over him, but he had to admit, it had its perks.

He'd show her those perks soon.

Sooner, rather than later.

Actually, as soon as possible.

"Well, no one is getting a nursery," Roman said. "The licensing issues alone are ridiculous." He looked at his wife. "I'll buy one down the street."

"See, Adra?" Lola said. "You can—"

"Sorry," Adra said, getting up quickly, her eyes locked on Ford's. "I'm just… I'll be back."

They all fell silent while Adra walked away, Roman and Lola clearly having no idea what was going on. Ford wasn't sure he knew what was going on either, other than that Adra was upset.

Whatever it was, he would find out.

"Excuse me," he said, getting up to follow Adra. He ignored the quizzical looks of Roman and Lola; he wasn't interested, and he certainly wasn't interested in helping them play nice with the movie people. Besides, they could handle themselves just fine.

It was Adra he was worried about.

He found her in the hallway off the main corridor leading from the Volare dining room to the main room. She was leaning against the wall, her back arched a bit, her hands clasped behind her, her head tilted back. Jesus. She looked almost like she had when he'd bound her wrists with his belt. Was that unconscious?

It was fucking beautiful.

Down, boy.

She was upset. He could tell from her expression; she looked almost pained. Her eyes were closed. She thought she was alone.

"Adra," he said.

She didn't seem surprised. Just smiled, laughed softly. "Hi, Ford," she said.

"What's going on?" he asked, joining her in her wall leaning. It reminded him of high school, leaning against rows of lockers, talking to a girl. He smiled.

"Nothin'," she said, smirking up at him. "What's going on with you?"

"Adra," he said, laughing. "Come on."

She bit her lip and looked down at her feet.

"I'm not sure," she said. "I'm just… God, that was so overwhelming."

"Dinner?"

"Dinner with you," she said. "And the rest of them. I mean, we're keeping it secret right? Not that I'm ashamed or anything. Oh God, I didn't mean…shit."

Ford tried not to smile too hard.

"It might be better if we kept it to ourselves until we were more sure of its shape," he said carefully. "If that's important to you, I have no problem with it."

"I didn't mean…"

"I know you didn't, Adra," he said, pushing off the wall and turning to face her. He planted his hands on either side of her body and looked her over. The charge between them was immediate.

"I'm just… I mean, I keep learning all these things, and my family, and…oh God, you don't even really know about Charlie, *or* my Dad," she said, her eyes getting bigger, the words tumbling out in a rush. "And I don't know anything about your ex-*wife*! I have *no* idea what's going through your head, except that I think I do, and that makes no sense at all. And isn't that already more complicated than this is supposed to be? Like, by hour three? I mean, are we doing this wrong? And the whole time, the whole time, all I can think about, all I can even…breathe…is—"

Adra stopped talking when Ford kissed her.

He took her mouth in his again, the way he had back in his office, the way he'd been wanting to all damn night. He kissed her until her body started to go slack and then pressed into his, until her hands came out and around his neck, on his chest, his back. Until he was sure she'd forgotten she was freaking out.

"You're thinking too much," he said as he pulled away. She reached for him, and he pushed her back against the wall, just hard enough to make her squirm.

She was breathing hard.

"I'll tell you whatever it is you need to know," he said, and realized, as he said it, that it was completely true. He wouldn't hide anything from her. There wasn't anything worth protecting more than her.

He held her face in his hand.

"No secrets," he said.

He slipped his hand down her neck.

"No games," he said.

His slid his hand over her breast and savored the noise she made.

"No pressure," he said.

His hand crossed her abdomen, leaving fluttering waves of contractions in its wake.

"And I can tell you right now," he said, slipping his hand beneath her second skirt of the day, between her legs, and under the fabric of her underwear where he could feel her wetness. "We're not doing this wrong."

She moaned.

Ford watched her face, watched the change in her. She'd gone from overwhelmed and vaguely panicked to the kind of calm that only a submissive seemed to achieve, and he knew that he'd been right: she needed order imposed on the chaos. So did he. This was something he could do for her.

He removed his hand, and licked her juices from his fingers. Then he leaned forward, and whispered into her ear.

"Right now you're going to go home," he said. "Immediately. You're not saying goodbye, you're not bothering with anyone else. You're getting away. You're going to run yourself a bath, and you are going to soak until you start to relax. And then you are going to touch yourself. And you're not going to come until I call and tell you to. Understood?"

Adra let out a long, soft sigh, her hands digging into his shoulders.

"Yes, sir," she said. She looked relieved. Happy. She looked perfect.

"Don't forget your phone," he told her.

chapter 11

Adra drove home in a kind of daze. In fact, she'd been doing everything in a kind of daze since it had happened.

Holy mother of God, they had really done it, hadn't they?

It was like she had moments of lucidity when she was sure that, the rest of the time—the rest of the unbelievable, blissful time—she must be hallucinating. Or drunk. Or some combination of the two.

Ford was her Dom now.

And he was perfect. He was better than perfect. She hadn't even let herself imagine him like this; she was one of those people that had to fantasize realistically, for some annoying reason, with flaws and plausible situations and the whole thing. And she'd always given Ford plenty of flaws, because maybe it felt safer to think about him that way.

She'd been wrong.

Well, so far she'd been wrong. Fingers crossed that there was something wrong with him, because otherwise…

Adra shook her head again, trying not to feel dizzy remembering how he'd "checked" her in the hallway. She was driving at the moment. Not a good time to be overcome by…

Whatever this was.

And whatever it was, it had worked. She'd been mildly freaking out, just overwhelmed by all of these things happening all at once. Now? No more freaking out. Now she was just horny as hell and wanting to get home so she could obey Ford's orders.

She grinned into the pale blue light coming off the streetlights as she sped down Santa Monica Boulevard. Maybe there were some benefits to being dominated by your best friend after all. Ford couldn't possibly know all the different things Adra had to freak out about—like, for a very stress-inducing example, that she was terrified of falling in love with him—but he had known that she was stressed. And he'd done something about it.

He was still doing something about it, in fact. Adra could barely wait to get home and take that bath. And get his phone call.

Which is why she was more than a little thrown off when she turned the corner onto her street and was confronted with a throng of photographers.

Not just photographers. Photographers who were waiting for her. Photographers who already knew her car. Photographers who swarmed around as she slowed down to enter her building's garage, blocking her view, forcing her to stop, blinding her with flashes.

It was like a zombie movie, only the zombies were armed with digital cameras.

"Are these people serious?" she said to herself, not really believing it. Then someone jumped across the hood of her car and a flash went off in her eyes. Instinctively Adra slammed on the brake and put her hands up over her face. "What are you doing?" she yelled.

And then, stupidly, oh so stupidly, she lowered her window. As if the problem was that they hadn't heard her. It was just a reflex. A stupid, human reflex, because she was worried.

"Get away from my car!" she shouted, and she heard the fear in her own voice. What if that guy had slid off the hood, under the wheels? What was wrong with them? "Someone could get hurt!"

"Adra! What's it like working on the movie with your ex?"

"Adra, tell us about Club Volare!"

"Adra, are the rumors about you and Derrick Duvall true?"

Adra had never been on this side of it before. She'd always just tried to comfort clients when they'd done something stupid and the tabloids picked up the scent. She always told them to hang tough, that it would blow over.

She'd had no idea.

She was trapped. Completely, utterly trapped under this assault.

And for a moment, she was frozen with fear.

Then she said, "Oh, screw this," turned off the car in the middle of the garage entrance, opened her door, and hurled herself through the scrum of photographers.

She ran all the way to her building's entrance with the pack in tow, somehow outrunning a bunch of grown men who were wearing comfortable shoes—it was the adrenaline, maybe? Or maybe the photographers were just soft; you couldn't be a wimp and wear Adra's kind of shoes—and slipped inside the door held open by Greg, her building's lone doorman.

Greg locked it behind her.

That didn't stop them from shooting pictures through the glass.

"Ms. Davis, get to the elevators," he said. "I called the police, but they weren't breaking any laws. If I'd known they were here for you, I would have called you. Come on, get away from the glass."

Adra didn't want to give them the satisfaction of seeing her run away. Well, anymore than she already had, anyway. That first sprint was kind of unavoidable. But now? She'd conduct herself with dignity, damn it.

She smoothed down her hair, her back to the glass doors behind her, pretending there weren't any men outside, screaming lies about her framed as questions.

"Greg, I left my car in, like, the exact middle of the garage entrance," she said. "Do you think you could…?"

"No problem," Greg said, taking Adra's keys. "I'd be happy to do it."

"Thanks," she said.

The relief was almost palpable. It felt...it felt weak. Like the moment she stopped to rest, she might be pretty upset about this whole thing. And she didn't want to be upset. She didn't want this to be a big deal.

Really, she just didn't want it to be true.

"Ms. Davis, you know they're not going to go away right away," Greg said. He'd come with her to the elevator bank, and was standing between her and the doors, obstructing any view the photographers might have had.

Greg was a good man.

"I just hate the idea of letting them get to me," Adra said. "I don't even know what the story is yet."

But right as she said that, she realized it was a lie. Of course she knew. She'd been in this industry a while; she knew, suddenly, exactly what had happened. That photographer who'd broken into the Volare grounds and snapped pictures of her—he hadn't been checking his camera for damage before Ford knocked it into the koi pond. He'd been removing the memory card.

And once he had pictures, it probably took all of ten minutes to find out that Adra and Derrick used to live together. Every gossip rag in the city kept a file on stars like Derrick; Adra had probably been just a single line in a long biography.

Well, not anymore. She might have her own file now. The story practically wrote itself. Kinky ex-girlfriend and movie star on kinky film set—what could possibly happen?

Adra grit her teeth.

"You sure you don't want to go somewhere else?" Greg said, gently.

"And go through that again?" Adra said, looking back at the photographers gathered outside. "They know my car, so they'd just follow me. I just…I just need to get upstairs."

"Call down if you need anything, all right?"

Adra smiled. She'd stayed in this building for years, even buying the unit next door to hers when it became available rather than move to a bigger place, because somehow it felt like a big enclosed neighborhood and not an impersonal apartment building. Greg was a big part of the reason why. He'd been there over twenty years.

"Thanks, Greg," she said, beginning to feel a little better about the whole thing. "They'll probably lose interest."

Greg waved as the doors started to close.

"I'm sure you're right," he said.

Well, except that she wasn't, and she knew it. It was wishful thinking. Derrick Duvall had become a huge star, and now that they thought Adra was sleeping with him, they'd look into his private life and discover that Derrick had a long term girlfriend, and that he'd actually left Adra for Ellen way back when. Now that she thought about it, one of the only decent things Derrick had done once he got famous was keep his private life private. It wasn't an option for everyone, but Derrick had definitely tried to protect Ellen, as far as Adra could tell.

And now that was all coming to an end.

"Shit," Adra said as the doors opened.

She was exhausted. She had no idea how she was going to handle this. How she was going to handle getting out of her freaking apartment and over to Volare in the morning, how she was going to handle the inevitable horrible story that would run on the blogs starting any second now, how she was going to handle Derrick on the set when he caught wind of the whole thing.

All she wanted was the privacy of her own home. For the safety. For the comfort.

For the bathtub.

Adra laughed out loud, letting herself into her apartment. She was still, *still*, thinking about Ford and his orders. Her mind clung to it like a life raft. Somehow it was like having him with her, and she felt…safe.

Not just safe. Wanted. And wanting.

Which was a whole lot better than terrified. She decided to go with it.

She ran the bath first thing, wondering how much time had elapsed, wondering when he'd call. And she was smiling. Smiling as she undressed, as she tested the water, as she poured her favorite bubble bath. And definitely as she carefully set her phone on the edge of the tub.

And then her doorbell rang.

Adra jumped. But she tried to be rational, she really did. It was probably Greg, checking on her, or her neighbor, Theresa, trying to find out what had happened. There was absolutely no reason to freak out. There was no reason to ruin the mood.

She put on a robe, and went to the door.

"Who is it?" she said.

"Delivery came downstairs," the muffled voice said.

Adra frowned; normally Greg called up. Maybe he was just trying to be nice.

She opened the door.

The flash was immediate and blinding.

"Adra, what—"

She slammed the door in the photographer's face, lights dancing in front of her eyes as she leaned against the door and tried to block out his shouted questions. How? How had they gotten in?

How could this be happening?

What was she going to do?

Adra had fought all day to keep from panicking. No, she'd been fighting for longer than that; it had been creeping up on her since she'd screwed things up with Ford, since Charlie had started to let his marriage unravel, and then with the movie...

There had been a lot of things. And she'd managed to keep it together, for the most part.

Until now.

She couldn't breathe. No, she could breathe, she was breathing, but no matter how fast she inhaled it felt like she couldn't get enough air. She was starting to sweat, and she felt hot, too hot, so hot that she actually took off her robe, standing there next to her front door buck naked, trying not to listen to the jerk shouting questions on the other side of it.

She was having an actual panic attack. And *then* her phone rang.

~ * ~ * ~

Adra could tell that Ford had known right away that something was wrong. He'd spoken calmly, his deep voice enough to drag Adra out of the panic attack, and he'd asked for only the barest facts. He didn't tell her what he was going to do; he'd only told her that he'd handle it, and to pack a bag.

She'd thrown one together in about thirty seconds flat. She suddenly didn't want to be anywhere near this building that had been her home. Even Greg could tell she was upset when she called down to tell him about the photographer; she'd never heard the poor guy sound so upset, himself. She bet that photographer was going to have a bad night after this.

And then she'd only had to wait about five more minutes. Ford must have set a new land speed record.

"Ms. Davis, there's a Ford Colson asking to see you," Greg said over the phone. He sounded suspicious. Good man.

"I'll come down," Adra said.

And then, not for the first time, she took a moment. She'd dressed herself well, in a simple, beautifully cut black dress and a white shawl, for the same reason she'd stopped in front of the doors downstairs. She wanted her dignity back. As soon as she'd gotten off the phone with Ford, she'd felt embarrassed about the whole thing. She really had gone straight from the verge of a panic attack to being embarrassed about said panic attack in about a minute.

She hated that other people could make her feel like that.

She hated even more that, for the second time—for the third time?—Ford was coming to her rescue.

No, that wasn't accurate. She didn't hate it. She secretly loved it, loved that he didn't demand to know anything other than how to fix it, loved that it was his first thought—but it scared her. So she'd dressed in what, for her, was battle armor. Pity she didn't have time to properly do her makeup.

The elevator doors opened, and she held her head high, prepared to step out and face the whole thing all over again.

And then there was Ford. Holding the doors open, his big, muscular body dressed perfectly in that suit, his dirty blond hair tousled across his forehead, his worried blue eyes searching her face for anything, anything at all...

She couldn't look away.

He stepped in, and she stepped back.

The doors closed.

Gently, he touched her face. "Are you ok?" he asked.

Why couldn't she speak? She opened her mouth, she tried, she just...

"I don't know," she said finally. It was the truth. He always got the truth out of her, in the end.

Ford smoothed his thumb across her cheek and Adra turned into it, unable to help herself, her body just...it had a mind of it's own, when it came to Ford. She could feel her shoulders begin to relax with just that touch.

He dipped down and kissed her lightly, gently, just once. And then he wrapped his arms around her.

And Adra gave in.

"I'm not going to let anything happen to you," Ford said, as she cried softly into his chest. "Ever."

Adra pulled herself together, and raised her head, trying not to think about what she must look like. She had just needed a good cry. That was all.

Nothing more.

"Well, I'm not going to let anything happen to this suit," she said, trying to smooth the now wrinkled material. "Anything else, anyway."

Ford smiled at her, kissed her once more on the nose so that she had to swat him away, and then picked up her suitcase.

"Having you on my suit will always be an improvement," he said, winking. Adra opened her mouth in mock outrage, but couldn't quite stifle a smile.

"That is one dirty mind, Ford Colson," she said.

"You have no idea," Ford said, pressing the button for the garage. He smiled brilliantly. "But I'll tell you more in the car."

Oh, of course. Adra hadn't thought of it. Ford could drive her out in his car; they photographers would never know the difference. And of course she'd need to stay somewhere with actual security. Her building was generally not designed for the needs of the famous or even the temporarily infamous.

She sighed as practical thoughts invaded her brain all over again.

"What am I going to do?" she whispered.

"Right now, you're going to step to the side of the elevator so that you aren't visible from the garage," Ford said, herding her into the corner. "You're going to let the doors close and then you're going to press the emergency stop button so the elevator doesn't go anywhere. I'm going to get my car, and I'm going to drive up here, in case any of those vultures are hanging around. And then I'm going to get you into my car."

Well. That was good enough for her.

And it worked. She didn't know why she was surprised, and she definitely didn't expect Ford to simply ignore the existence of a curb and pull his truck right up to the elevator—and it was his truck he'd brought instead of the Jag; somehow she loved that—but it all worked. And when he drove out of her garage, all she had to do was duck down.

"Are we clear?" she asked after a few minutes.

"It was a brilliant escape," Ford said.

"You think very highly of yourself," Adra said, smiling as she sat up straight.

Ford looked at her.

"Sir," she added.

"Damn straight."

Adra leaned her forehead against the cool glass, already feeling calmer inside. Still, like a glass lake. Like he'd quieted the storm, however briefly.

"So where are we going?" she asked.

"Where do you think?"

Adra looked out at Sunset Boulevard—they weren't going to Volare or any of the hotels that knew how to handle celebrity circuses.

"Oh, Ford," she said quietly.

"They'd find you in any hotel in Los Angeles, except possibly the Chateau Marmont, and Derrick and Ellen are staying there while their place is being renovated," Ford said.

How did he know that? Was that at dinner? Adra hadn't paid attention to anything but Ford and the aftershocks she'd occasionally had to hide.

"And Volare is a mess while they're shooting," Ford went on.

"Ford…"

"I have a guest room made up for you," Ford said, looking at her so she'd catch that 'guest room' part. "And I have a play room you'll be spending most of your time in anyway."

In spite of the nervousness growing inside her, Adra laughed. "Don't tease me."

"I'm not," Ford said.

That smile was positively carnal. He was completely serious.

"You don't think this is… I mean, what about the rules?" Adra tried. "Our rules?"

"I'm not compromising on this, either, Adra," he said, turning the truck into his gated drive. "That man could have forced his way into your apartment. He could have hurt you. He could have—" he stopped himself abruptly, his jaw tense, and shook his head.

The truck came to a stop in front of the house, and Ford turned his full gaze on Adra.

"I'll go somewhere else if you want, and I'll take you anywhere you want to go, but you will damn well be somewhere safe, even if I have to hire people to watch over you. Understood?" he said.

Adra blinked. "I'm not kicking you out of your own house," she said.

Ford nodded. He didn't say anything else until he'd come around to Adra's side to open the door and help her down. And then when he did say something, it was…well, it was something.

"Well, then," he said, carefully setting her down on the drive. "Welcome home."

chapter 12

It wasn't just what he said to her. It was that he'd already prepared a place for her. It was the way he held her hand as she picked her way through the gravel of his drive to the broad slate squares of the walk to his front door. It was the way he carried her bag, without a second thought, without a chance that he'd give it up even if she fought him for it. It was the way his hand on the small of her back made her feel completely *safe*.

Which, ironically, meant danger. Adra knew she was about to freak out.

Ford held open the door for her.

She liked walking through it way too much.

"You don't have to take care of me, you know," she said, stepping over the threshold.

She hadn't been in this house in so long. She had missed it. She'd missed this ridiculous masculine decorating scheme, all these dark stones and dark polished woods and high-end electronics. She'd missed the scent: the wood-burning fireplace, and Ford himself.

"There aren't very many things I have to do," Ford said. "Some things I just want to do."

Adra stopped, the final *click* of her heels echoing softly in the high-ceilinged foyer, and closed her eyes. She took a deep breath.

"I don't want you to take care of me," she said.

That echoed, too.

She hated that she'd needed to say that. She hated how defensive it sounded, how ridiculous, how scared and uncertain. She was a grown woman; she didn't have anything to prove to anyone.

No. She *shouldn't* have anything to prove to anyone. But that didn't necessarily make it so.

She opened her eyes, and found Ford watching her. Studying her. His eyes searching, his expression intense, his whole body primed, alert—just like her own.

Damn.

She felt exposed. Naked. Far more naked than she'd ever actually been before, if that was possible.

Oh God, what if she was in way over her head?

She felt the panic begin to brim, and it felt like a breath taken underwater. And then Ford was there.

Her Dom was there.

"I *am* going to take care of you," he said. "Right now."

He kissed her back against the wall, put his hand between her legs, and squeezed until Adra moaned helpless into his mouth. By the time he pulled away she was weak-kneed and feverish, her mouth searching mindlessly for his, her hands gripping at his shoulders.

Jesus, this man…

As her eyes started to focus, she latched on to the heat building in her core with what could only be called gratitude, and looked up at him.

"I'm not done with you," he said.

Adra swallowed. She didn't know if she was done freaking out, either. She didn't know if she could…

"Go into the living room, strip naked, and wait for me on all fours," Ford commanded.

Her breath hitched.

"*Now*," he said.

His voice snapped her back into herself, and away from all that over-thinking, overwhelmed panic. She thought about what he'd said, where he'd touched her, and how wet she was. How she felt the pressure pulsing inside her, how it was drowning out everything else, even the panic, distilling her down to this one, pure thing that she could handle.

Jesus *fuck,* this man…

"Yes, sir," she whispered.

And she practically ran to the living room, her heels echoing off the polished floors until she crossed another threshold, and nearly tripped in the soft, deep carpet of Ford's comfortable living room.

Shoes were the first to go.

He hadn't turned on any of the lights yet, and so Adra undressed in the dark. The dress slipped right off of her; bra and thong followed. She hadn't worn stockings or garters, though she'd thought about it. She was glad now that she hadn't. She went from dressed to the nines to dressed for one thing in particular in about three point two seconds.

One thing left to do. She shivered slightly in the dark.

Then she walked to the middle of the room, in front of the huge, dark fireplace, slowly lowered herself to her hands and knees, and felt her mind begin to empty.

The thing about waiting was that at first the world would shrink down to a size just big enough to hold the thing she waited for. And then, as the seconds—minutes? Eons? Who could tell?—ticked by, slowly the world kept shrinking, until the thing she waited for, the man she waited for, was too big for it. There wasn't room in Adra's head for anything else but Ford. For when he would arrive. When he would touch her. What he would do.

She waited, and the only passage of time were her rapid, shallow breaths, and the wetness she could feel spreading between her legs.

Adra listened. She listened so, so hard.

But the thing about carpet over a stone floor is that you can't hear a damn thing.

She didn't know he was behind her until he was inside her.

Her breath came out in a long, soft cry as he slid into her, his hands holding her steady at the hips while her arms buckled beneath her. He felt big, bigger than she remembered, stretching her to where she almost thought she couldn't take it anymore. Her eyes flew open while he paused briefly and her body adjusted. And then she leaned her head against her forearms, now flat on the floor, and pushed up against him, wanting more, so much more, as much as she could take.

Ford slapped her ass and drove into her again.

And again.

And again.

She was moaning, she was sure she was moaning, just driven to it by the feel of him thrusting inside her relentlessly, when he reached forward, grabbed her by the back of the neck, and brought her up to where he could grab her breast.

"Oh fuck," she said.

"You know the rules," Ford said, pounding into her again. "You don't come unless I say so."

This was different. This was anything but gentle. This was perfect.

He held her down, toyed with her nipple, fucked her mercilessly, and all the while all she could think about was that she couldn't come. Her whole body tightened around him, around the impending orgasm, the shape of the thing she could already feel building inside her, and she could only think: *Oh God, don't come, don't come, don't come...*

Then she felt his hand leave her breast, only to snake downward, his fingers searching out her clit, and she almost screamed in denied agony. He thrust into her, hard, and she went mindlessly blank.

"Please," she begged. She was babbling. "Please, please, please..."

"Come," he ordered, and she exploded.

He stopped, kept himself motionlessly inside her while she came hard around him, the man apparently having an iron freaking will, something Adra could now appreciate more than ever. By the time the contractions subsided, Adra's face was wet. Tears? Sweat?

Oh God, he was still inside her.

She shuddered, another aftershock tearing through her. She groaned, bit her lip, moved her hips.

Ford slapped her ass again.

"That one was just because I'm feeling nice," Ford said. "Now I'm going to have some fun with you. Remember you don't come until I tell you, or you're going to feel it."

And with that he slid out of her. He was only gone a second, maybe two, that might as well have been forever. Adra only noticed that she didn't dare to move out of position until he came back and stroked the back of her thigh.

"Good girl," he said.

And then he attached the nipple clamps.

Adra hissed, then felt herself start to float away as the sting faded into pleasure. This would keep her close to the edge for however long Ford deemed fit. This would...

The clamps were attached to a lead.

She knew because he pulled on it.

"Pay attention," he said.

Adra whimpered. "Yes, sir," she said.

"Which hand do you masturbate with?" he said.

"My left," she said.

"Use it," he said. "Touch yourself."

Adra groaned even at the thought. The second she touched herself, knowing it was his order, knowing he was watching, knowing he would do whatever he wanted, it would be a constant battle not to fall over the forbidden edge. And still, she did it. She gingerly shifted her weight, moved her hand. Winced in anticipation.

And then she touched herself, and she started to shake.

"Adra," he warned.

"I know," she panted. "I know, I'm trying, I'm trying…"

"Try harder," he said, and trailed the cool leather end of a riding crop up the inside of her leg.

She almost lost it.

Instead she moaned and turned her head to hide in the crook of her arm, closing her eyes, turning all her concentration on what she wasn't allowed to do. Even though she knew what was coming.

The first strokes with the crop were light, feathery, like little stinging bites all over the backs of her thighs and her ass. Then sharper. Longer, not letting the crop dance off her skin quite as fast, letting it linger instead. Each one spiked sensation all over her body, each one struck nerves that seemed directly connected to her clit, each one threatened to send her over.

"Move your hand," Ford ordered.

Adra did as she was told, and moaned.

He struck her with the crop and she cried out.

"Touch yourself," he ordered, his voice hoarse.

And then he hit her again.

"Keep at it, Adra."

And again.

And again, until she was actually dizzy, moaning aloud, incoherent. Begging. Definitely begging, though she didn't know if she had real words anymore, just that pleading tone of voice, that desperation that not even the best actress could fake, that base, animal *need*, her fingers working, her other hand balled into a fist, her teeth clenched...

He flipped her over quickly, easily, like it was nothing at all, and settled her shaking legs on either side of him. She opened her bleary eyes, blinked up at him, gripped at the carpet with her hands.

He removed the nipple clamps and for a split second she felt the painful surge of blood returning and cried out—and then he replaced them with his fingers, pinching, rubbing, slowly letting up on the pressure. Letting her feel every, long second of it while he kept his eyes locked on her contorting face.

"Please," she begged again, writhing under him. "*Please.*"

Ford positioned his cock at her entrance, the head nestled in her folds, and it was so close she wanted to cry—and he paused.

"Your orgasms belong to me now," he said, and his voice was different, rougher, more raw.

"Yes," she said.

"You are mine," he said.

"Yes!"

"Now come as many times as you can," he said.

With a growl, he plunged into her again, and Adra screamed. She came immediately. She came insanely. She wasn't sure if she ever stopped, or if that low, buzzing hum was just the base note of the longest orgasm of her life, or if what would happen next was that she might actually die. She had no idea what was happening to her. And she didn't care, as long as Ford kept doing it to her.

And he did, until sweat began to trickle down his forehead, until his own fingers dug into the carpet beneath her, until he dropped his head and kissed her roughly. Then he pinned her hands above her head and, with a feral growl, gripped her neck with his teeth and finished them both, fucking her with wild, senseless abandon until they both lay sweaty and limp on his living room floor.

Adra loved that feeling, with Ford on top of her. Loved how he covered her, how she could bring her hands up the broad plans of his back and never quite reach everything, how she could barely see over his shoulders while he breathed her in. It was the first time she felt like she was drowning and enjoyed it.

She had no idea how much time had passed.

She didn't care.

It was Ford who moved first, Ford who would have been waking up to his Dom responsibilities. Adra was content to lie there for the rest of time, really, but Ford stirred, nuzzled her, licked her neck, pushed himself off of her so that he could see her face.

So that he could stroke her cheek.

So that he could kiss her.

So that he could take care of her.

Adra was still floating somewhere high in subspace when he gathered her up, carrying her again to a comfy couch, wrapping them both in a blanket. Even as things were still kind of fuzzy, she remembered being gratified by the fact that they were both naked this time, and she found herself burrowing into his chest, toying with the fine hairs she found there. She didn't even remember to worry about it all.

"How are you?" he asked, after a while.

"I'm excellent," she said, and sighed softly.

"Still coming down?"

"I don't even know," she said. "It feels different. Easier. The drop isn't so hard."

"This was intense," he said, stroking her hair. "Was it too much?"

Just like him to make sure.

"It was perfect," Adra said, looking up at him. She meant it. "It was exactly...it was perfect. I would tell you, Ford. I wouldn't hide it just for your approval. I'm not that sub."

"I know you're not," he said gently.

"How did you come up with that, on the fly," she murmured.

"I'm that good," Ford said, shrugging.

She smacked his chest, but what was she going to do, argue with him?

"How are you outside of the scene?" he asked, suddenly serious again.

And she was now very, very aware of their closeness, all over again. Only this time, it didn't bother her. She knew it would later, but at the moment her body simply did not have the energy to freak out anymore.

Ford was a very smart man.

"I'm ok," she said. "I am, really. This was...this was perfect, I meant it. I feel kind of amazing. You may have killed a whole bunch of brain cells, but they were all the bad kind, so I think it's a win."

"Is that how that works?" Ford said, and snaked his hand up her stomach to play with her breasts. Adra sucked in her breath but couldn't fight a smile. "I'm going to have to kill a whole lot more."

"We're outside a scene," she said in mock disapproval.

"We are well into cuddle time," Ford said, gently rolling a nipple between his fingers. "And you are mine, anyway. I'm gonna do this whenever I want."

God, that sounded good. How could she fight that?

She bit her lip.

"You keep doing that, we're going to be in a scene again pretty quickly," Ford said.

"Oh my God, you're going to kill me."

"We'll die happy, though."

"Hush," Adra said.

He smiled at her.

And then they sat like that, together, Ford holding Adra, the two of them wrapped in a blanket. Together. And it was…it was comfortable. It was peaceful. It was nice.

No, it was beyond nice. It was—

"I have to call it," Ford said softly.

"Hmm?" Adra said.

"The cuddle clock."

Had it been ten minutes since he'd first asked her if she was ok? Really? It felt like…it felt like nothing.

Then Adra remembered what he'd said. "The cuddle clock?"

"You heard me."

"You're making fun of me."

"Of course I'm making fun of you." Ford smiled.

Then he kissed her on the cheek and lifted her up, gently setting her on her feet.

Adra got to keep the blanket. Which meant that Ford didn't.

She let her eyes wander.

Jesus Christ.

"Let me show you where you'll be sleeping," he said, and took her by the hand.

Adra didn't take her eyes off his perfect ass even once. She kind of just...couldn't believe it. That he was real. He was one of those mythical people who actually looked better naked. Better than "better," even—he was perfect. He was her ideal.

Adra shook her head. That was not a helpful thought.

"Here you are," he said, opening a door to a large bedroom that was, objectively, lovely. Soft lighting, white on white high-thread count sheets and a comforter that looked like an actual cloud, a sitting area with those plush chairs that made you want to take a nap. And a bathroom. A beautiful en suite bathroom with a standing tiled shower and an oversized hot tub.

"This is your *guest* room?" she said.

"Get used to it," he said. "Hey, did you actually remember to pack any comfortable clothes?"

Adra tore her gaze away from the bathroom and was confronted with Ford's nudity again. She lost her train of thought.

"Eyes up here," Ford said.

"What? Um, no, now that you mention it," Adra said. "I was just kind of..."

"I'll put something out for you," he said, smiling down at her while she made every effort to make eye contact. "I thought we could do a movie."

"Nothing sappy," she said, perhaps a little bit too quickly.

"Really? You think I'm gonna pick out a sappy movie? Me?"

"I've seen your DVD collection, you bleeding heart."

"You know I'm gonna remember that, right?"

Adra smirked. "I was hoping."

"Get your ass in that shower before I regain my strength," Ford said, and whisked away the blanket. Adra ran into the bathroom laughing.

And when she got out, the first thing she saw was a pair of Ford's sweatpants and one of his t-shirts, both of which she would be swimming in—and she didn't care. They smelled like him, and they were the most comfortable things she'd ever worn. And when she wandered back to the TV room, she found that Ford had fixed them some food and had the movie all set up.

"Here," he said, handing her a bowl of stir-fry. "You like spicy beef, right?"

"When did you learn to cook?"

"I didn't. I learned to dial."

"Well, good job dialing," she said. It smelled amazing, and Adra realized she was starving. She took her bowl and a fork and plopped down on the world's most comfortable couch, ready to relax.

"So what are we watching?" she asked.

In response, Ford sat down on the other side of the couch and picked up the remote.

It was *Clueless*.

Adra stared at him. "You own *Clueless*?" she said.

Ford looked at her haughtily. "It's an American classic," he said. Then he smiled. "Someone told me that."

Yeah, Adra had.

The thing was, Ford had never seen it before she'd made him go. And she really had gone through his DVD collection back when they used to hang out together all the time. Ford definitely hadn't owned *Clueless* before they'd had their…little mistake, and stopped being friends for far too long.

She was still staring at him.

"You want something else?" Ford asked, frowning. "It's this or *Die Hard*."

"No, this is fine," she said, blinking back the world's stupidest tears. "This is great. It's perfect."

"You sure?"

"I'm sure."

"Ok, then," Ford said, and leaned back in his corner of the couch, his feet up on an ottoman.

Adra suddenly had no idea what to do with herself. It was obviously very important to observe the rules of the cuddle clock for mental health and general sanity reasons, but she found that she was almost terminally conscious of the physical distance between them. She wasn't watching the movie; she knew it by heart anyway. She was watching Ford out of the corner of her eye.

It was torture.

It was worse than not being allowed to come.

Why couldn't she think about anything else but how far away his leg was from hers?

She must have been sitting up ramrod straight, the tension obvious in every line, because when Ford looked over at her he kind of laughed, reached over, and pulled her into the crook of his arm.

"Friends are comfortable with each other," he said.

"Right," she said. "You watch movies with Roman like this?"

"I'd watch movies with Lola like this," Ford said.

"And then you'd be dead," Adra said.

"I didn't say it would be a long-term plan. Are you gonna relax?"

Adra sighed, heard it turn into laughter, and shifted down until her head was in his lap.

"I guess so," she said.

She lay like that through one and a half movies, with Ford's hand in her hair, alternating between a kind of nervous, aroused tension and utter contentment, until finally, finally, she fell into what must have been the least restful sleep ever.

Only when she woke up she was in that beautiful bed, and it was morning. And she was alone.

She felt enormous relief paired with a vague kind of grief. She didn't know what to call that weirdo feeling, but felt certain that there must be a word for it.

Staying with Ford was going to be interesting, to say the least.

chapter 13

Ford allowed himself a smile as he walked through the Volare compound on his way to Adra's office. He'd left her a surprise there, and he wanted to be there to see her reaction. It had been a good couple of weeks for both of them.

Well, not entirely. The tabloid fascination with Adra and Derrick hadn't let up, fueled by Adra's apparent disappearance and Derrick's refusal to talk to the press. That part sucked, in theory. In reality? It didn't seem to bother Adra too much. Or maybe she just didn't have time to think too much about it.

Possibly because Ford was doing his best to make sure she didn't have the time to think much about anything.

They'd managed to keep their arrangement a secret, too, though Lord knew how. The sex was fucking insane. Each and every time Ford thought they couldn't get higher, couldn't get any closer, and then they did. It was a miracle it wasn't stamped on their faces every morning.

Nights were another matter.

Ford was being careful. So, so careful. He was so attuned to Adra that reading her was easy for him, and he knew when to back off. He could feel her boundaries. And one of them came up every night.

She needed her own bed. Ford didn't push it. He didn't like it, but he understood it, and he didn't push it. She would come around. She hadn't even tried to find another accommodation; she didn't want to go anywhere.

And Ford was damn grateful for that.

Because he'd been around long enough to know when he was falling in love. Whether that was a good idea or the stupidest thing he'd ever done was another question entirely. They both kept their distance, Ford because he was being careful with Adra, Adra because she was scared. They danced around the biggest facts of their lives, of their pasts, almost as if their pasts—and the scars that came with them—were the final frontier. After that, what the hell was left to keep them apart?

Ford wasn't even convinced it mattered now, at least not to him. The time he spent with Adra was so special that it was like all that other crap, the stuff he'd carried with him for years, it just ceased to exist. Boom. Gone. Like the past was some long forgotten country that he'd finally gotten to leave.

He was smart enough to know that it was crazy, in a way. But he'd be damned if he questioned it too long. And he fervently hoped that it would be his privilege to give her the same gift, if she'd let him.

If she'd talk to him.

Because there was something still getting to her. He knew. He could see it eating away at her.

But he wouldn't push. He cared too damn much to push. Adra would come to him when she was ready.

If that woman only knew how much effort that took…

Well, she was about to find out, in a way. Ford knew she was stressed, even if she wasn't talking to him about what was upsetting her, and that she needed a release. And she was about to get it.

Time to see if she'd found the present he left on her desk.

Ford smiled again.

~ * ~ * ~

Fucking Charlie.

Adra could swear *she* had actually felt the stress building over the past few weeks. Like she was directly tied to the pressure cooker that was Charlie Davis's head and she knew, just *knew*, when he was about to blow. It had set her on edge lately — it was like when animals knew there was an earthquake coming and the dog just started whining and hiding under the kitchen table. Only Adra had tried to talk herself out of it, because, let's be honest, that was the sane thing to do. It was so irrational, there was no way, she was just making it up.

And then Charlie called her.

"I'm just calling you so you don't freak out," Charlie said. "But I'm going away for a few days, up to Big Sur. Just taking a break. Nicole knows, and her parents are coming down to help out with the kids, so it's not…I'm not doing a runner. Ok?"

What could she say?

"Thanks," she said. "Thanks for checking in, and planning, and…thanks for doing it the right way."

"You were right, little sister. Safety valve, you know?"

Adra smiled into the phone and told him to have fun, but really, what she was thinking in the back of her head was this: *The itch doesn't go away. He still has the itch.* Having Nicole's parents come down to help with the kids wasn't a long-term solution, either.

It shouldn't have been such a big deal. A long weekend away was not abnormal or anything. And it wouldn't have gotten to her if Charlie didn't have that habit of just disappearing, sometimes, and if it didn't seem like he always had one foot out the door, but what was she going to do? It wasn't even really her right to get upset about it.

It just made her sad. She wanted at least one of them to manage to have a family.

It really just made her sad, was all.

And she had collapsed into her comfy, oversized chair, feeling sorry for herself and her brother, when she saw the box.

A nice little black box with a red ribbon and a card.

And then she couldn't help but smile just a little bit.

Slowly she pulled on the ribbon, watching the red curls unfurl, and then she gently lifted the lid of the box. She was never about reading cards first;

the anticipation always killed her, and she wasn't able to really appreciate sentimental words until she'd opened the present itself.

Which, apparently, Ford knew.

Inside was a silver bullet. A vibrating bullet. Larger than normal, with a cord—something that attached to underwear?

She'd never seen this particular one before, but she was a lady of the world. She knew the basic idea. And it made her...

It made her a lot of things.

She sighed, and rubbed her legs together, unconsciously trying to get at some of that *want*. Ford made her crazy. Every day, every night, he made her absolutely crazy. He was the only thing in her life that was constantly good, even if sometimes the intensity of what went on between them frightened her, and even if she sometimes wished she could tell him about Charlie and Derrick and all her personal fears, the way she might have done if they hadn't been sleeping together.

Well, no, that couldn't entirely be true. She'd had plenty of time when they hadn't been sleeping together to tell him about all that stuff, and she hadn't done it. And they weren't sleeping together, technically. They were having sex; sleeping together didn't have anything to do with it, Adra made sure of that. She had to. Maybe for the same reason she'd never confided those things to Ford: there had never been a time when she hadn't wanted him, and confiding in him, showing those parts of herself? It would erase the last boundary.

She'd be over the edge. The man would have all of her then, wouldn't he?

So here she was. Stuck "only" having the most amazing sex anyone had ever had, in the history of ever, with a man any woman would kill to have. The kind of man who would leave surprise sex toys for her with the most exquisite timing, just when she needed something to take her mind off things. The kind of man who could dominate the hell out of her and then go another ten rounds just as Adra thought she'd pass out, then make her dinner later.

And the card?

All it said was, "Keep your door unlocked."

Goddamn, was she grateful for that man.

She didn't have to wait long for him to arrive, either. In only a few minutes Ford strode in like he owned the place and closed the door behind him, while Adra was still sprawled across her chair in a mild daze, checking out her new toy.

She looked up at him through her eyelashes and smiled.

"Hi," she said.

Ford was silent. Watchful. He got that look on his face when he was doing his Dom thing, but also when he was studying, considering. It was part of what made him such a good Dom, and part of what made him so terrifying as a guy she couldn't let herself fall in love with—he really *saw* her. He did it purposefully. He paid attention.

It always made her feel so naked. And she was always afraid he'd see too far into her.

This time he came around her desk and sat on the corner, bending down to take her ankles and lift her legs onto his lap. Gently, he stroked the delicate skin on her ankle—her *ankle*—with his thumb, and it sent small waves of pleasure rolling up her leg.

"What's wrong?" he said.

Damn it, how did he *know*?

And he didn't ask to know what was wrong, he demanded. It was Dom voice. It was the only context in which Adra felt ok being taken care of—a scene. Being dominated. It was actually being with Ford that had taught her that, because he was so good at it, and because he was so careful to curb his natural instincts to keep doing it outside of a scene since that wasn't part of their arrangement.

Which, on its own, was amazing. She'd gone her whole adult life without knowing this fairly important fact about herself—that BDSM provided her with the only framework in which she could let herself be taken care of without having an anxiety attack—and Ford had figured it out and showed it to her in a manner of weeks.

It would be infuriating if she didn't enjoy it so much.

But this wasn't a scene. Not yet. This was still personal.

She shook her head.

"It's nothing," she said.

"It's not nothing," Ford said.

"Ok, it's not nothing," Adra agreed. "But it's not something I can do anything about, and thinking about it just makes me sad, so I don't want to think about or talk about it if I can help it, I just…I want to think about something else."

Adra was afraid to look at him at first. She hadn't even acknowledged that something was up with her until now; she'd just kind of let it go, let him treat her with kid gloves, because that's what she'd needed to do. Saying it must change things somehow. Right?

She looked up.

Ford had that face, that concerned, intense face, those hard lines and those soft eyes. It was how he looked when he checked in in the middle of a scene. And now he leaned forward, outstretched his hand, and gently, so goddamn gently, cupped Adra's face.

He brushed her cheek with his thumb, leaned over, and kissed her forehead.

Then, in that unmistakable Dom voice, he said, "I can arrange for you to not think at all."

Adra closed her eyes, and took a deep breath.

She felt his other hand slide between her ankles, still on his lap. Felt him lift one of her legs and place it on the other side of him, spreading her to him.

Felt him take the silver bullet out of her hand.

Adra shuddered as Ford's hand lightly caressed the inside of her leg, his fingers dancing on her skin, spinning a trail of sensation that threatened to overwhelm her. The teasing—he knew it killed her. Like the anticipation of wondering what was in the box, it drove her insane. Only without Ford, she would never have the discipline to ride it out.

"Eyes open," Ford said.

She obeyed.

"Eyes on me," he said.

Again, she obeyed.

Fuck, he was mesmerizing. Coming toward her with the slow intensity of a hunter. Of a man with a purpose.

His hand was on the inside of her thigh now, his other hand pushing up her skirt while she panted in short little breaths and gripped at the ends of her armrests. Her lower belly was already contracting, like it knew what was coming. Jesus.

He stroked her, outside her underwear. Her eyes almost closed.

"I can feel how wet you are," he said.

Mutely, she nodded.

"Good," he said.

Then he pulled aside her panties and pushed the cold silver bullet inside her.

Adra gasped, then shivered, then gasped again. She lifted her hips to accommodate it, to help him slide it up inside her, and he watched her the whole time. She was breathing hard by the time he finished, wishing he wouldn't take his hand away, wishing…

Ford dug something out of his suit pocket, held it up.

It was a remote.

"You'll go about your day like any other," he said. "I'll call you when I want you."

Adra stared feverishly at the remote. At any time, in any place…

Except apparently here and now? When she was already so wet, so worked up, so…

Suddenly Ford was on her, one hand gripping between her legs, the way he liked to do, putting pressure on her, the other slipping inside her blouse, mauling her breast. And his mouth on hers, taking her in.

Adra moaned.

Then he turned on the bullet.

The vibrations rocked through her, sending echoes through out her body, echoes all centered on the growing storm in her g-spot, the…

They stopped.

Ford pulled away.

Adra blinked up at him, bewildered and probably disheveled.

"Be available," he ordered.

And then he walked out the door.

Well, it had worked. About the last thing she was feeling right then was sad.

chapter 14

The day only got crazier from there.

It had only been about an hour, give or take, but Adra had spent that entire time in a constant state of oh-my-fucking-God *need*, and that meant it had been an eternity.

The actors had needed less and less coaching as the shoot progressed, and Derrick had a late call time today so he wasn't around to try to get her attention, which meant that not too many people bothered her while she was walking around like a woman in heat wondering where Ford was. Which was good, because he'd turned the bullet on twice already.

The first time she'd had to steady herself against the wall.

The second time she'd gripped the sides of a chair and closed her eyes.

Both times, he'd left her hanging.

What the hell was the *range* on that thing?

Her nipples were at the point of pain. There was no way at all to hide it; every man she passed had to tear his eyes away, and some of the women, too.

She was so past caring.

All she cared about was an orgasm. All she cared about was when Ford would finally relent, and fuck her. For one blissful, torturous hour, he'd made her life incredibly simple.

Which might explain why she was so off her guard when Lola showed up.

Well, waddled up.

Adra smiled and tried to force her brain to switch gears. "You look great, you know."

"I feel like a whale. It didn't hit me until this week, and suddenly, *boom*: whale. I have no idea what's going on."

"Your due date is what's going on," Adra said.

Lola looked at her. Adra couldn't help it.

"Hey, don't *you* cry!" Lola said. "I'm the one who's pregnant! And holy crap, do I want to be done being pregnant. I just want the baby already."

"I know," Adra said. "I'm just…how soon?"

Lola took a deep breath. "Twenty-two days," she said. "What? Why are you smiling like a lunatic?"

"I'm just really happy," Adra said. Seeing Roman and Lola start a family, seeing them in love—it was almost as good as seeing Charlie happy. Adra knew it didn't necessarily make sense that she didn't believe in happy endings for herself while she believed vehemently in those happy endings for her friends, but she was ok with being a woman of contradictions. Mostly she felt very lucky.

"C'mon, you goofball," Lola said gently. "There's some sort of entertainment TV show here, and they want to do an interview with you, and I figured…"

"Oh God, seriously?" Adra said, suddenly alarmed. "Which one?"

"*The Daily Tattle*," Lola said. "Someone named Brooke Kenner?"

Adra made a face. "Yeah, I know her. Or know *of* her. Which is enough."

"Yeah, she's definitely going to ask about the rumors about you and Derrick," Lola said. "Roman and I thought that, given all the bad publicity, we need to put a fun, warm face on Volare, you know? It's better to jump out in front and try to take control of it at this point. And I'd do it by myself, but they won't do it without you."

"Of course they won't," Adra sighed. "You know they're going to edit it ruthlessly, right?"

"Yeah, but they underestimate us," Lola grinned. "But you really don't have to do it if you don't want to, kiddo. I'm serious."

"I know you are, but you're right that we kind of need it," Adra said. "Besides, I can do these in my sleep. I mean, probably. I coach clients through it all the time, so it's gotta be the same thing, right?"

"Huh," Lola said, sounding slightly less than confident. "Well, you look great. New moisturizer?"

Adra felt herself start to blush. There was definitely only one thing responsible for her recent glow.

"Sure," Adra said.

Lola laughed and looked at Adra sideways. "Yeah, how *are* those new living arrangements working out?"

Oh, goddammit. Of course Lola knew about her and Ford. Or at least knew that there was something to know. Adra was staying with the man for crying out loud, and they hadn't been fighting at all, and instead there'd just been lots of smoldery looks and long stares...

Of course Lola knew *something*.

But the idea of having to explain to Lola what she couldn't even explain to herself made Adra's insides twist together in unholy knots. Still, she also hated lying to a friend.

"Um, it's great," Adra said.

Smooth.

Lola laughed again. "I'll bet it is."

"Hush."

"Well, you let me know if things get complicated," Lola said. "I know you can't go back to your place until this all blows over, but you always have a home where we are. And people willing to listen. You know, friend things."

"If things get complicated?" Adra whispered. The idea of 'complications' was, of course, terrifying. That was what she was trying to avoid entirely. That was the whole point!

Don't think about it.

Lola just smirked all the way to where Brooke Kenner had set up her little interview area. Adra decided to pretend 'complications' were just things that happened to other people, and focused on the evidence of just how good the simple stuff was — she felt the bullet every time she took a step. By the time they got to the interview area, she was already fighting back thoughts of Ford.

The lights were already set up, and Brooke was going over her notes, perched near the couch they'd all share. She looked up and smiled about as wide as a human being could smile and waved them over.

"Ladies, thank you so much!" Brooke said, ushering them onto the couch. "I am *so* excited to do this interview!"

I bet, Adra thought to herself as she sat down.

And then she stopped thinking for a little bit as the remote-controlled silver bullet pressed firmly into her g-spot.

And then she thought about how it had gotten inside of her.

And about what Ford might do to her later.

And she was right back where she started, barely capable of finishing a thought, squirming in her seat. Only this time someone was powdering her face for camera while Brooke Kenner tried to chat them up.

"Adra?"

It was Lola's voice. Adra tried to snap out of it, but to no avail. She had to cross her legs on this couch, and that meant…

Oh God.

"Adra, you ok?"

"Yup," Adra said, shaking her head. "Sorry, just lost in thought for a second."

"You ready?" Lola asked.

"What are we supposed to do again?" Adra whispered while Brooke talked to a production assistant.

"Make us not look like some sort of den of iniquity," Lola said. She paused. "Well, not the bad kind, anyway."

"Right," Adra muttered. "The good kind of den. Got it."

And she actually might have been able to handle it.

Might have.

The interview started off soft, the way they were supposed to, warming both her and Lola up. And Lola, as always, was formidable, taking charge of the interview almost immediately, representing Volare. And Adra followed along perfectly at first.

At first.

But then, somewhere around Lola's third witty remark and Brooke's surprised laughter, the bullet started to vibrate.

Adra's eyes half-closed and her mouth opened. Jesus Christ. Could he see her? Did Ford know what he was doing to her right now? She couldn't move, except she had to. She couldn't…if she didn't let it out…

Oh fuck.

And just before she thought she might lose it, it stopped.

Adra's eyes came back into focus on a skeptical-looking Brooke Kenner. She hoped to God her brain would start working again soon, too.

"Adra, you've been working so *closely* with the actors on this project," Brooke said. Adra didn't like the emphasis, but at least she already knew where this question was going: the rumors that she was having an affair with Derrick Duvall.

Normally, thinking about those rumors made her vaguely sick. Now? She wasn't able to keep her attention on it long enough to care. Every fiber of her being was focused on the bullet inside her, and what it might do next.

Adra licked her lips, and tried to ignore the wet pressure between her thighs.

"That's right," she said. "I'm one of the consultants they've brought on."

"Well, I'm sure you've heard there are rumors swirling around," Brooke said, leaning in and smiling, like they were old friends. "This is *such* a hot project, and everybody wants in, and you're one of the only people that's read the script! What can you tell us about the rumors that the movie involves the 'other woman?'"

Adra took a deep breath, and forced her brain to go into gear. This was sneaky. Making it seem like the question was about the movie, when everyone and their mother would know what this was really about.

Focus, Adra. Take control.

"Oh, that's false," Adra said. "I mean, there's no cheating in the script I read, and I'm grateful for that, because I don't know how comfortable I would have been in that situation. I'm sure you've heard the other rumors, Brooke?"

Brooke stumbled. Then she smiled, raised an eyebrow, and said, "Well…"

"Those rumors in the press are so mean-spirited, and they make me so sad," Adra said, realizing how true that was for the first time. "I mean, Derrick and Ellen are committed to each other, and I hate to hear anyone disparaging their relationship. Derrick and I were involved *ages* ago—"

Lola laughed. "Hey, don't date us. I'm still twenty-nine and holding."

Adra elbowed her friend, getting a giggle out of Lola. She was grateful for the levity. It made Adra seem less defensive, which was probably Lola's intent. That woman knew how to work a camera.

"Anyway, back in the ice age," Adra said, "We found out we were just wrong for each other, you know? And Derrick and Ellen are *so* right," Adra went on, telling herself it wasn't actually a lie. Maybe they were? Ellen definitely put up with Derrick, and he'd protected her, so far. "I love seeing my friends happy and in love. I love seeing them end up with the person they're supposed to be with. It just…it fills me with joy."

That part, at least, was true.

Lola squeezed Adra's hand. And Adra thought about how, in real life, even though she really wasn't the other woman, they were still sneaking around. It wasn't real. But Ford had had a wife, an actual *wife*, once…

Jesus, where did that come from?

"So who *are* you with, Adra?" Brooke said, coming in for the kill. "Inquiring minds…"

Adra opened her mouth to answer—and the bullet turned on.

She nearly yelped out loud.

Instead she dug her fingers into the couch, pressed her lips together, and tried desperately to remain still.

They were all staring at her.

Ford…

God, she wouldn't care if he showed up right then and there—that would be an answer to that question, wouldn't it? If he showed up right now, she'd do whatever he wanted...

"We keep our personal lives personal here at Volare," Lola said, stepping in. "We're not going to disclose anyone's personal business unless they consent to it. House rule."

"Oh, that's no fun," Brooke laughed.

"Depends on whether you're a member or not," Lola said, smiling.

And the bullet finally stopped.

Adra exhaled suddenly and took a long, deep breath. She had to leave. She had to go, right fucking now, and find Ford. She had to.

"Are we all done?" she asked, breathlessly.

"Um, yeah, I think—"

"Thanks," she said, and got up to go find the man who held her in the literal palm of his hand.

chapter 15

Ford decided to have some mercy. He sent Adra a text ordering her to come meet him.

He'd been in her office for about fifteen minutes, wondering how long it would take her to come looking for him, but he didn't want to torture her needlessly. Over an hour should be more than sufficient.

His favorite part was when he heard her rush up to her own office door, stop, and then knock. On her own door: she knocked.

She was *his* sub.

"Come in," he said.

Adra opened the door, entered, and quickly closed it behind her, leaning back against it after she did so. She looked a little breathless, a little flushed, a lot turned on. She couldn't take her eyes off him the whole time.

She looked fucking amazing.

"Where were you?" he asked.

"Giving an interview," she said.

Ford threw his head back and laughed. "On camera?"

"Yes," she said, eyes flashing. "You made me look like…"

"Like what?"

She didn't answer.

"What were you thinking about?"

"You," she whispered.

Ford pushed himself back from her desk. He was sprawled in her big chair, feeling very much lord of the realm, and he wanted her to see it. Besides, she'd need room.

"Be specific," he ordered.

"You, fucking me," she said, without hesitation. Then she licked her lips. "Your cock."

Ford heard himself growl.

"Come here," he said.

Fuck, just the way she walked. He could tell she was so swollen and primed that she could feel every step. He'd make her feel a whole lot more in about a minute.

Adra stopped right in front of him, her back straight, her breasts out, her head slightly down. Beautiful. Everything about her was always so damn perfect.

He pulled her closer, between his sprawled legs, and said, "On your knees."

Adra bit her lip, smiling, and then obeyed.

There was a beat. A moment. She was staring at his erection, already so visible through his slacks. Ford wanted to see what she'd do.

Finally she looked up at him, through those long eyelashes, and he just couldn't fucking wait anymore.

"Suck me," he ordered.

"Yes, sir," she whispered.

And she freed his now aching cock with an expression approaching actual awe. The pure lust he saw there made his cock jump, and Adra smiled as she bent down and took him in her mouth.

Ford groaned.

She felt fucking incredible. Just like he knew she would.

His body moved on its own, thrusting gently into her mouth, moving with her while her tongue worked a fucking miracle. Ford threaded one hand through her hair and took hold, wanting her to know who was in control, as if she could forget.

"Be careful," he managed to rasp.

And then he turned the bullet on.

Adra moaned long and loud and the vibrations carried through to his dick, driving him higher. Jesus, she was good. He had been thinking he'd come in her mouth, but watching her, feeling her on him, knowing she was feeling it too—he wanted to bury himself in her.

"Get up," he said, and pulled her off of him, pulling her up to her own desk.

He pushed her down on that desk. He looked at her wet lips, her lidded eyes, her flushed skin.

And then he thrust his hand between her legs.

Adra jack-knifed forward as she moaned again, her hands going to his arm instinctively. She was so sensitive by now, so goddamn sensitive.

He was gentle as he could be, even though his hard-on demanded he be quick.

He reached between her legs and pulled out the bullet.

She looked up at him, brows furrowed, apparently past the point of thinking and only missing the sensation. He was almost there, himself.

Fuck waiting.

He pushed her flat on the desk, held her down with his hand between her breasts, and entered her.

Slowly.

So fucking slowly.

So slowly they could both feel every single inch, and Adra's expression went from desperate to delirious, her hands pulling at him, her *body* pulling at him.

And then, when they were both on the point of setting fire to the world if they didn't get what they needed, he started to move.

He angled himself to hit her g-spot and thrust as deep, as strong, as long as he could, watching her writhe and moan and beg as he held her down with his thumb on her clit, like she was speaking in tongues, like she'd lost all sense. She came almost immediately, and she came hard, so hard that Ford had to grab hold of something, force himself not to come with her. And then after that, Ford let go.

He buried himself as deep in Adra as he could get, and he just let go.

By the time he was done, they'd cleared the desk. The chair was tipped over. The office in shambles.

Both of them laid out, done.

Happy.

When he had the strength, Ford propped himself up on his forearms and kissed Adra deeply before pulling out, hating to lose contact with her. She rewarded him with one of those little sounds, like a mix between a whimper and moan, one of the many things she did that drove him wild.

He brushed the hair out of her face and said, "You ok to walk?"

Adra laughed, looked off to the side, covered her eyes with her hand. "I don't know. Probably?"

Ford kissed her again. Couldn't help it.

When Adra finally caught her breath again, she said, "How about you?"

"I'll manage," he said. "Barely."

A strong man could always admit weakness, after all. And this woman was his kryptonite.

He touched her face, and she looked up at him. She looked different now than she had this morning. He'd knew he'd done that, or at least he'd helped. He'd do it all the time if he could.

"You ok?" he asked.

"Yeah," she said, and smiled up at him.

Fucking heaven.

Then he remembered what she'd said about her morning, and he gave her an evil grin. "So how was the interview?" he asked.

Adra pushed him back into her own chair, laughing, and did her best to fix her near ruined skirt.

"You are a brute," she said, grinning back.

"Only when it counts," he said.

"You're lucky I always keep a change of clothes here."

"You should start keeping two."

Adra paused, and gave him a sidelong glance.

"I don't know how you can still make me blush, Ford Colson," she said, shaking her head while she quickly changed clothes.

"I'm good at it, that's how," he said. He watched her carefully. "So how was the interview?"

Adra shrugged. "They wanted to know about Derrick."

Ford stifled the impulse to go hit the nearest member of the media. Of course they asked about Derrick. They didn't have anything on the movie production, because it was kept so under wraps, so that was all they cared about—those rumors of an affair. Rumors that had no basis in fact. Rumors that only hurt Adra.

"I'm sorry, Adra," he said. "I should have guessed."

"I told them..." Adra paused and looked at him. Questioning. Like she was hesitating, trying to figure out if she should say whatever it was she was thinking.

He didn't like that.

"What?" he said.

"I told them I'd never be the other woman," she said quietly. "Which is true, obviously. But I meant more that...I don't know. I have my pride."

It was the look on her face that got him, though. The look on Adra's face. Because he couldn't read it. Not entirely. All he could see was that uncertainty, that wariness, that expression she had when she was guarding something painful.

And he had no idea why.

"What's wrong?" he said, standing up. His strength had come back full force; all he wanted to do was hold her.

But Adra backed away. A half-step, but in the wrong direction.

"Ford," she said, again like she was trying to pick her words. "Your wife…"

"My ex-wife," he corrected.

"Your ex-wife." Adra nodded.

They stood in silence.

Finally, Ford said, "Adra, what do you want to know?"

"You never talk about it," she said, picking another blouse out of her office closet.

"I told you why."

"You said it wasn't relevant," Adra said, looking up at him while she did up the last buttons.

"Exactly," Ford said.

"Ford," Adra said, softly. "Is that really possible?"

It was hard to tell if Adra was asking about Ford's life, or her own. Ford figured it was a little bit of both. Whatever it was that was getting to her, whatever it was that had been bringing her down — whatever was going on with her brother, most likely — it was something she dearly wished was no longer relevant to her life.

That, and maybe she wondered whether Ford had really moved on from his disastrous first marriage. That last possibility was, for various reasons, bittersweet. He didn't like having his motives or mental state questioned in any way, shape, or form. But he damn well liked the idea that she cared about it.

"Is it really possible?" she asked again. And this time she sounded hopeful.

Ford smiled, and pulled her in so he could kiss her on the forehead.

"Anything's possible, Adra," he said. "And I promise you, Claudia is not part of my life. I'll see you later tonight."

***

In fact, Ford saw Adra again almost immediately. And for fuck's sake, he wished he hadn't.

At least not the way it happened.

He left her office, intending to make sure everything on this godforsaken production was still running smoothly so that they could get out of his club on schedule, and the first thing he saw was his ex-wife.

Of all the damn luck.

Claudia was dressed to intimidate, her eyes hidden behind giant sunglasses, her mouth smiling and flirting with some production assistant. Standing next to her, looking bored, was Jesse.

His ex-wife, and his ex-best man, standing in the middle of Volare.

He'd been prepared for this, and he was gratified, if not surprised, to see that it didn't really affect him directly. But he was surprised that it affected him at all. Because his first thought was to get these people the hell away from Adra.

He'd just left Adra looking contemplative and vulnerable, and wondering about his ex-wife, and then, like his ex had been summoned by some demonic ritual, here Claudia was. And Ford was gripped by the absolute need not to have this ugliness ever touch Adra. By the need to protect her from…all of it. From his previous life, from the ways people could treat each other, from the cold, hard fact that most people in the world just couldn't be trusted.

He didn't even care that it didn't make sense. He just knew he'd left Adra feeling wary again, knew from how scared she was of love that she must already have reasons not to trust people to treat her right, and he'd be damned if she ran into another one of those reasons. He'd be absolutely *damned* if he let these two ambush Adra in the one place she should be comfortable.

Yeah, it wasn't his most rational thinking. But Adra had that affect on him.

So he walked over there, and excused the production assistant.

Claudia and Jesse stared.

Claudia spoke first. Jesse still couldn't look him in the eye. All these years, and Jesse still couldn't look him in the eye.

"Ford," Claudia said. "It's nice to see you."

"I wish I could say the same, Claudia," Ford said. "But this isn't a good time. What are you doing here?"

"Well, we were looking at schools for Andrew in the area, and we thought we'd stop by to check the club out in person," Claudia said.

The name 'Andrew,' said so casually, like it was just another name of just another child.

It pierced through Ford like a stiletto.

And it took Claudia a beat or two to remember why, but the exact moment she did was clear on her face. There was an uncomfortable silence.

"We were just looking around," Jesse finally said. "We apologize for the intrusion—we should have realized, with the movie—"

"How did you even get in?" Ford demanded. Security was still a joke.

"Jesse called one of the producers," Claudia said. She sounded subdued now. "Remember I told you he did some work on the financing."

"You'll have to come back another time," Ford said. He was done with this. "We offer tours for exactly this purpose, and we'll be in touch with new applicants as soon as filming is complete."

"Of course," Jesse said. For a moment it looked like he might extend his hand.

He decided against it.

Claudia stayed back while her husband turned to leave, her eyes locked on Ford's. Then, hesitantly, she reached out and touched the back of Ford's hand.

"I'm sorry," she whispered.

It didn't help that Ford knew she meant it. Claudia might have been a bad wife to him, but she wasn't a bad person. Real people were never that simple. She could be supremely selfish, and had made more mistakes than many, but the woman had a working heart.

None of that mattered anymore to Ford. He'd made his peace with it.

But when he turned around and saw who'd been watching the entire time, he saw that it apparently mattered to Adra.

chapter 16

It *shouldn't* matter. Adra knew that. It really, really shouldn't.

But it freaking did.

It was obviously her own fault for obsessing about Ford and his ex-wife the past few days. Adra hadn't asked Ford about it partially because she almost didn't want to know, and partially to protect the boundaries of whatever the hell this arrangement had become. Or, if she was being honest, to protect herself.

It had shocked her to find out Ford had an ex-wife, and she'd been hurt at the time. But in the end? It had put this distance between them that made her feel safer, like it would be easier to keep herself from falling in love and then inevitably getting her heart broken. And the longer this went on, the more Adra needed to feel safe, because Ford was anything but safe.

Besides, it made her feel less crappy about not telling him about Charlie and her family. She *liked* that Ford was like this blissful island in the middle of her otherwise chaotic life, untouched by all the garbage she had to deal with.

That is, until she saw him with his ex-wife.

So *that* was what jealousy felt like. It wasn't necessarily a stabbing pain; it was like this great, yawning gulf opened up inside of you and then slowly filling with despair.

Oh man, be more dramatic, Adra. See if you can do it. Go for the gold.

She felt like a freaking teenager. She hated feeling like a teenager. She had been almost universally stupid as a teenager.

Worse, it was absolutely one hundred percent unfair that she felt like this. This was explicitly against the rules, wasn't it? They were under no romantic obligations, which was the way it had to be. He was technically free to fall for someone else, or even to not be over his ex-wife. And yet watching the evidence of intimacy between Ford and his ex—how she'd put out her hand to touch his and revealed years of history, of emotion, of things Adra knew nothing about, in one tiny gesture—had made her insane.

And it had made her realize how much she missed emotional intimacy with Ford. It wasn't just that she was afraid to tell him about Charlie, or afraid to ask him about his ex, it was that at the same time she desperately *wanted* to do both. She wanted to know him, and share with him, and...

She was right between a rock and freaking hard place. And it was her own fault, since she was the one who couldn't handle the real thing. Adra had exactly zero right to complain.

And, conveniently, she had no one to complain to, not if she didn't want the intense scrutiny of Lola to fall on her and Ford.

Which was why she'd already been on shaky ground when her brother's wife called her. And why, after they'd talked, and Nicole had sounded so tired and defeated, and had said in that flat voice, "You know you can't take care of us all the time, Adra," Adra had decided to hide in one of the playrooms during a break in shooting. Here, she could cry and feel sorry for herself and only feel mildly silly about it, because she was alone.

Well, she was alone for about five minutes.

Then the door opened.

It was funny. Adra's first thought was that it must be Ford. She'd been trained by a million romantic comedies, maybe? Like in the world of Hollywood, it absolutely would have been Ford, no doubt about it.

Instead this was real life, which meant she got Derrick.

"Shit," Adra said, and tried to dab at her eyes. Wouldn't do much good; mascara was a bitch on a day like this.

"I thought I saw you come in here," Derrick said.

He sounded different. Gentle, almost? Adra had forgotten that he could be gentle, she'd gotten so used to his asshole Dom performance. But they had been together for almost two years all those years ago. He hadn't been an asshole *all* the time.

Still, she was wary. Especially because Derrick had been taking every opportunity to either hit on her or remind her that they used to have sex since the shoot began.

"I came in here because I wanted a moment alone," Adra said.

Screw being polite. She didn't have the reserves.

"Yeah, you do that when you're hurt," Derrick said. "You hide like a wounded animal."

Adra turned away. She didn't need to be reminded that he knew her so well. "Derrick, I'm not trying to be rude, but I really can't handle any crude jokes, or inappropriate flirtation, or…I just can't, right now. So please leave."

The door didn't open. Which meant he didn't leave.

Adra turned around to find Derrick standing there with his hands in his pockets and an absolutely miserable hangdog expression on his face.

"I am probably the world's biggest asshole," he said.

"You are at least in the running, yes."

"I know it won't help to say I'm sorry," Derrick said. "But I am."

"Derrick…" Adra shook her head. She thought she was past being angry at Derrick for his behavior and had just moved into this dismissive, stoic sort of attitude, but it turned out that his admission of asshole-ness actually made her angry all over again.

She glared at him. *"Why?"* she said.

Derrick ran a hand through his artfully messy hair and stared at the ground. "Fuck if I know,

Adra," he said. "It wasn't even about you, it was just this stupid fucking dominance thing, like territorial, you know, and—"

"I'm trying to decide if you were this bad a Dom when we were together," Adra said.

Silence.

Derrick stared at the ground, angrily this time.

Mostly, Adra found it sad.

"You don't treat people like objects in some sort of Dom competition," Adra said. "What kind of person treats someone they used to love like that?"

And as soon as she said it, Adra found herself wondering: *Well, maybe he never did love me.*

That would explain a lot. It would explain how he left, for one thing. It would almost make things easier.

And like he could read her mind—maybe because he could, in that way you get to know someone you've lived with—Derrick went from angry to saddened and contrite in about the space of a heart beat.

"Damn, Adra," he said. "I really am sorry. About all of it. About the way I ended things. I was young and didn't know how to handle it, but it's not excuse."

Adra shook her head. "Ancient history. I'm over it."

"I really am sorry about being a jerk the past few weeks, too," he said, taking his cue to come sit beside her. "I guess I'm just not used to being around you and not being…"

Adra looked at him. He was thoughtful. He was the way she remembered him in the beginning, when they first became close. The way he was when she decided to trust him.

"I'm not used to *not* being the most important person in the room to you," he said, smiling ruefully. "Fucking childish, when I say it out loud."

She stared at him.

"Yeah, it is," she said. "Jesus, Derrick."

He shrugged, not particularly bothered by his admission. He'd always had an ego. It had always been what drove him—you couldn't become a successful actor without that, honestly. Adra had never understood how Derrick had withstood the countless rejections that came with working his way up, but now she kind of got it: an impenetrably thick skin made of pure ego.

Well, whatever worked, right?

"That's not even why I'm here," he said finally.

"You're not here to be a jerk while I'm crying?" Adra laughed. "I don't know if congratulations are in order, I'll be honest."

Derrick nudged her with his elbow, laughing.

"No, shockingly," he said. That old charm coming back. "I'm here to see if you're ok. Obviously, you're not."

Adra paused. "Obviously."

"You going to tell me about it?"

"Derrick…"

The thing was, Derrick knew about Adra's screwed up family. He knew all about it, because Adra, in her youthful exuberance, had decided to trust him. No, it was more than that: Derrick had known about the walls Adra put up, he'd known about the limits she set on her relationships, and he set out to get around them. And eventually it had worked. And she'd told him everything.

"Is it your dad?" Derrick asked softly.

Adra sighed.

The thing about people you once trusted was that you couldn't take it back. They'd always have that part of you; they'd always know. And most days that made Adra crazy. But right now, mostly what she kept thinking about was how good it felt to have someone to talk to.

Even if it wasn't the person she wanted.

"Not exactly," Adra said, staring at her hands. She didn't want to look at Derrick, for some reason. "We haven't heard from Dad in years. It's my brother, Charlie. He's just…pulling the same old stuff."

As soon as she said it, it felt wrong.

It felt wrong to be in this room with Derrick Duvall. It felt wrong to be telling him anything about her life, anything at all, but especially about something she couldn't bring herself to share with Ford.

"You haven't told him, have you?" Derrick asked.

Adra snapped her head up. "Who?"

"Ford." Derrick put his hand on Adra's shoulder. "C'mon, it's obvious there's something going on there. But you haven't told him about this."

Red fucking alert.

Adra stood up suddenly and stepped away from the bench she'd been sitting on.

"I should get back to work," she said.

"Are you sure you're ok?" Derrick asked. What had sounded sweet before now felt...

Ugh. Manipulative.

Goddammit. She should have seen it. Derrick was exactly narcissistic enough that he could be sympathetic and manipulative all at once.

"I'm fine," Adra said. She was already reaching for the door. She just needed to get away, be alone. Think about why she was almost ready to talk about the things that hurt her with someone who actually *had* hurt her, rather than the man that she...

Fuck. She'd almost let herself think it.

"You sure?"

Adra ignored Derrick and stepped out into the hall, eager to put as much distance between herself and everything as she possibly could.

But Derrick grabbed her hand and pulled her short.

"Adra," he said. "You know I'm always here if you ever need me."

It was a lie.

She knew at once, in that way she knew him so well, that it was a lie. But it was a lie he might actually believe, right up until it was no longer convenient.

She had been sad and stupid, to give this man credit. She knew him too well for that. She *saw* the goddamn look in his eyes at that very moment. Derrick Duvall was about the chase, the hunt, just as he had been all those years ago. If she sobbed on his shoulder, it would mean Derrick had won whatever little fantasy competition he had going on with Ford in his own head. And then, after that, Derrick would go back to being Derrick.

Adra pulled her hand away. "I'm fine," she said.

And she turned around to see Ford watching from the other end of the hall.

"Oh, come *on*," she whispered.

That, at least, would have made the Hollywood version of her life.

chapter 17

Adra made a beeline for Ford.

It was a weird reaction, technically. But she felt gross, having almost allowed herself to be manipulated by Derrick because she was feeling…whatever she was feeling about Ford, and, even weirder still, she felt somehow disloyal for having done so, even though that made zero sense. And now she was presented with a situation in which she was literally in the middle of a hallway with Derrick on one end and Ford on the other.

Nothing else in her life made much sense, but this, at least, was pretty simple. Even if no one else got the metaphor.

She walked toward Ford as quickly as she could.

Ford was staring past her in Derrick's general direction, a truly frightening look on his face, right up until she got close. And then she had all of his attention.

And, like it always did, the full strength of Ford's focus nearly bowled her over. Only this time, she couldn't read everything she saw there.

He looked worried. Concerned. But there was…

It almost stopped her. Somehow not knowing what was going on in Ford's head as he saw her have a supposed "moment" with Derrick was worse than if she'd seen something disappointing. Which was when she realized she had hopes that could be disappointed.

And she was hoping for jealousy. She was actually *hoping* to see jealousy in his face, since she'd just had a big fat heaping taste of that herself. And that, of course, was horrible and petty and juvenile, especially considering that Adra had been the one to set the limits on their relationship in the first place.

On the other hand, everything else about her behavior was starting to seem pretty nuts — really, crying alone in a storage room? — so what was one more thing to add to the list?

Besides, she might have been the one to initially set limits on their relationship, but everything since then indicated that Ford was now perfectly happy with those limits. He may have wanted her — all of her — at one point in time, but then he saw how flaky she could be, how terrible she was with relationships, and…well, he didn't seem to want the same things anymore. He seemed content with their current arrangement. Which was a *good* thing, because it would protect them both, but it still kind of made her feel like…

"Crap," she muttered.

"What's wrong?" Ford said.

Adra looked up, got hit with those blue eyes, and was momentarily stunned.

There were so many things she wanted to say to him.

But how would she figure out how to say them? There weren't words for them all, for all those conflicting feelings, for all the context, and so instead they just swirled around inside her head, overwhelming her, drowning her. Until she couldn't think of a single thing to say at all, because not one thing was the truth, and not one thing told the whole story, and they were all hopelessly inadequate to tell Ford what he meant to her and why she couldn't be what he deserved.

So instead she said, "Hi."

She *really* hated feeling like a teenager all over again. Seriously, one ride on that hormonal hell train should have been enough. Adra ran a successful business in a cutthroat industry, she managed a high-profile club, she took care of everyone in her life, but Ford just made her ridiculous. All he had to do was look at her, or…

"Adra, are you ok?"

Or say something like that, like that was his only concern in life at that particular moment.

God. Dammit.

"I'm fine," she lied.

Ford stepped closer, close enough that she could smell his cologne, close enough that she could see the stubble coming in, close enough to…

"Are you sure?" he said. Then he looked up, past her, where Derrick had been, and his eyes went hard. "What did he do?"

"What?" Adra said. He thought Derrick had hurt her? "Oh, of course I'm ok. I can handle him, Ford."

In fact, she could handle pretty much everything, except apparently Ford. It kind of irked her that he thought otherwise. Or maybe she was just looking for an excuse to be mad at him so she wouldn't have to feel…all these other things.

Ford looked down at her again, his eyes searching. "Of course you can," he said. "But that doesn't mean you always have to, you know. Sometimes I might like to do it for you."

Then he smiled.

Adra forced a laugh, and hoped that covered up how that had taken her breath away. She was constantly having to remind herself not to take Ford's protectiveness too personally. He'd always been like that, with everyone he cared about. It was just who he was.

He was also apparently pretty unaffected by seeing her with Derrick. Which was the way it should be. Even if she'd felt like she'd gotten punched in the stomach when she'd seen him with Claudia.

But what weighed on her at that moment, standing so close and yet so far away from Ford Colson, was that what bothered her the most was how much she wanted to share everything with him—and how much she knew she couldn't, and still keep things as they were: safe. Well, safe-ish.

So close, and yet so far.

But mostly so, so far.

And what once felt safe now felt like that great, yawning gulf, opening up inside her. Before it could overwhelm her, Adra smiled back up at him, gave him a peck on the cheek, and went back downstairs.

~ * ~ * ~

Ford ran hard.

He hadn't taken his truck up to the canyons for a cross-country run in what felt like a long time. He'd gotten everything he'd needed lately from playing with Adra, but today required more, at least if he was going to be able to help the woman he cared about the most.

The sweat poured off him in waves, sucked up greedily by the dry ground as he ran harder and harder.

It was the only way to clear his head after Roman had told him that he was giving Adra an early ride back to Ford's place. Hell, just running into Adra earlier had put him on high alert, but getting confirmation that there was something upsetting her, something she wouldn't tell him about—again—just made it worse.

Every time he looked at Derrick Duvall, for example, he wanted to punch that pretty boy through a wall. Ford was self-aware enough to know that wasn't even about Derrick. Adra was right when she said she could handle him, even though it pissed Ford off that she ever had to.

No, he was pissed off because Derrick knew what was going on. Derrick was still close to her in a way that Ford wasn't.

It was straight up jealousy. Which was beneath him, and it was beneath Adra, and more importantly: it was fucking dangerous. Ford had kept it under lockdown, not even letting himself think it. The last thing he wanted was to spook Adra further.

She was already so frightened. So torn up. And so clearly anxious about their arrangement, with those questions about his ex-wife. He could see it—he could fucking *feel* it, like he had nerves tied to hers, and he couldn't do a damn thing about it.

He ran harder.

He ran until his lungs burned and his legs ached and thought he might, just *might*, have worked the worst of it off. And by the time he drove home the sun was already setting and he was thinking clearly. His priority was Adra. Which meant he couldn't take his own baggage into any conversation with her; he couldn't think about it his own past with a woman who didn't know what she wanted and eventually left him for another man. He couldn't push Adra into something because it was what *he* wanted.

He had to be strong enough to wait for her.

Which actually felt easier than it should. Easier than he would have expected it to feel. He thought about that, as he drove through the winding canyon roads, knowing he was getting closer and closer: this kind of situation should be setting off all kinds of alarm bells, reminding him of what happened with Claudia and Jesse, looking like the exact kind of thing he'd always said he'd avoid. It was the reason he'd avoided Adra for a while after she'd told him she couldn't really be with him. It should have had the same effect now.

Only it didn't.

He could kind of feel that in the background, weak and irrelevant. But it was like a shadow compared to what he felt when he thought about Adra now.

So much so that he knew he wouldn't feel good until she did too. Fact. All he wanted to do was help her be happy, and it killed him when she wasn't.

Yeah, he was one hundred percent, absolutely screwed in love.

And he was happy about it.

So happy that when he got home and found Adra already sleeping, her body curled up into a tiny little ball and her expression anything but relaxed, he knew enough to leave her alone. But he gently, slowly, draped a blanket over her first.

chapter 18

The next day, Adra felt…off.

No, it was the entire world that felt off. Just *wrong*, somehow, like there was a major imbalance somewhere, something that would explain why she kept bumping into things, or dropping things onto other things, or just generally screwing up. Or why she had actually snapped at one of the production assistants.

She *never* did that.

She'd brought the poor kid a cup of coffee later because she felt so badly about it—really, if anyone knew how terribly people were treated at the bottom of the entertainment industry ladder, it was Adra, and she'd always promised herself that she would never treat anyone that way—but she'd still *done* it.

The kid was maybe twenty, and had just looked confused and suspicious when she'd apologized.

It was really not her day.

She tried not to think about why.

So, of course, she pretty much *only* thought about why. She'd realized around two in the afternoon that the previous night was the first night since they'd started having sex that she and Ford…hadn't. Not even plain old vanilla sex. That was clearly her fault for running away in the middle of the day and falling into one of those deep sleeps she only managed when she was emotionally exhausted, but she still felt the absence.

She'd woken up with a blanket tucked around her and she'd wished it had been him instead.

And then, right on schedule, she'd had a mini freak-out about wishing it was him.

She was actually *incredibly* tired of freaking out. Really, how long could she keep it up? She was only human. It felt very much like she was on some kind of treadmill with an ever increasing speed, and she was reaching the end of her limit.

"Hey, crazy lady," Lola said. "Whatcha being crazy about?"

Adra turned around to find Lola standing there with a giant, heaping plate of baked goodies stolen from the film catering table.

"That obvious?" Adra asked.

"Mmmhmm," Lola said. "That's why I bring you treats. Well, treat, singular. As in one. The rest are for me."

Adra actually studied her options for a second, trying to make a considered treat-related decision, before Lola burst out laughing.

"Oh my God, I'm kidding," Lola said. "I can't make a pregnancy joke?"

"You ordered an entire page of appetizers. Remember that?"

"That was just indecision," Lola said, waving her hand. "You helped."

Adra laughed. "You are really milking this pregnancy thing, aren't you?"

"Hell yes," Lola said. "Wouldn't you?"

Adra didn't mean to give anything away, but she must have. Maybe her emotions were just running too close to the surface. She watched Lola's expression fall, and felt terrible.

Man, I should come with a warning label today.

"Oh, honey," Lola said. "I didn't mean…"

"Of course you didn't," Adra said. "And I shouldn't… I mean, I'm just weirdly sensitive today, it's not anything you said. I'm just a big ball of feelings lately and I'm starting to feel…"

"Worn out?"

"Yeah."

They sat down in one of Adra's favorite little hidden areas, a little nook where you could see over the second floor balcony onto the chaos below and still have some privacy. Plus, the couch was super comfortable.

"So you want a family," Lola said.

She said it gently, but it was still a statement.

Adra took a deep breath. "It's more complicated than that."

"Not really," Lola said. "I mean, yes, the getting one part is pretty complicated, and so is the having one part, but wanting it…that's often pretty black or white."

Adra tried to stare her friend down. She should have known that never would have worked.

"Fine," she said finally. "Yes, in an ideal world, which this one is not, I would want a family."

"Of course you do," Lola said, tearing into a cinnamon roll.

"What do you mean?"

It was strangely alarming to think Adra's most secret desires, the things she desperately wanted but knew couldn't have, the things she almost never let herself think about, were totally, completely obvious. Like finding out your favorite dress was transparent in the wrong kind of light.

"You're the most maternal person I know," Lola said. She put down the now deconstructed cinnamon roll to give Adra her full attention. "And it's not just maternal instinct, or whatever. You don't treat people like children, but you take care of everyone, Adra. All the time. Like it's your job. Like they're your family."

"You guys are my family," Adra said quietly.

"But you don't let us take care of you," Lola said. "So, *kind* of. But it's not the same, and you know it."

"Lola, please don't make me cry," Adra said.

"At some point you have to let it out, Adra," Lola said. "Whatever is eating at you, whatever this thing is with Ford—"

"Shit," Adra said.

"Oh please, you know I know," Lola said, and shoved a piece of sugared, cinnamoned, doughy heaven at Adra's face. "Eat before you cry."

"Don't have to tell me twice," Adra said. "Sticky fingers and cinnamon tears. You ready for that mess?"

"Always. It'll give me practice for the baby."

Adra laughed until she nearly choked, which, as it turned out, was also a pretty effective way to keep her from crying.

"I hate to tell you this, but I'm pretty sure they don't smell like cinnamon," Adra said.

Lola was not deterred.

"You going to tell me, Adra?" she said, serious now. "I worry about you. I worry about you keeping this inside. I worry—"

"I can't fall in love with him," Adra blurted out.

There was a silence.

Lola carefully picked out a chocolate cupcake and handed it to Adra.

"And why not?" she said.

"Because…" Shit. This was one of those things, where, when she tried to explain it, she just sounded like an idiot. She'd never been able to put together the words to convey the feelings that came over her when she thought about allowing herself to rely on anyone, or have them rely on her, even though it was probably the single biggest guiding principle of her life. If she could even call it that.

Oh, who was she kidding? It wasn't a principle; it was a fear. She should at least own up to it.

"Oh damn," she said, and put down her cupcake. Her appetite was suddenly gone. "Because I'm not really built for it. Other people…I don't know, they seem to manage it. But I never have. I get left, over and over again, and people in my family, they leave, and they hurt people. And I'm not strong enough for it anymore. I know that's a pathetic reason, but it's true, and I just…I would break, Lola. That's the truth. I'd break, and I'd break him, and it would be awful."

"That's…"

"What?"

"I mean, I want to say that's totally crazy and you've just had terrible luck," Lola said. "But somehow I don't think that will help."

"Maybe it's just bad luck, but it's made me like this," Adra said. "I mean, I've gotten used to the idea that I'm not able to have committed relationships. Fine. But if I tried it with Ford and it went to hell the way it always does…oh God, it would just destroy me. And I don't want to lose him entirely. Selfish, I guess, but, well, there it is. So I don't know how to manage the whole thing."

"Who would?" Lola said, picking out another cupcake. "Sounds like a nightmare."

"Well, it's not *all* bad," Adra said.

Lola grinned in a manner that could only be described as "saucily."

"Uh-huh," she said.

"There's actually a *lot* of good."

"There would pretty much have to be," Lola said. "Hey, I have a question. If Ford's your best friend, how come you're not talking about this with him?"

Well, that broke Adra's brain.

She opened her mouth. Closed it. Opened it again. But nope, she still had nothing. Because Lola had a point. If Adra couldn't talk about this with Ford, he wasn't really her best friend. It meant she'd already lost him in a way. It meant the current situation wasn't working.

Lola raised her eyebrows like, *Mmmhmm, I thought so.*

Adra tried to untie the knots in her brain and took another cupcake.

***

It didn't happen like she planned.

It wasn't even meant to happen at all.

Adra had gone back to Ford's early again. She'd paced, and thought, and argued with herself out loud. She'd tensed up when she heard him come home and then she'd waited, both nervous and dying to see him, until she heard his footsteps outside the door of her room. "Her" room—it was *his* house; that she thought of it as her room was kind of ridiculous.

He'd only knocked, and then when she flung open the door, insanely anxious because she still didn't know what to say or what to do, he'd taken one look at her and asked if she was ok.

"No," she'd said. "But I will be. Give me time?"

And then he'd asked no more questions, and made her dinner.

Now it was late. It was past late; it was that hour of the night that felt like a separate island from the rest of the world, at least up here in the Hills. Back at Adra's place, she could always hear some sort of city sounds. But here, in Ford's private house, she felt like she was in another world.

Maybe that actually helped what came next.

She'd been up all night. Trying to figure out how to maintain her friendship with Ford and keep the sex, because, well, she had to face it: the sex wasn't going anywhere. The sex was like a force of nature. Which obviously wasn't sustainable, right, if Ford was going to one day…

She couldn't even think it. Which was screwed up; if she was his best friend, she should want him to be happy. She should want him to find someone to love and build a life with.

And she didn't.

But she couldn't be in love with him. Or, if she was, she couldn't act on it.

Adra went around in these circles for hours, until the moonlight crept across her bed, until the night settled on everything like a deafening blanket, until she had actually driven herself out of her mind.

And it was at that point that she got up.

She walked, shaking, down the hall.

She knocked on his door.

She let herself in.

Ford was sitting up in his huge bed, rubbing his eyes, his bare, muscle torso a pale blue in the light from the window. Adra smiled softly at the sight of him waking up, the gentleness of it, this rare moment of softness. It only lasted a moment and then he was up. Fully present. Full attention on Adra.

It was like a spotlight.

"Adra," he said. "What's wrong?"

She twisted the ends of the shirt she'd worn to bed in her hands. It was one of his old button downs, worn soft and smooth—that's why she'd told him she'd taken it to sleep in. But it was also because it smelled like him, ever so faintly.

Fuck, she had no idea what to say.

"Adra," he said, and he got out of bed, his face worried, his body…

Oh God. His body.

Boxer briefs.

Adra snapped out of it, remembered what she was here for. "Wait," she said.

"Whatever it is, we can fix it," Ford said.

Adra closed her eyes.

"Just…be quiet for a second?" she asked.

"Ok," he said.

Now or never.

Adra opened her eyes. "I came here to say…"

And she couldn't do it. She just couldn't do it. She tried to speak, and realized that she still hadn't pulled a coherent thought out of all that mess, still didn't know what she could say to herself, let alone him. Because once again there weren't really any words that did any of it justice, not words she could say, and so she choked.

She didn't want to be talking. She didn't want to screw up anymore by saying things that weren't true or only half true or just a shadow of the truth.

She could have cried in frustration. Because there he was, Ford Colson, watching her from just a few feet away, and it felt like he was a million miles away. It felt so far, and the distance made her cold, and it made all those words weigh down on her when she already felt too damn heavy. She knew she couldn't tell him how she felt.

She just wanted to show him.

"Adra…" he said again.

"No," she said. "I can't talk. I'm sorry, but I can't…I just…"

Fuck it.

Slowly, Adra worked at the buttons on her shirt. Ford's old shirt. He was watching her, his expression still worried, his brow furrowed.

One button.

Two.

"Adra," he said again. This time his voice was hoarse.

"I'm not good with words," she said. The buttons were done. The shirt hung open. She wasn't wearing anything underneath. "Let me show you."

Silently, Ford put his hand on the side of her face. She leaned into it, savoring the feel of his hand on her cheek. And then she shrugged the shirt off, stood on her toes, and kissed him.

And after that, she didn't know what came over her.

She'd never been too much of a sexual aggressor. She wasn't lazy, either—she was adept at the ways a sub could initiate and contribute to the game. But she'd never felt the need to take; she'd never wanted to leave a mark.

She did now.

She'd never felt *hunger* like this.

She'd been starving. These days without him, these days without his touch, without that feeling of *being* with him—she'd starved. She kissed him with such manic desire that it took them both by surprise. Adra threw her arms around his neck and pressed her whole naked body against him. She felt him come alive, inch by delicious inch, felt him grow hard and huge, felt him match her hunger with that insatiable force that she'd come to crave.

Felt him pick her up with a growl and throw her on his bed.

He stood over her for a second, running his eyes over her body while she panted. Taking it in. Taking her in. Taking *her*.

And then he was on her.

He ran his hands down the length of her body like he was claiming every curve, every hollow, every dip. Ford was the one who would leave his mark, and holy God, did Adra want him too.

He kissed her again, roughly, deeply, his hand in her hair, his weight between her thighs, and then he entered her. There wasn't anything controlled about it. Nothing formal. There was no game, no rules. He just took her with a ferocity that mirrored her own, and as he slid inside her, she found relief.

As they began to move together, Adra brought his head down to hers, his forehead against her own. She felt tears come to her eyes and this time, she didn't fight. She let them spill down her cheeks as her back began to arch, as Ford drove her higher, tighter, brighter.

And the world went back to right.

chapter 19

Ford came awake slowly. Truth be told, he thought he was still dreaming.

Adra was asleep on his chest.

Adra, who usually fled to her own bed each night like some modern-day Cinderella who was afraid of intimacy instead of…what the hell was Cinderella worried about? Pumpkins?

Yeah, he woke up slowly.

His brain wasn't doing much anyway. Everything he had was focused on the woman in his arms.

He'd known it was something big when she showed up in his bedroom in the middle of the night. He'd had to stand there and watch while she shook where she stood, while she tore herself up on the inside trying to tell him something.

The goddamn self-control that had taken, not to just sweep her up. She would never know. But she had obviously needed whatever it was she was doing, so that meant it was going to happen. Whatever she needed, he'd make sure she got it.

And then he had done exactly that.

It had been so *raw*. So naked and honest. If Ford had had any doubts about the way Adra really felt about him, they were gone now. They hadn't fucked—they'd made love. That's what she come into his bed to do. Ford hadn't needed to hold back; he'd been able to show her exactly how he felt, too. He'd loved her like he'd always wanted to and then held her while she clung to him, listening to her breathing as it slowed, as her body relaxed, as she finally let herself fall asleep. He'd laid awake for a long time after that, just to listen to her, to feel her. And while they were both old enough to know that sometimes love wasn't always enough, he figured at least they'd have that night.

At least they'd given each other that.

Now he was awake, and trying to figure out how he could give her more. Because he knew this woman, and he knew she was due to be stressed about the whole thing. And he also knew exactly what he wanted.

Her.

"How long you been awake?" he said.

Adra curled her fingers on his chest. Her breathing had gotten shallower.

"A little bit," she said. "Thinking."

Ford couldn't help but laugh. "Yeah, I figured."

Adra propped her chin up on his chest and narrowed her eyes.

"Are you making fun of my tendency towards anxiety? Implying that I perhaps, sometimes, on occasion, *over*think things?"

"Of course I am."

She blew her hair out of her face, and smiled slightly. "Well, I suppose that's fair."

"Don't think I don't like it," he said, smoothing his hand over her hair. "You start freaking out, it gives a Dom something to do."

Adra laughed softly. "I…had not thought of it that way."

"So you going to tell me?" he said.

"What I'm freaking out about now?"

"Of course," he said again.

She was silent for a while. Almost long enough for Ford to push her, because this time, now, he was going to push her. She was too close to give up now, and if she needed his help, so be it.

But instead Adra pushed herself off his chest, wrapped the sheet around her, and gave him the most earnest, vulnerable look he'd ever seen.

"I'm just going to talk for a while, and I need you to be quiet, because there are things I have to say and I don't know why they're so hard to say to you, but…"

She stopped, and managed to breathe. Good. He wouldn't have to remind her.

"But that's already a lie," Adra said. "Already I'm lying. Jesus Christ."

Ford sat up, leaned against his abused headboard, and pulled Adra closer to him.

"Be nicer to yourself than that," he ordered gently.

"But I do know why it's so hard to say things to you," she said. "It's because you're *real*, and telling you things makes them real. You *matter*, Ford. You're…"

Ford kissed her forehead. He'd never seen her like this, not since they'd had sex. No, not since ever. If he could have taken away every painful thing she felt, every fear she had, every little thing that was screwing with her head, and put it all on himself, he would have done it. It was worse to see her hurt.

"You're my best friend," she said, looking away. "And you deserve better than a coward, even for just a no-strings-attached sub."

"Hey," Ford said. "What did I say about being nice to yourself?"

Adra finally looked at him again, hitting him square in the goddamn heart with those big doe eyes.

"Please just listen," she said softly.

And then she told him all about her brother, Charlie.

What was weirdest about the whole thing was that Ford could tell, even as she was telling him about her brother's tendency to do a runner, even as she kind of glossed over her family history and her dad in a way that made it clear that that whole part of her life was way more relevant than she let on, it was clear that she was skirting around something else. It was clear that the reason she was scared to tell Ford this stuff wasn't because it made her fears about her brother real. That situation was what it was, no matter who she told.

It was because it made her fears about Ford real. Because now they were close again. Because now they talked about personal things, in bed, naked. They made love. They cared about each other.

That's what she was afraid of.

But that was nothing new, not really. It just put a name to some of it. What struck him the most, while she sat in his bed, a sheet wrapped around her beautiful body, her fingers worrying the fabric while she tried to keep herself calm—what struck him the most was how much she freaking apologized for being upset.

Adra didn't even believe she had good reasons to feel the way she did. But a while ago Ford had reason to read up on child psychology and child-rearing and every other child-related thing like it was his damn job, and he knew that habitual neglect or repeated trauma was often worse than a single painful event. That kind of thing never made for a good story or an easy personal narrative, but it would leave its imprint on a person just the same, and they'd have no idea why. Until years later, when they found it so hard to do anything different, so hard to snap out of a groove they'd worn down over the years of learning the same dumb thing, over and over again...

Watching Adra, the most beautiful heart he'd ever met, talk her way through exactly that while she fucking *apologized* for it, damn near broke his own heart.

What he wanted to do was fix everything. He wanted to love her until she forgot about anything that had ever hurt her. He wanted to go knock some sense into Charlie, give him some money, just do *something*. And years ago, when he was younger, he might have tried that.

Now he knew it wouldn't work, because people don't work like that.

So he just had to sit there, against every instinct he had. He listened. And he planned ways to take care of the woman who was prepared for everyone she cared about to screw her over at all times.

"Anyway, that's what's been upsetting me so much," Adra was saying. She was over the worst of it. "I really believed Charlie could make it. That of the two of us... I don't know, maybe that's a lie, too. Maybe I just really wanted to believe, you know?"

It was a rhetorical question they both knew the answer to. They both knew the answer to the implied follow up, too: Adra didn't believe in love for herself or her brother. For other people? Sure. But not for herself.

Ford shook his head, slowly, and pulled Adra to him, knowing he couldn't do anything other than hold her tight at the moment. What he wanted to do, beyond fixing everything, was find every lowlife asshole who had hurt her, who had made her believe that there were no happy endings, and put their heads through the same wall he imagined putting Derrick's head through.

It was so much easier to feel angry, and it didn't do her any damn good.

"That's not all that's been upsetting you," Ford said.

Adra stiffened in his arms. He felt her stop breathing, start again.

"But let that go for now," he went on. "Just know that I'm not going anywhere. *Anywhere*. You got that?"

Adra was too quiet.

"Adra," he said.

"That's not necessarily true," she said quietly. "People have hurt you. They've lost you."

Ford blinked.

"You're talking about Claudia?"

Adra sighed softly. "Yeah."

What in the actual fuck? Ford wasn't usually stumped about what was going on inside Adra's head, but this was like be smacked in the face with a freaking mackerel. Comparing herself to Claudia made no goddamn sense.

"You are not a cheater," Ford said.

"And we don't have that kind of relationship," Adra added, sitting up to look at him. "But it's just…I know it's complicated, but…"

She looked down for a second, and he missed her brown eyes. And when she looked back up, Ford could tell that she knew there was more.

She knew there was something he wasn't telling her.

He felt that pang of grief he always felt when he thought about Andrew, only this time, it was different. This time it felt, for a second, like a thing that kept him from Adra. He hated that. *Hated* it.

And he couldn't fucking tell her.

He looked at Adra's sweet face, thought about how hard this had all been for her, to be this vulnerable and come this far, and how she still didn't want to talk about what they really were…and all he could think was how much more freaked out she would be if he told her about the child he almost had.

~ * ~ * ~

Well, this was unexpected.

She'd done it. Somehow she'd pushed ahead and jumped off a cliff—ok, a mini-cliff, the smallest cliff she could find—and she'd told Ford about Charlie, and the world hadn't ended.

It hadn't ended, but it had confirmed one thing: she felt immeasurably better having confided in Ford about Charlie. Like she'd stopped wearing the wrong size shoes or something. He was her best friend, after all.

And it wasn't like she'd gone ahead and confessed everything that had been stressing her out, because wow, that would be crazy. She hadn't just casually dropped bombs about maybe, possibly already being in love with him and how that would ruin everything. Or about how deathly afraid she was of losing him. Or about how no matter how hard she tried, she couldn't think of a way that this situation ended well, because in the end, Ford deserved to be happy, and if Adra couldn't give him what he deserved because she was such a mess…

But Adra was kicking all those habitual, worrisome thoughts aside now that she was looking at Ford while he very clearly kept some worries of his own to himself.

Part of her wanted to laugh. She wondered if it was this obvious when *she* kept stuff from *him*, and if so, how they'd both managed to avoid being main characters in a comedy of manners so far. It was ridiculous. She could *see* it in his eyes.

What a terrible liar. Call that a quality, though.

And, bonus: This gave her something else to think about. She wasn't panicking about how making love with Ford had been the most honest experience of her life, or about how the rules she'd so carefully insisted upon had pretty much gone out the window, or about anything else.

She was thinking about what had really happened with Ford's marriage.

And while part of her wanted to laugh at how ridiculous they both were, another part of her managed to be both simultaneously hurt *and* relieved for the exact same reasons. Namely: here he was being all distant again, and that sucked, but wasn't it safer? If she was never pressed, if he didn't push her into admitting what she really felt, maybe she really could do this best friends thing. Right?

Best friends who had amazing, perception-altering sex. She could totally do that, right?

What was it they said—'fake it 'til you make it?'

"You don't have to tell me about what happened," Adra finally said, and still couldn't tell if she was hoping he would or if she was hoping he wouldn't. "Boundaries are good."

On the plus side, she was getting pretty used to feeling like a total nutcase, so she had that going for her.

"Adra..." Ford said, and she let herself savor that deep, low rumble, because she looked at him and knew he was far away.

She didn't have to suffer that long, though. When Ford's phone rang at the side of the bed, Adra practically leaped for it.

"It's for you," she said, smiling up at him as she handed him the receiver. She'd actually sprawled across his hard, muscled body to get at the phone. She didn't plan to move.

Ford grinned, took the phone, and then pulled away her sheet.

She was naked from the waist up again, and he was going to take full advantage of it. Adra sighed as his hands played lightly with her breasts. What was it about being fondled by a man who was otherwise occupied? She didn't know, but whatever it was, it was magic.

So she noticed when it stopped.

Adra looked up. Ford's expression had changed. It had gone dark. Medieval. Like the expression he'd had that first day of shooting, when he'd gone after Derrick...

"You've confirmed this?" Ford said into the phone. "I'll need to meet you at the club in an hour. Bring whatever materials you have."

Adra watched him carefully as he cradled her in one arm, and leaned over to hang up the phone with the other. She'd almost never seen him so upset.

"Ford, what happened?" she asked.

"That was the private investigator I hired," Ford said, gently covering her with the sheet, bringing her closer before tucking her into the bed as he got out. He quickly pulled on some jeans and a t-shirt, his face serious.

"Private investigator?" Adra asked. What the hell was he talking about?

Ford looked at her like she was a very precious, very breakable thing.

"He knows who's responsible for all the security leaks," he said.

chapter 20

Ford was on a fucking *tear*.

Adra was at home. Adra was safe at home, and yes it was a goddamn home, it was *their* home now, whatever anybody called it, and that was where she was staying, because it was safe.

He had put his foot down on that one. And then he'd still had to remind her that if he didn't know she was safe, under the circumstances, no one else would be safe, either, and that was a very bad idea.

She'd relented.

"But only because I don't really want to see him," she'd said. She'd laughed a little. "I'm not even surprised."

Ford had said nothing.

"What are you going to do?" she'd asked.

"Fix it," he said.

"Ford, you can't fix it," she'd said.

"I can damn well try."

Which was bullshit, obviously, and they both knew that what was done was already done. But fuck, did Ford want to make just *one* thing in her life better. He'd only realized once he was halfway out the door that there might be more than one way to do that.

He'd stopped dead in his tracks, turned around, and looked her in the eye.

"Tell me you need me to stay and I won't go anywhere," he'd said.

Adra, still wrapped up in his sheets like a present—good God, that woman, with her hair all messed up and curling around her shoulders—reached up, and rubbed her thumb along his chin.

"Will you think less of me if I say that I might actually enjoy it a little bit if you scared the crap out of him?" she'd asked.

"No."

"I'm pretty tired of the filming anyway."

"Yeah."

"And you'll come back soon?" she'd said, biting her lip.

He could practically feel the heat of her body. He'd gripped the doorframe with punishing force.

"God, yes," he'd said.

He'd come back. He'd figure out what to do next, he'd figure out how to deal with what had changed between them, he'd blow off steam. He'd make sure this movie never had the power to hurt her again. And then he'd come back and show her everything he felt.

Which was why he was speeding. Or had been, until he'd hit Venice, and now he was stuck in traffic. It was that damn broken stoplight again, the one on Abbot Kinney right by Volare. Looked like there was another accident.

Ford did not have the patience for this.

He turned his truck down a side street, locked it, and ran the rest of the way.

When he got to Volare he was sweating slightly, his blood was pumping, and he could feel the adrenaline start to surge. Normally this would be where he'd take a step back, tell himself to watch it. Normally.

Ford stopped a startled production assistant in his tracks and loomed over him.

"Tell me where Derrick Duvall is," Ford said.

It wasn't the kind of question a PA was supposed to answer, necessarily, even if he knew the answer. This one stammered it out immediately.

"Upstairs in his dressing room," the PA said. "He doesn't have a call for another hour."

"It's not his goddamn dressing room," Ford growled. "It's a playroom. He was borrowing it."

He took the stairs two at a time.

The door was unlocked, which was good, because Ford would have hated to break it. And Derrick, not the quickest on the uptake, was sprawled out on the couch, one foot on the ground, only half-awake.

"What the hell, man?" he said. "I was taking a nap."

Ford closed the door behind him.

"Get up," he said, walking toward the lazy movie star.

"Dude, what is with—"

"I said get up," Ford said, and hurled Derrick off the couch. "You're going to stand up so I can knock you back down again, as many goddamn times as I feel like. Stand *up*."

Derrick jumped to his feet, doing his best to posture with his shoulders back, his chest out, like he was a big man. He looked ridiculous.

"What the hell is your problem, man?"

"I know," Ford said. "I know it was you, Derrick."

There was a silence.

Derrick chewed on his lip, watched Ford. Ford waited. He wanted an explanation before he dealt with Derrick. He wanted something to bring back to Adra.

"Well, so the fuck what?" Derrick finally said.

Ford clenched his fists and took another step forward. "You leak the location of the shoot, you spread false rumors about your relationship with Adra, you make her home unsafe, you put her in actual danger, and you still don't understand why I'm going to beat the shit out of you?"

"You don't have the balls," Derrick sneered.

Ford just smiled.

"You touch me, and my lawyers will have a field day," Derrick said.

Ford smiled again. He fucking loved his law degree. "Lawyers don't scare me. I know too many of them."

Derrick ran a hand through his hair and laughed.

"You know how much publicity this got for the movie? For your stupid club?"

"For *you*," Ford said. "It got a lot of publicity for you."

"Yeah, that's right. That's my job. I play the goddamn game. Jesus, how naive can you be?"

"You better start talking," Ford said. Now there was just an end table between them. Ford kicked it aside. "The only way I get to fix the damage you've done is if I *know* what you've done, so fucking *talk*, you piece of shit."

"I already told you," Derrick said.

"I'm not just talking about the leaks," Ford said.

The look on Derrick's face really deserved to be punched. Ford opened and closed his fists, and kept it steady.

"Tell me what happened between you and Adra," Ford said.

"You want to *know*?" Derrick said. "You kinky son of a bitch."

That was it.

Ford grabbed Derrick by his two hundred-dollar shirt and threw him against the wall like a rag doll. Derrick worked out, but he did it for appearance; Ford lifted for performance. It was almost embarrassingly easy.

It was embarrassing in general, if Ford were being honest. He knew Adra would be horrified if he lost control. With immense effort, he reined himself in again.

Of course, Derrick didn't need to know about that.

"Derrick, I know I give off an impression of cold reserve," Ford said, cracking his knuckles. "And normally I am a consummate white collar professional. But I didn't grow up that way. And where I'm from, we have very specific ways of dealing with people who hurt family. You wouldn't believe the shit I'd get from my brothers if they knew you still had all your teeth," Ford said, shaking his head. "I haven't beaten down anybody who deserved it in a long time. But don't for a fucking second think that means I've forgotten how."

Derrick slumped his shoulders and began a long, slow slide down the wall.

"Jesus Christ, you're serious?" he said.

Ford was silent.

"Nothing happened, man," Derrick said. "I don't know what she told you, but—"

"Before that, Derrick."

"What?"

Ford crossed his arms. "Start with what you did to her before, when you were together."

Derrick looked up at him, mouth open. "Dude."

"She trusted you?" Ford asked.

The very idea made him itch to hit things.

"What the fuck kind of question is that?" Derrick said, running his hand through his hair again. This time his palms were sweaty.

"You knew about her family, about her father, her brother," Ford said, his voice dangerously calm. "She trusted you."

"We lived together. Kinda hard not to—"

"And then you left her, the exact same way? Disappeared?"

Maybe it was something in the way Ford said it. Maybe it was something in his eyes. But whatever it was, all the color drained out of Derrick Duvall's face.

It wasn't just fear, either. It was anger, too.

That was interesting.

At this point, Ford had Derrick Duvall down to rights. He knew the little worm, knew what made him tick, and he was in no way gratified to know he'd seen through the other man from the beginning. Derrick was powered by a raging insecurity that drove him to treat people like fuel for his constantly starved ego. He was a fucking narcissist. That was why he needed to be a Dom, that was why he leaked damaging info to the press, that was why he'd harassed Adra until Ford scared him into stopping.

And Ford could just see it. He could just see Derrick worming his way into Adra's heart, getting her to trust him, not because he cared, but because it was a challenge. Because if someone who was already damaged could bring herself to open up to him, it was a big win for that monster ego.

And then he'd be done with her.

"You've only heard her side," Derrick finally said. He sounded bitter.

Two things: Ford didn't expect the bitterness. That was also interesting. And he hadn't heard Adra's side at all; he'd only guessed. And this asshole had just confirmed everything.

Ford took a very deep breath and rolled his neck.

"Tell me your side," he said.

"You think she really trusted me? She never went all in, man," Derrick said. "She always had one foot out the door. She was always waiting for me to run, or fuck up, or whatever. You know how much that sucks? If you care about someone, and you fucking try, and you *know* they're not buying it?"

Ford blinked.

He took a step back.

Did he know how much that sucked? Yeah, he did.

But he wasn't thinking about his ex-wife, or even Adra and all the times she kept things from him. He was thinking of Adra's face, just that morning, when she'd asked him about his divorce and she'd known, she'd *known*, there was something that Ford wasn't telling her.

He was thinking of how hurt she'd looked.

He was a fucking idiot.

Ford had spent all this time convincing himself that he'd moved on from his marriage, that he was over what Claudia and Jesse had done. And he was, in the sense that he no longer wanted anything from them, that he was over being angry. But that didn't mean he'd moved on. He'd just killed the part of him that they'd hurt, cauterized that wound, and called that getting over it.

Only Adra had made him come alive again. And that had hurt, for a while, and made him cautious, because maybe he didn't trust people like he used to. He hadn't trusted Adra because of one screw up early on. And then this morning he hadn't trusted her to learn the truth about the divorce and stick around. He hadn't trusted her not to freak out. To be the kind, caring person that she always had been.

And she'd known. And that had hurt her.

"Christ, I'm an idiot," Ford muttered.

Derrick laughed, like now they were friends. "Yeah—"

"Shut the fuck up," Ford barked.

"Jesus, what is your deal?"

"You rationalize your behavior because you're a coward," Ford snarled and shoved Derrick back against the wall. "You did the thing that would hurt her the most, and you did it knowingly. And she was *right* never to fully you trust you, because you're a piece of shit."

"If I was so bad, why does she still trust me?" Derrick said, standing up a little straighter. "You saw us yourself, the other day. Didn't you want to know what we were doing?"

"Watch your mouth," Ford growled.

Derrick straightened his shirt and laughed, covering up his injured pride. Then he pretended to dust some dirt off of Ford's shoulders and said, "Hey, relax. I'm not even really into her anymore. It's just a nostalgia thing. Plus, she's hot."

Ford closed his eyes, slowly shook his head, and thought, *Fuck it. She'll let me have this.*

"You're going to want to brace yourself for this, Derrick," he said softly. "So you won't suffer any internal bleeding."

Ford looked the other man in the eye. Waited.

And then he punched him in the stomach.

"Now get the fuck out of my club," Ford said. "Your goddamned movie can figure it out, or not, I don't care. But you are out on your ass."

Adra would be pissed he got violent, but at least he could tell her he pulled his punch. And then he would tell her that she had her club back, because Ford was done with this nonsense.

Now he just had to figure out what to do about Adra.

chapter 21

A lot of things happened then, all at once.

Adra found herself thinking seriously about her feelings for Ford, and, most importantly, somehow not having an anxiety attack about the whole thing. He let her skirt around it, so they were spending time together, sleeping in the same bed, but not saying the words. The words were still too much.

But they were getting closer, those words. They were definitely getting closer.

And she didn't even have too much time to freak out about that, because the movie was in the final, whirlwind stages of production. And that was because Ford had laid down the freaking law. He'd banned Derrick from Volare and told Santos the director to just figure it out, and that if he had any complaints he could bitch about it in his deposition for the lawsuit Volare would file for multiple breaches of contract.

The end result was that the film crews were leaving. They'd frantically gotten in all the shots they could in the meantime, but today was the last day, and the relief from everyone was palpable. Adra would miss Olivia, and much of the crew, but she was happy to have her club back.

Everyone was happy to have their club back.

So happy, in fact, that they were going to throw a giant, informal wrap party just to show there were no hard feelings—with the one obvious exception—and to welcome all the members back to the club they loved. Adra figured this was also an excuse to introduce some new people to the real Volare life, but hey, that was a good thing. She liked Olivia. It would be good to see her stick around and figure out what submission meant to her.

The world was mostly right again.

She sighed.

So why did she feel so ill at ease?

"Adra, honey, where's your head?"

Adra looked at Lola, who was busy going over a caterer's menu. The wrap party would be last minute, by their standards, but Lola wasn't about to scrimp on the food.

"Never mind," Lola said lightly. "I'm pretty sure I know where your head was."

"You're wrong, for once," Adra said. "My thoughts were perfectly innocent."

"Then Ford's not doing his job."

Adra threw a napkin at her.

"Ford is *excellent* at his job," she said, which only made Lola burst out laughing.

"Oh, please, tell me you've figured it out," Lola said. "Does he actually have a job title yet?"

"No," Adra said, sitting back in…well…confusion. "I don't know. It's still too…"

"Unsettled?"

"Unsettled."

Really, though, the word she was thinking of was "disoriented." Disoriented, and nauseous.

Adra had never been a roller coaster person. Her brother, Charlie, though? Loved roller coasters. Had been on every roller coaster in California, even the old, rickety wooden ones that looked like they were particularly effective methods of tempting fate. To Adra, they just looked like overly elaborate nausea machines.

And Ford was a freaking roller coaster. The man had no idea what he did to her brain. Since he'd made her realize that submission was the only way she felt comfortable letting another person take care of her, the only time she felt ok needing anybody, the whole notion of needing him in particular had…crept into the rest of her life.

Oh, who was she kidding? She already needed him. She couldn't begin to imagine her life without him, or the world without him in it. She was a mess. But the weird part was that she hadn't lost her mind over it yet. For the first time in recent memory, there was a part of her that wanted this. That wanted to be able to open up outside of a scene, to…

No, not just to "open up" in general, indiscriminately, to whoever would have her. It was to Ford. It was always just Ford.

"Oh God, I can't think about this," Adra said.

"Then don't," Lola said. "It'll come. In the meantime, help me plan a party."

"Easy for you to say," Adra said.

Because the flip side of reveling in the wonder of sort of, sometimes, letting Ford take care of her was feeling like she wanted to take care of him, too. In her defense, that was her natural state. She was a nurturer. She couldn't help it; it was who she was. But with Ford, it was different. She wanted Ford to be hers. She wanted to know he was ok, she wanted him to be happy.

And she didn't know what was bothering him.

"Adra, your head went missing again," Lola said.

Adra looked up.

Fuck it.

"Give me a time line of what happened with his ex-wife," she said.

Lola put down her menu.

"Why aren't you asking Ford that question?"

Oh, damn.

"Can we just pretend I have a good answer to that and move on to the part where you tell me everything you know?" Adra asked.

Lola raised an eyebrow.

"Ok, let me ask you something," Adra said, knowing she was doing something crappy, and not being able to stop herself. "If you thought something was bothering Roman, or hurting him, or whatever, but for some reason he hadn't told you…"

"Adra."

"You'd do whatever you had to in order to help him, wouldn't you?"

Lola picked her menu back up and looked at Adra over the edge. The woman had a flair for drama.

"That doesn't mean it would be a good idea," Lola said. "In fact, prying might be a freaking *terrible* idea. Think about how upset you'd be."

"I know, I just…" Adra sat back, defeated. If Lola hadn't convinced her, her own conscience would have. "I just hate feeling so powerless."

"You sure about that?" Lola asked. "You sure you're just not freaked out by being on the other side of that whole taking-care-of arrangement?"

Adra looked for another napkin and realized she was all out of ammo. Besides, throwing things at Lola never seemed to work—she'd tried it with a number of things.

It did usually indicate that Lola had a point, though.

Adra hated the idea.

It *hurt* to think about Ford being hurt. To think she might have already lost her chance to be there for him.

"I just want to help him," Adra said.

"Assuming there's anything actually wrong with him," Lola said, putting down her menu, "I'm pretty sure the only thing that will make Ford feel better is you."

"Now you get your mind out of the gutter," Adra said ruefully.

"I don't mean it like that," Lola said. Then she smiled. "Though that can't hurt."

Adra laughed it off, but she couldn't shake the self-doubt that had wormed its way into her head, ever since she'd confided in Ford and seen that he couldn't trust her back. It wasn't a big thing, not to normal people. But Adra couldn't help but notice it.

And she decided not to care. Because even if Ford didn't trust her because she'd already proven herself to be a screw up, or because he was trying to protect her, or even if it was because he wasn't really over his ex-wife, it didn't matter. She wanted to help him however she could.

And she was about to get the chance.

***

The wrap party was magnificent.

It wasn't even the planning, which was bare bones, or the preparation, which was scatterbrained, but just the sheer enthusiasm. People were so, so happy to have Volare back, to be able to unwind and relax without the pressure of a film shoot, to just be able to enjoy each other's company. You could see it in the faces of the movie people who were there for the first time as guests, and you could definitely see it in the faces of the members who were just happy to have their playrooms back.

It was a happy place.

Adra, of course, was wandering around with her head in the clouds. She was pretty sure she didn't used to do this, pre-Ford situation. Yeah, she definitely wasn't this angsty pre-Ford.

She wished she could hold that against him, but nope. Overall she felt stronger. Angsty, but only because she was actually dealing with…

Feelings.

So she was wandering around the Volare gardens, lost in thought about what came next, when she heard the voice.

"Adra!"

She spun around, trying to figure out where Olivia was hiding. And why. Why would Olivia Cress, famous actress, be hiding?

"Adra, over here!"

Adra had been walking along the perimeter of the garden, away from most of the revelry, and now she saw that Olivia had been taking a breather by one of the catering tables, abandoned by the catering staff for the moment. Just a few feet away, there was a gaggle of laughing guests, but the tables provided a barrier that made it seem like another world.

"What are you doing out here?" Adra asked, smiling. "I'm pretty sure you're meant to be meeting a whole bunch of people."

Olivia blushed almost immediately.

"Wait, you already have met someone?" Adra asked.

"Yes," Olivia said. "I mean, no. Not that. Later. Right now, look under there."

She pointed frantically at one of the tables.

Adra was dubious. No, not dubious: she was apprehensive. What on earth could possibly be hiding under a table?

Well, there could be a small boy. That could happen. A beautiful, brown-haired little boy of about three or four, hiding under the table and sticking his tongue out at Adra.

"Oh my God," Adra said.

"Yeah, exactly," Olivia said. "I think he's playing hide and seek."

"I mean, just, oh my God," Adra muttered again and then smiled at the child. He smiled back.

He was so sweet.

"Go get Ford," Adra said without looking up.

And then, when she heard Olivia walk away, Adra took off her shoes, hiked up her dress, and sat on the ground.

"What's your name?" she whispered.

The little boy just smiled again and covered his mouth with his hands, which were full of grass he'd pulled up from the ground.

Adra laughed.

"I'm Adra," she whispered again. She pulled out her own handful of grass and pretended to eat it.

The little boy laughed, delighted. He tried to pull on the table cloth to hide himself away from Adra, and nearly brought down a row of champagne flutes.

Then he crawled out from under the table and tried to put a handful of grass in Adra's mouth.

Adra fell half over, laughing, while the boy climbed into her lap and tried to feed her more grass. She knew enough that she should be stressed out by the fact that there was a child running around unsupervised at Club Volare, with all the champagne and leather everywhere, and she knew Ford would know how to handle the club's liability…but in the moment, she just let herself feel the joy of hanging out with a child. She'd forgotten how different it was when they were small, how much more innocent and unguarded. Her nephews were all starting to become little tough guys, but this little angel—she missed this. She wrapped her arms around the sweet little boy, blew a raspberry on his cheek, and tried to figure out how she was going to find his parents without causing a panic and scaring the poor kid. Or, for that matter, why his parents weren't panicking.

Which was why she didn't notice when Ford arrived until he was practically standing over them, and the little boy threw a handful of grass at Ford's shoes.

Adra looked up, unable to contain her smile. And then she saw Ford's face.

She'd always thought the expression "like he'd seen a ghost" was an exaggeration. Nope. Ford was dumbstruck. He was staring at the little boy in her lap, and he was…

He was a statue. Rigidly still, he was a statue with an expression, this slow moving drama playing out across his face. He was like a monument to loss and grief, the only time she'd ever seen anything like that in his eyes.

Adra could feel it all in the pit of her stomach.

She scooped up the little boy and stood up, her eyes searching Ford's.

"He won't tell me his name," she said, while the boy toyed with her hair.

Why wouldn't Ford say anything? He was staring at the boy.

"I know his name," Ford said. "It's Andrew."

And then he looked at Adra, standing there with Andrew in her arms, and he touched his fingers to Adra's face. So softly, so gently, but the impact was enough to take her breath away.

What was happening here?

"Do you want to take him?" Adra asked.

Ford flinched. Barely perceptible, but he did. He shook his head, and said, "No, he seems to like you. Let's get him back to his parents, though."

"Yeah, about that…"

"I'll deal with it," Ford said. He walked Adra over to a chair by one of the catering tables. "Can you wait here for a second?"

"Of course, Andrew and I are buddies," Adra said. She held up her hand and Andrew slapped it. "We'll be fine."

Ford really was gone only a moment.

In retrospect, Adra realized he must have seen the parents right away, in that group of people chatting just a few feet beyond the catering tables. Andrew had never been too far from his parents, thank God, but that wasn't really the point.

But it was only when Ford brought them over that she started to put the pieces together.

"Adra, this is Claudia and Jesse Gifford," Ford said. He was even more distant than he had been before. "They are Andrew's parents."

Holy shit.

His ex-wife, and her new husband. Ford's old friend.

It was their kid.

Adra instinctively hugged Andrew in some futile, protective gesture, just as a response to the sudden tension. Then she realized she was hugging someone else's child, in front of them, and handed Andrew over to his mother.

That didn't make things less awkward.

"I thought you were watching him," Claudia said to her husband. Her tone was sharp. She looked tired.

Jesus.

"Um, this might not be the best place for Andrew right now," Adra said as gently as she could.

Adra felt like crap as soon as she spoke up, but she still wasn't gentle enough.

"Do you have children?" Claudia snapped.

"No," Adra said, taking a half-step back. "No, I don't."

"Well, when you do, then we'll talk," Claudia said, holding her son in one hand and rubbing grass stains off his face with the other. "Sometimes sitters cancel at the last minute. It happens. You do what you have to do."

Damn it. That wasn't what Adra had meant at all. The problem was the club's licenses, not Andrew. Roman had made that very clear at dinner not too long ago, but Claudia thought Adra had just gone after her for being a bad mom.

Adra cringed. She had somehow managed to fit both feet in her mouth.

Ford moved slightly, and all attention went to him. Adra could never figure out how he did that, just commanded a room or a group. But then he put a hand on her arm and drew her to him in that protective way, his eyes on Claudia and Jesse, his face calm, and she stopped caring. She just wanted to melt into him. She wanted to hug him and be held by him at the same time.

She had no idea what else was going on between these three, but this was obviously a mess.

"She's right, Claudia," Ford said in that low rumble. "This is a sex club, not a restaurant. It's no different from the New York rules you already know. Our licenses are very restrictive, this place isn't childproofed, and there's unsecured equipment and alcohol everywhere. And more importantly, the club isn't legally permitted to admit minors under *any* circumstances. This could get us permanently shut down."

"Don't lecture me, Ford," Claudia said.

"I'm not," Ford said. "I'm telling you the club's limits. I'm sorry."

"This is petty," Claudia said. She was modulating her voice so she wouldn't upset her son, but her expression was—it was emotional. She had bags under her eyes, and she was looking at Ford with something approaching desperation. "You don't want us—"

"You know that's not fair, Claudia," Ford said. "If I were being petty, your application never would have been accepted in the first place."

"He's right, honey," Jesse said.

Adra looked at the other man, startled, and it occurred to her that he seemed afraid to speak in front of Ford.

This was all kinds of screwed up. She looked at Andrew anxiously, but the little boy seemed to have no idea. Thank God.

Claudia pressed her son's head to her chest and covered his exposed ear with her hand and said, to no one in particular, "Shit."

Then she sighed, hefted Andrew up, smiled at her son and rubbed his nose with hers.

"C'mon, little man," Claudia whispered.

And then she walked off toward the garage.

Adra was…well, confused was one way to put it.

"What the hell?" she said aloud.

"She hasn't slept in about a week," Jesse said, looking at them both with this sort of imploring eagerness. "Andrew's been…well, it doesn't matter. This was our one night off, and then the sitter canceled, and we were going to leave in a few minutes. She's just…you have to understand what it's like…"

He looked at Ford, his former best friend, and trailed off.

Oh God.

Adra recognized the expression on Jesse's face. It was the same expression her nephews had when they got caught doing something really, really bad, something they knew would be met with disappointment instead of anger—something *that* bad. It was like Jesse Gifford was asking for forgiveness. Not just for bringing a kid to the club without asking first, but for everything. That was what Claudia's desperation had been about, that was why Jesse was still here, talking to them, trying to explain the kind of easily avoidable, not-calling-ahead mistake people only made when they were trying to operate on no sleep and no breaks.

That's why they kept coming around. That's why they inserted themselves into Ford's life when they'd moved back to Los Angeles. That had always seemed unbelievably, pathologically screwed up to Adra, but now it made perfect sense.

They were living with the guilt of what they'd done to Ford, and they wanted to be forgiven.

Adra didn't know whether to hate them or pity them. Maybe a little bit of both?

But Ford just shook his head slowly. And then he said, "Everyone makes mistakes."

Jesse blinked silently and nodded, the first glint of moisture in his eyes.

And then Jesse was dismissed.

Adra stood there with Ford as he watched Jesse walk toward the garage to meet his wife and son. Neither of them said anything for what seemed like a long time until Adra delicately slipped her hand into his, her heart swelling to the bursting point with every ounce of love she had for this man.

"There's somewhere I need to take you," she said.

chapter 22

"You're going to rob me, aren't you?" Ford said, grinning. "This was all part of a plot to get me to some deserted canyon where you and your gang of hot accomplices are going to rob me blind and take my truck before I have to hunt you all down."

"Damn. You figured me out."

"At this point that seems the most plausible explanation."

"First of all, I did not get us lost."

"Agreed. We're not lost because I know exactly where we are," Ford said. "*You* don't know where we're going."

"It's around here somewhere, I promise. Oh, try that turn, go, go, go!"

Ford hung a dangerous-feeling right turn into another narrow, winding road and flicked his high beams on while he slowed to a crawl. He had no idea what they were looking for, but he might as well try to find it.

"My gang of hot accomplices, huh?" Adra said, looking at him out of the corner of her eye. "I bet they're all female."

"I assumed you'd be the leader of a kick-ass girl gang, yeah," Ford said. "You'd each have your talents."

"Like the A-team, only hot lady thieves?" Adra said.

"What?" he said. "You're telling me Hollywood has lied to me?"

Adra swatted at him, laughing, and Ford was seriously considering just pulling over so he could make her moan, just for a little while, just because she'd already done so damn much to lift his mood after what happened back at Volare—when Adra suddenly hit him in the arm, hard.

"There! Right there! I swear to God, it's exactly like I remember it!"

It wasn't even a road. It looked like an opening in the brush.

Dutifully, Ford turned into that brush, knowing his truck could handle it, and found an unkempt dirt road. And then they came upon a dead end, and he suddenly understood what they'd been looking for.

It was fucking beautiful.

The entire city laid out before them, glittering, shining, pulsing with the beat of millions of people living their lives. It was huge and humbling. It was Los Angeles at peace.

"This is what I wanted you to see," she said softly.

Ford didn't have the words.

Instead he turned the truck around, carefully, in this tiny little enclave, so that the bed of the truck faced out on the opening in the canyons that gave them that view. Then he grabbed the blankets he always kept with him, helped Adra down, and set them both up in the bed of his truck, looking out over his adopted city.

"This is beautiful, Adra," he said. They were both sitting in the back of his truck with their legs hanging over the edge, side by side. He reached over and put his hand over hers.

She was so warm and small. After a moment, she turned her hand over, and laced her fingers with his.

"No one knows about it," Adra said. "I found it by accident once in high school, getting lost on my way to a party. After that I came up here all the time."

Ford grinned at her. "You and your high school boyfriend?"

"No," she said, nudging him. "Just me. This spot was always just for me. I came up here whenever I needed to feel...I don't know. Like it could all work out."

She was staring hard out at the city when she said that.

And then she looked directly at him, with her heart in her eyes. It made Ford ache to his core.

"You don't have to talk about it if you don't want to," she said. "I just wanted you to feel differently than I saw you feel back there."

It washed over him, the weirdest sensation, knowing this woman he'd kill for was trying to protect him. It was like being in a dream world, some place he hadn't really let himself think about, he'd been so focused on taking care of her. He hadn't even conceived of how he might let her in, and here she was, knocking on the door.

For possibly the first time in his life, Ford didn't know what to say.

Then Adra smiled a little shyly. "Ok, you kind of had me. I did come out here after the first time I got my heart broken."

"And?" he said.

Adra started to laugh. "And I promised myself that I would keep trusting people, no matter what happened, no matter how much it hurt. God, did *that* turn out to be stupid."

Ford threw his head back and laughed harder than he had in years.

"Christ, the both of us, messed up in the head," he said. "It was that obvious there was something up back there, huh?"

"Not to anyone else," she said.

"Yeah, I bet not," Ford said.

He couldn't stop looking at her.

The truth was, seeing Adra with little Andrew had hit him in a place he'd thought was long dead, and it had woken him the hell up. It was like being jerked out of a dream. He'd known he loved Adra, but this…

He'd seen the woman he loved with the child he'd thought would be his, and all of a sudden he saw a future for himself again.

It wasn't even a decision. It was a realization. He was helpless before this woman.

Ford impulsively lifted Adra up and pulled her sideways into his lap, wanting his arms around her, and felt a low, satisfied rumble in his throat as she relaxed into him. This was better. He looked at her troubled face, and then he kissed her.

She'd need to feel steady for this.

"When Claudia was pregnant," he said as he pulled away, telling this story for the first time in years, "I thought the baby was mine. Up until she gave birth, I thought he was mine. We'd separated by then, but it was only after that I found out how long the affair had been going on. Andrew is Jesse's natural son, but I thought…"

"Oh, Ford," Adra said softly.

"I thought I had a son," he said simply.

"Ford," she whispered.

Her doe eyes were full of tears, and that he hated to see. He knew it wasn't pity; it was love. And more than that, it was Adra. Adra felt everyone's pain even more than she felt her own. It made her the best friend on the planet to everyone she met, and it made Ford want to wrap her in his arms and take her away from anything bad that could ever happen.

"I'm ok, Adra," he said. And he realized it was true. "I wasn't, for a while. Claudia and me, we weren't right. We never should have gotten married, but we were young and dumb and it happened. I got over her and Jesse. But Andrew…"

He shook his head, and kissed a tear off of Adra's cheek.

"I had a hard time trusting people after that," Ford said.

And he realized suddenly that he was using the past tense. There was only one reason for that, and she was sitting in his lap at that very moment, her fingers toying with the lapels of his jacket. That's why he could see a future for himself: he didn't just love Adra, he trusted her. He trusted the person he knew her to be.

He hadn't been all that different from Adra, really — they both had all these scars from experiences that taught them not to believe in anyone. Those scars just showed up in different places. But Ford was done being the walking wounded. He fucking *loved* this woman, more than he'd known was possible, and that made it easy to do whatever he had to do.

Even if that meant putting it all on the line.

"Adra," he said gently.

"Yeah?"

"I don't have that problem anymore," he said. "I trust you."

Wait.

Watch her.

Adra exhaled a slow, shaky breath.

"So we're doing this now?" she said.

"Not all at once," he said.

He brushed her hair out of her face, flying around in the breeze, and kissed her again.

"You're scared," he said.

"I'm fucking terrified," she said. She looked up at Ford, her eyes shining. "You have to be the brave one, ok?"

Ford didn't hesitate. If he'd thought it was about bravery, it would have been done ages ago. But it was about letting them come into their own. And maybe they were finally ready.

"You are the love of my life," he said. "I didn't know I needed anybody, but I need you. I need you to be happy. Whatever else happens, Adra, I need to know that you're happy. The rest doesn't matter."

Adra blinked, and tears fell down her cheeks. She shuddered in his arms and he held her tighter.

"You know I love you, too," she finally said, her voice small. "And, oh God, I need you, Ford. I do. It scares the crap out of me, but I do."

"I'm never going to let anything happen to you," he said.

He had never meant anything more in his entire life.

And then Adra began to cry.

He couldn't hold her tight enough.

"But I don't know if it will work," she said. "I don't know if I can do it. What if it doesn't…what if we—"

"Shhh," he said. "We have time. We have all the time in the world to figure it out. Slowly, ok?"

"Slowly," she said, nodding against his chest.

"Snail's pace," he said.

"Geological time," she said, and he could feel her smile against him.

"There will be stalagmites that give us a run for our money."

She breathed deeply, let it out, and looked up at him.

He wanted to preserve that moment. The look on her face. The naked love there, and yeah, the bravery. Ford might never know what he did to deserve having Adra in his life, but he'd damn well make sure he lived up to privilege.

"So this is really happening," she said.

He laughed. "I was wondering how long it was going to take you to figure that out."

"We've both got...I mean, we've both got issues, let's be honest. And I've hurt you already—"

"No, we hurt each other, because we were idiots." He shrugged. "And nobody makes it to thirty without some sexy battle scars."

"You are pretty damn sexy," she admitted, and smiled.

Fuck, that smile.

He could look at her face all day, every day. If he were lucky, he would get to. But right now, in this moment, he let himself fall a little bit more in love with her. He let himself look into her eyes and see that she was feeling the same thing, that they both knew they stood together on the cusp of something, that she was scared and thrilled and everything in between, and that Ford...

Ford couldn't feel anything but love. He could see that she was scared, he could see that she was wound up, that she felt out of control, but all he felt was love.

And he knew exactly what Adra needed next.

chapter 23

Holy shit. Holy, holy shit.

Adra kept repeating it to herself on the drive back to Ford's house, her arm resting up by her window, her head in one hand while Ford held the other. She couldn't stop smiling, either, looking over at him occasionally.

Yeah, this was happening.

It was that same feeling you got on a roller coaster that moment when you knew it was really happening.

Maybe not the best analogy.

She squeezed his hand and tried to calm herself down, but it was no use. Of course it wasn't. She'd spent years trying to make sure she never felt the things she was feeling right now; she was totally out of practice at it. It was like a giant weight had been lifted off of her, a weight that she'd carried so long that she'd forgotten it was there — pretending that she wasn't in love with Ford. The feeling of suddenly being free was almost like subspace.

It was amazing.

She could handle it. Probably. She was overloaded, but she could handle it.

Adra shared a look with Ford then looked down at her hand. It was shaking.

He saw it, too.

"Oh my God," Adra said, laughing lightly. "I am such a nutcase. Did you know that, falling in love with me? Total nutcase?"

Ford smiled at the road. "It's part of your charm," he said.

"Then I have got plenty of charm for you, mister. Get ready to be charmed. I will charm you to within an inch of your life."

Adra heard the distinctive crunch of Ford's gravel drive and looked ahead to see his house illuminated in the distance by the headlights.

"No, that's not what we'll be doing," Ford said.

It was the voice. That easy confidence. That utter certainty.

Without another word, Ford got out of the truck and walked around to her side. Adra didn't move. By the time he opened her door, she was breathing quickly. Shallowly.

He had that look.

"Get out of the car," he said, and offered his hand.

Adra tried. But as she swung her legs out, Ford stopped her, looking at her heels and frowning.

Then he picked her up.

Now she was overloaded.

He carried her like that, heart thudding against her chest so hard that she was sure he felt it in his, her arms around his neck, her body melded to his, up the front walk and…

Around to the back gardens?

She hadn't spent a whole lot of time out there since she'd been staying with Ford. In fact, she'd spent more time with Ford, usually naked, than anything else, and they'd both been so busy that she never got to use the pool or anything else.

She didn't know the grounds very well in the dark, but she definitely recognized that fire pit between the Jacuzzi and the pool. And the crazy modern sculpture thing right next to it.

She'd always wondered about that sculpture. It was like a giant burnished circle of metal that pivoted, tilting with the sun, or…

Oh.

It wasn't a sculpture. Or it was, but it was also…functional. You could see the restraint attachments if you were really, really looking.

Ford put her down right in front of it.

"Step into it," he said.

Hesitantly, Adra stepped under the upper arch of the thing and looked up. It must have been seven foot in diameter, fixed on the sides to support poles so that it could…spin.

Ford had taken the lid off a nearby bench that apparently doubled as storage. Adra recognized the restraints he removed—soft leather, strong chains.

She took a very deep breath.

He didn't speak as he tied her up. Just his hands on her body, positioning her where he wanted her, making sure she stayed there. Her arms were above her head, bound by wrist cuffs attached to chains. Her legs were spread, her ankles bound the same way, her dress riding up almost to her ass.

Every cuff brought her a little higher. Every restraint…

She was panting by the time he was done.

And then he walked away.

Not too far, but far enough that she ached with it. That the anticipation, as he patiently lit the fire pit, became unbearable. That when he finally looked at her again, the flames high and warm behind him, she actually moaned softly.

Oh God.

He studied her for a moment.

Then he came back, his eyes locked on hers, pulled her head back, and kissed her.

Rough. Hard. Deep.

His hands invaded every inch of her while the fire roared behind him, his fingers tracing gentle lines, then pinching. Squeezing, kneading, then slapping. Every change, every sensation, driving her higher, further and further away from the ability to worry about the future.

This was about giving her her release. This man knew exactly what he was doing.

This man…

Adra groaned as his hand settled between her legs, stroking her absently while he kept eye contact.

This man was the end of her.

"I've never used this ring before," he said, his mouth hovering inches away from hers while his fingers stroked her the soaked fabric of her underwear. "I had it put it in just after I met you. I've always wanted to see you in it."

Adra opened her mouth to speak, but nothing came out. There were fleeting thoughts of all the time they'd wasted, of all the nights she'd spent wanting him, of all—

And he put them all to bed with another kiss.

"I love you, Adra," Ford said. "You are mine. Do you understand?"

"Yes," she panted. "Oh God, yes."

"Say it."

Adra closed her eyes, and sighed as she felt the left strap of her dress pull to the side. It all seemed so clear when she was like this, bound, on the verge of subspace, her body thrumming with pleasure. It was all so simple it almost made her want to laugh.

"I'm yours," Adra said. "Always have been."

Then she opened her eyes.

"And you're mine," she said.

Ford paused, his eyes locked with hers. He smiled. Then he pulled a pocketknife out of his pocket and cut away her dress.

Adra gasped as it fell to the ground.

Ford let his fingers trail down her naked torso, dallying over her nipple, teasing down her abdomen, until he reached the thin fabric of her underwear. He never broke eye contact.

And then he cut her last remaining piece of clothing away.

"Mine," he said.

That was when Adra started to slip away.

She loved that feeling. Loved it and knew it well, that moment when she started to fall up, somehow, into subspace. Only this time, it was different. This time, as she watched Ford go back to the cabana to retrieve a bag of toys, as she felt the warmth of the fire on her bare skin, as she simply waited to fall fully into submission...she did it all with her heart, too. It wasn't locked off; it wasn't hidden away so that her mind and body could go on a little temporary vacation.

It was all of her.

He had all of her.

And he knew it. He had her, and he loved her.

She knew because of the way he whispered to her as he dragged the tails of the flogger over her exposed skin. The things he murmured in her ear from behind as he penetrated her, briefly, with the handle and told her to hold it in place, one hand slapping her ass, the other holding her head still, his fingers in her mouth while she moaned. The way he never broke contact, not once, the way he orchestrated her every sensation, her every feeling, her every emotion. The way he knew when she was highest, when he'd filled her with so much sensation that she was ready to burst.

All of it, all of it made it impossible for her to be anything other than his. For her to keep even the last, most frightened parts of her safe and separate. He owned all of her. And when he'd shown her that, he released her legs, lifted them over his shoulders, looked her in the eye, and slid slowly into her.

"Mine," he said again, and her head dropped forward to his while he moved inside her, waiting helplessly for the mind-obliterating orgasm that he'd built inside her.

She didn't really have words for the rest.

He filled her, completely. He owned her, completely. He was hers, completely.

And for the first time in her life, Adra really let herself go.

She didn't really come back to reality until he had taken her down and carried her, limp and exhausted, to the Jacuzzi. And she didn't know how long they spent in the hot, bubbling salt water before she was cogent again. But she did know he refused to let go of her.

He had her in his arms, on his lap with her back to him, kind of floating, the way you do in a Jacuzzi. Adra laid her head on his shoulder and just let the aftershocks ripple through her, wondering if she'd ever really come down from this.

Probably not.

Definitely not, if he kept moving his hands over her thighs like that.

"Did you think I was done with you?" he said into her ear.

chapter 24

Neither of them really cared when Adra lost her phone. In retrospect, Ford wished he'd cared. He'd just been so happy to have Adra to himself for an entire long weekend that he didn't give a crap about anything else.

Anyway, it turned out that carrying your woman to the backyard, tying her up, teasing her to the point of delirium and then making love to her until neither of you could stand up without ever dropping into the house to drop your stuff off was an excellent way to lose a phone.

Neither of them even noticed for a few days, and when they did, it didn't matter. Adra was fucking incredible. He had watched her go back and forth from blissful to frightened, from serene to scared—and he got it now. It wasn't just her family and her past experiences; it was that the stakes were so damn high. Falling in love always felt like winning big, but when it was with your best friend, you were all in. They were both risking it all.

He could see it haunted her even though she was happy. Sometimes she'd look at him with those big doe eyes and he'd see all those fears, clear as day, and that was his cue to step in. And he made a point of it: he would never not be there for her. Hell, he couldn't get enough of her anyway.

It was one of those times, lying out by the pool at night, Adra on his chest pretending she hadn't just tensed up, that he decided to push her.

"Adra, what are you afraid will happen?"

She sighed.

"I don't know."

"Bullshit," he said, and he hauled them both up so he could see her face—and more importantly so that she could see his face.

"Look at me," he said. "I'm not going anywhere. I love you."

She smiled at him. "Drama queen."

"Watch it," he growled, his hands on her ass. He let her run her fingers through his hair for a while, and just watched her.

"I'm serious, Adra," he said finally. "If you believe one thing…"

"I know," she said, and she touched his face.

He believed her. She did know. But that didn't stop it from feeling too big to handle.

So they took it slow.

And it was fucking wonderful.

And it wasn't until Sunday that Roman finally called Ford.

"My wife wants to know if she should be worried that Adra hasn't answered her phone in two days," Roman said.

"Adra is...very well," Ford said, smiling at the beautiful woman who was currently destroying his kitchen. She'd caught the end of a *Top Chef* marathon and she'd been inspired.

Then Ford remembered who he was talking to.

"Wait, is the baby coming?" Ford asked. "She'd kill me if we missed the birth of your kid."

"You haven't yet, unless something has changed in the last five minutes."

"Well, tell Lola not to worry. We're just fine."

"She wants to come to dinner."

"Shouldn't she be—"

"Ford," Roman said, his voice only slightly strained. "My very pregnant wife wants to come to dinner, and she wants to see her friend. So she is coming to dinner. And even if you have to get Adra down from an overly complicated suspension harness, she will be at dinner so that my wife can talk to her."

Ford laughed. He knew all about the impending stress of fatherhood, in a screwed up way, and what it was like having this great big responsibility and not being able to *do* anything in the meantime. Just waiting drove most men crazy. Roman had found something he could make happen, so it was going to damn well happen. The poor bastard.

"Done," Ford said.

"Thank you."

"Anytime."

And as Ford went to go tell Adra that she could either make an overly ambitious meal for four instead of two, or she could order from a three-star restaurant and just put it on some plates and he'd never tell, he made a mental note to look for her phone.

***

Dinner was mostly a chance for Lola to gloat.

"I *knew* it!" she said. "Oh man, I *knew* it, knew it, knew it!"

"Knew what?" Ford said innocently.

"I'd kick you under the table if I could reach," Lola said.

Ford laughed, but he was watching Adra to see if any of this spooked her. It didn't. She looked...she looked wonderful. She looked dazed by how wonderful everything was.

Hell, so was he.

Which set off his Dom sense a little bit. Nothing was ever so perfect or so easy. But he ignored it.

Of course he fucking ignored it. He couldn't take his eyes off of Adra for more than a few seconds.

"Ok, I'm just saying maybe next time listen to me and save yourselves the angst," Lola said. "Where's food?"

"Please, the angst was the best part," Adra joked. "And food is...complicated."

"Tell me there's food," Lola said.

"Tell her there's food," Roman repeated.

"No, there's food, it's just..."

Ford couldn't help from laughing.

"The appetizer came out ok," he said. Which it sort of had. She had "plated" it forty-five minutes ago and it was kind of sad and droopy looking, and Ford never had the heart to ask what it actually was, but it did actually exist.

Adra had dumped the main course before he ever got a chance to see it and then she'd informed him that they would never speak of it again.

"Hush," she said to him, smiling.

"We ordered delivery," Ford said. "Should be here any second."

"*You* ordered delivery," Adra said. "Did you ever find my phone?"

They both smiled at each other, remembering how it was lost.

"Yeah, it's dead," Ford said. He'd found it in the bushes lining the walk from the drive to the back yard, but he'd forgotten about it as Roman and Lola arrived. "Let me plug it in."

He thought about that later. If he'd used the charger in his bedroom instead of the one in the living room, would it have made a difference? Would it have made it seem less urgent, given Adra more time, made it less of an overall clusterfuck?

They'd only just torn into the Chinese food when Adra's phone sucked up enough juice to turn itself on. And that's when the notifications started.

That distinctive little *ping* went off just once at first.

"That message is from me," Lola said. "Probably the next five, too."

They'd all laughed, and then laughed again when Adra's phone kept pinging. It was kind of hard to pinpoint the moment when it stopped being funny, but it was Lola who put it into words.

"There is no way I called you that many times," she said.

Ford watched the anxiety start to seep into Adra's expression. They'd had a few days cut off from the rest of the world, and it had been almost perfect. But that wasn't real life.

Whatever was happening right now: that was about to be real life.

Wordlessly, Ford got up from the table and walked over to Adra. He knew what she was thinking: Charlie. Or some other version of disaster. Part of Adra was always waiting for the other shoe to drop.

"C'mon," he said. "It's gonna drive you crazy."

He took her hand and walked with her over to her phone where it was charging in the next room.

"I feel ridiculous," Adra said, laughing slightly at herself as she picked up the phone. "I just have such a bad feeling, you know? I mean, obviously, it's..."

She trailed off.

Ford felt it like a punch to the gut. Her face — all the joy went out of it.

"Adra, what's wrong?"

"I have to go," she said.

"Charlie?" he said.

Adra nodded sadly. "I have to go."

~ * ~ * ~

The drive down to San Diego was miserable. Adra kept thinking about one thing: Ford's face when she told him she had to leave, and that she had to go alone.

She'd guessed he'd known it was kind of bullshit. Not entirely; she really didn't think that Nicole and the boys would benefit from having a stranger show up in the middle of all this, even if he was her stranger. But the truth was that wasn't why she'd insisted on going by herself. And she didn't entirely figure out why she'd done that until she actually got there.

In the meantime, she thought about Ford's face. And she thought about how unimaginably happy she'd been in the past few days, how she'd felt things she never, ever let herself believe she'd get to feel. And how what was so terrifying about that wasn't that she was afraid Ford would leave—when he told her he wouldn't ever leave her, she'd almost wanted to laugh, because it was like telling her the sky was blue. She had more faith in Ford than she'd ever had in anyone in her life.

No, what was terrifying about it was watching how happy *she* made *Ford*, and knowing she could break his heart. It was watching him talk to her about the son he almost had, and realizing that he needed her, in his way, just as much as she needed him. *That* scared her. She could hurt him as bad as he could hurt her. It blew her mind. And it terrified her, with that familiar kind of panic, which surprised her.

That man had taught her more things about herself in the past few weeks than she'd learned on her own in thirty years. And that last lesson was a total mindfuck, because she'd never been in a position where that was possible before.

And she was willing to deal with the mindfuckery—she *was* dealing with it—until she got those messages.

The first one was from Charlie. Just the first one. "I can't do it. I'll call you when I get where I'm going."

And the next bazillion were from Nicole.

She didn't need to call Charlie to know he wasn't answering his phone, so she didn't bother. She just called Nicole to tell her she'd be there in a few hours, and what she'd heard had frightened her.

Nicole just sounded…flat.

Adra broke every speed limit in the book on the way down. She told herself the whole way that she was overreacting, that this was obviously just her own neuroses kicking into hyper-drive again, that she'd get there and it wouldn't be a huge crisis, and she'd go back to Ford and resume the business of slowly changing her life.

She told herself all sorts of reasonable things.

One of the worst things about being prone to anxiety and freaking out and imagining the worst-case scenario in every little situation was when she actually turned out to be *right*.

The house was a little bit of a disaster. It looked like…it looked like one of those places she'd seen on television pre-intervention. The sink was overflowing with dirty dishes, so the boys had started putting them on whatever surface was available, piling them up into little statues of cereal bowls and cups that adorned the entire house like tiny little cairns. Someone had done a load of laundry days ago, but it had never been folded or put away, and was just taking up one of the seats on the couch, so the cat had claimed it as a bed. There was trash on the floor like a fine layer of debris.

Adra wouldn't have believed this level of chaos could build up in only a few days, except she had seen those boys at work herself. In two days they could level the place down to the studs if they wanted. So this wasn't exactly as bad as it could be.

None of it was such a big deal on its own, not really. She could imagine things getting out of hand even if both parents were around; it happened with kids. But Adra knew her sister-in-law. And Nicole was a neat freak.

So this level of disaster was not good.

She picked her way through the house like it was an actual disaster zone, or like she had to be careful of destroying evidence, and didn't catch herself until she got to the kitchen. It was the silence, that's what was so weird. This house was never quiet. It spooked her until she saw the boys out in the yard, playing some sort of game.

And then she got to the bedroom and her heart broke a little bit more.

Nicole was lying in bed, surrounded by used tissues. Adra just stood there for a second in the doorway, trying to catch her breath. She had found her mother like this so many times. So many.

Except that Nicole, when she heard Adra come in, turned over, startled, and sat up. Nicole grabbed a tissue, apologizing, Nicole tried to engage, be normal, or as normal as she could be under the circumstances. Adra's mom...Adra's mom wouldn't have done any of that. She would have been drunk or too depressed to speak, or both. She wouldn't have moved from that mountain of tissues. She would have just kept staring at the wall with vacant, sad eyes.

"Oh God, you scared me half to death. I thought you were one of the boys," Nicole said, dabbing at her eyes with a clean tissue. "I just...I had to send them outside so I could have a cry. I'm trying to schedule it," she said, laughing through her tears.

Adra blinked.

Snap out of it, Adra. She's not Mom.

"What can I do?" she said.

Nicole leaned back against the headboard. "Give Charlie a brain transplant?"

Adra wanted to cry, but she made herself laugh instead.

"How are the boys?" she asked.

"Oblivious. Daddy is on a business trip again. I had to work from home, though, so that's why the place is a mess," she said. Then she sighed. "I don't know how long I can keep any of this up, though."

"When was the last time you slept?"

"Sleeping?" Nicole said wryly. "What's that?"

Adra flopped on the bed, feeling miserable and powerless. Just like she felt when she was a kid, and she had to watch her mother go through the same thing. Of course, Adra had gotten older and realized that, no matter how much Adra loved her, her mom had her own issues, that it wasn't all that simple. But the feeling was still there.

"I am so sorry, Nic," she said.

"It's not your fault," Nicole said. "I know what he's like, Adra. I know...I knew about this, kind of. I mean, I knew what I was getting into. I know that sounds completely insane, but…I love him." She shrugged.

Adra stared at this woman she'd thought she knew, and realized she only knew a very superficial part of her. "How are you not losing your mind?"

Nicole looked at her. "He always comes back, Adra."

Adra forced herself to smile, but inside…

Inside, she was screaming. Inside, she remembered how there was a time when their father didn't come back, and she felt ten years old again, powerless to stop it. Inside, she felt afraid.

***

As steadfast and sure as she was, Nicole was also just worn out, having gone through something like this countless times, and she'd reached her limit. And even though Adra had seen this so many times before, she still felt like a kid with no idea what to do.

So she did what she'd done when she was a kid — she took care of stuff.

She cleaned. She was like a whirlwind dervish of cleaning. She made the boys come inside and help, mostly as an excuse to check on them. They seemed fine, but she wondered. She wondered how long it would be before they figured out something was wrong, and that made her want to suit up and hunt her brother down. She would *not* let this happen to these boys.

And while she was thinking of ways to fix her brother's screw-ups, she made Nicole take a sleeping pill, because even an apparent stoic superwoman needed sleep. And she was relieved to hear that Nicole's parents were coming down from Seattle, the one piece of good news. They were retired, had all the time in the world, and were great with the boys. Nicole had plenty of people who wanted to help her.

Just not her husband.

So by the time Adra put the boys to bed, her heart aching when each one of them hugged her, she was a mess on the inside. She kept it together up until the rest of the house was asleep, and then...

Then it started.

She had let herself forget what this was like. She had driven down here in a total panic because she'd remembered, suddenly, she'd remembered the things she'd let herself forget. And just because Nicole wasn't broken by it, the way her own mother had been, that didn't change things, not really. She had let herself forget what her family was really like.

She had been so, so stupid.

So when Ford called her, she knew what she had to do.

"Adra, why are you crying?" he said.

She could already feel it in his voice. He was worried. She could imagine him pacing around that house, just looking for something to do, for somewhere to put that energy. She knew the only reason he hadn't insisted on coming with her, let alone tracked her down, was because of how much he respected her, but this would be driving him crazy. Causing him pain. Adra was perversely grateful that he was far away, that it was just his voice tugging at her heart over the phone, because she knew that if she had to see him in person she could never, ever do this.

"Because of what I'm about to say," she said.

There was a pause.

"Tell me what happened," he said.

"He left," Adra said. "Nicole says he's coming back, but I don't… I'd forgotten what this is like, Ford. It's bad."

"Does she have anyone else? How long are you staying?"

"Her parents are coming. I'm staying as long as she needs me."

"I'll come down."

Adra closed her eyes and stifled a sob.

"No," she said.

"Adra," he said, after a moment. "Don't."

"I've been so stupid," she said. "So, so stupid. You don't understand. If you knew…"

"I'm coming down."

"No!" she said, suddenly desperate. She really couldn't do this if she had to see him. She didn't care if that made her coward so long as it didn't make her the woman who made promises that she couldn't keep.

"You deserve so much more, Ford," she said quietly.

"So do you," he said, and she could tell he was saying it through gritted teeth. There was nothing that annoyed him more than when he thought she disparaged herself. She smiled sadly.

"Not that," she said. "I know I deserve more too, but it's not…it's not that simple. I'm not *capable* of this. I'm not. But you are. I can't do that to you. I can't risk it."

"That is *my* risk to take," he said, and it was the first time she heard him sound angry. "*Mine*. You're afraid, Adra. I'm not."

"Yeah, no shit," she said.

"Adra, I love you. I don't care about anything else."

"That's exactly the problem," she said. "Don't love me. Please, don't love me, don't be hurt by me, don't trust me. I've been so afraid of being hurt by you, because I love you more than I ever thought I could love someone, but the truth is, I've been hurt like that before. I know what it would do to me. But if I ever did this to you…"

She stopped, and covered her mouth while she sobbed.

"Adra," he said.

"If I ever did this to you, I couldn't handle it. I couldn't survive this. I can't be this person. I can't. I can't risk it. I'm not as strong as you are, Ford."

"You don't have to be, damn it. I can be strong for the both of us until you're ready."

"I want you to have a family," she said. "I want you to have all the things that you want… Ford, you know I have complete faith in you, don't you?"

He paused.

"Yeah," he said.

"Thank you for that," Adra said. "I honestly never thought I'd be able to say that about anyone."

"Adra, I know what you're going to say, and you are wrong."

"I'm not wrong," she said. "I *don't* have faith in myself. How can I? I can't…I can't do this to you, Ford. Please. I just can't."

There was a silence. An aching, ageless silence where Adra was alone in her misery.

And then he said, "No."

It was the voice. The Dom voice. Even then, even at that miserable moment, it made Adra sit up straighter.

"This is wrong, Adra," he said. "You are scared, and that is understandable, but saying you are not capable…"

He actually sounded angry.

"You are wrong," he said again. "And I am losing my patience. I will be damned if I let you think those things about yourself."

Adra closed her eyes again, and felt fresh tears glide down her cheeks. She loved him so much that it hurt, and she had to do this one thing right. What was it that she'd learned through this mess with Charlie? She couldn't fix it.

"Not even a Dom can fix everything," she said quietly.

"This one can," he said, his voice like iron. "Watch me."

"No, you can't," Adra said. She took a deep breath. She had to burn this bridge once and for all. She had to go for the jugular. "And you're not right about everything, either. You can't be this perfect, Ford. No one is. And I am the worst person in the world to use to fix your life."

There was a silence. A long, cold silence. Adra held her breath to keep from crying. She'd just tried to hurt him in order to do the right thing, and the worst part was, it had worked.

"That's what you think I'm doing?" he finally said. "Using you to fix my life?"

She couldn't even bring herself to say it again. But she couldn't do this, either.

When Adra finally spoke, her voice sounded as dead as she felt inside. "You can't change who I am, and you can't change who you are," she said. "You should find someone else, Ford. Because you can't have me."

chapter 25

Adra barely slept. It was one of those nights where it felt like she hadn't slept at all, just tossed and turned and tried not to think about Ford even while she missed him with a physical ache, until suddenly, too quickly, it was morning. And there was another day.

She actually didn't feel any better than she had the night before. Possibly that was not surprising. She was just…dead. A zombie. She was able to get up, go through the motions, but not one part of her felt alive.

So she was all set to spend the day with Nicole and the boys, just a way to fill the numb hollow where her heart had been, and she didn't even realize that that might be a way of distracting herself until Nicole's parents showed up.

There was a little bit of a chilly shoulder thing going on.

Adra thought she was imagining it until Nicole's mother, while helping to put away dishes, stared straight out the window and said, "So do you plan on looking for your brother?"

They wanted her out of the house, and that's what made Adra realize that she didn't want to leave. She didn't want to face what life would be like now. She didn't want to leave this cocoon of numbness and have to deal with a broken heart.

Yeah, maybe she really was running away from her problems.

And, to continue that grand tradition, she'd gone outside to supervise a game of touch-flag-soccer-football with the boys' own made-up rules while she tried to figure out what to do and why she was so messed up.

Luckily, she didn't have much time for angst before her phone rang.

She almost didn't pick up. She knew she couldn't handle talking to Ford, and…

It was Roman.

"Is everything ok?" she said, picking up immediately.

"Baby," Roman said.

"What?"

"Baby!" he said again.

"Roman, you sound like an insane per—Oh my God, the baby is coming?"

"Yes, the baby is coming, right now, this very second, we are en route to the hospital, and I order you back here right this second."

"Roman, you can't order—"

"Lola wants you here!" Roman barked. "So you will come if I have to send someone for you."

Adra had never heard anything like it. It was kind of charming in a way—the closest Roman would ever come to losing his cool. She almost felt like smiling.

Almost.

"Understood, sir," she said. "I'm on my way."

She could hear Roman smile. "I won't tell Ford you called me 'sir,'" he said.

Adra winced, and covered her mouth to keep from crying. It felt like she'd been hit.

Well, her best friends were having a child, and she'd broken up with the love of her life. She was going to have to go back and deal with real life whether she wanted to or not.

~ * ~ * ~

Ford and Roman were alone in a hospital waiting room, but Ford was the one pacing back and forth. Roman looked mildly agitated, which for him was the rough equivalent of a volcanic eruption. Ford knew in similar circumstances a normal man would have been reduced to insane gibberish; Roman just raised his voice slightly.

"I have to go, Ford," he said. "Lola was very specific about what she wanted. Labor is unpredictable, and at any moment she could—"

"You're sure Adra said she was on her way?" Ford said again. "You actually spoke to her? You didn't leave a voicemail?"

"I spoke to her," Roman said. "She said she was leaving right away."

"That was over seven hours ago."

Exasperated, Roman checked his watch and then looked up, startled. "It has been seven hours. It felt like thirty minutes."

"You don't understand," Ford said. "Seven hours. She was only coming from San Diego. That's two and a half hours, tops, even if you drive like Adra."

Roman paused.

"You're worried," he said.

"She should be here," Ford said, and ran his hand through his hair. Never mind that she'd left him. Never mind that she'd hit such a low with her family that she'd lashed out at Ford, trying to push him away. Never mind that she was miserable. For all her bullshit fears about what she was capable of, Adra would never put her loved ones through this, not in a million fucking years.

'Worried' didn't cover it.

"You haven't spoken to her?" Roman asked.

Silence.

Roman nodded, and put his hand on Ford's shoulder. "I'm sorry," he said. "But right now I have to go get Lola what she asked for."

"No," Ford said. "I'll do it. Go be with your wife. Unless she sent you out of the room because you were driving her crazy."

"That," Roman said, "is a distinct possibility."

Ford tried to smile. His own life might be a goddamn mess at the moment, and he wouldn't be right until he knew that Adra was safe, but that didn't stop him from appreciating his friend's happiness. There was no way Roman hadn't already commandeered the entire staff of the hospital in pursuit of whatever whims Lola might have. The man was probably looking for a new project already, when there was nothing to do but wait. And Lola probably just wanted to distract him.

"You should still stay nearby," Ford said. "Go back in and try not to act like Napoleon stuck inside on a snow day. I'll get whatever it is she wants."

"You're a good friend," Roman said, grinning back. Then his eyes softened. "I think it will be all right, you know. In the end."

Ford knew Roman wasn't talking about his wife or the baby.

"I'm going to make sure of it," Ford said, quietly.

"Good man," Roman smiled.

"What did Lola want, anyway?"

Roman shook his head, clearly baffled, which was a rare occurrence. "She says Declan Donovan baked her cookies and left them for her at Volare."

In spite of the way he was feeling, Ford burst out laughing. "What? There's no way they'd let her eat cookies right now. Even cookies baked by a rock star."

"It might be a trick."

"Hell, it's a good one," Ford said. "I'll go get the rock star cookies. You go get your wife."

He was halfway through the doors when Roman called to him.

"Ford," he said. "Adra will be all right."

Ford just nodded. If it was up to him, there'd be no question. He knew she loved him, even if she didn't know how to make that work yet. And he knew he would find a way for her to be happy, no matter what. He knew a lot of things. But he couldn't think of anything in the world that could keep Adra from being there for the birth of Lola's kid.

Seven hours was a long time.

***

Ford tried to calm himself during the drive over to Volare. He thought about how Adra was working through what was left of her hang ups. She'd come a long way already, and this blow up, coming right after her brother went nuclear, this was like the last struggling gasps of this great big beast of a fucking hang up that she carried around with her.

So maybe she just lost track of time.

He should have gone down there. Screw giving her space; he should have gone down there. He'd let himself get angry, and that was his mistake, and so he'd stopped himself from going down there.

"Goddammit!" he shouted, and hit his steering wheel.

No matter what he told himself, in the end, he knew that woman inside and out. And he knew there was nothing on this planet that could keep her from being there for the people she loved. Roman and Lola and their baby qualified in spades, and that meant something was *wrong*. Ford wasn't used to uncertainties wracking his brain; he was used to *knowing*. This was what anxiety was like. This was what Adra felt half the damn time. How did she do it?

Best-case scenario, what was wrong was that she'd broken her own heart. It fucking killed him.

Calm the fuck down, buddy. You're useless all amped up. You're on a freaking cookie run for your pregnant friend. Get it done, find Adra.

The drive from the hospital to Volare took twice as long as it should have, and all those extra minutes got eaten up in the last half-mile. Ford was so preoccupied thinking about Adra and where the hell she was that it took him too long to figure out what the traffic was all about.

Way too damn long.

He was almost there when he realized it was that stupid broken traffic light. Just like it had been all those weeks ago, on the day Roman had told them about the movie project. Another accident at that damn light.

He was practically on top of it when that feeling hit him: a sinking pit of dread opening up in his gut. A certainty that somewhere, something in the universe was dead wrong.

And he was out of the truck and running by the time he saw Adra's car on the side of the road, blocked off by yellow police tape.

There was blood on the ground nearby. A lot of blood. Blood on the ground, and paramedics on walkie-talkies, talking about airlifting a woman out.

And yellow fucking police tape around her car.

He ran past it.

He ran until two cops restrained him, and then he just started shouting. They didn't understand.

It was *Adra's car.*

chapter 26

Adra woke up slowly, the kind of wake up where she fought it, except that something was telling her to wake *up*, damn it.

That something was her ribs. Her ribs, and her head.

When she opened her eyes, it hurt. Her head: it *hurt*. It wasn't the kind of headache you'd take Tylenol for; it was the kind of headache you'd stay home for. She closed them again, and tried to remember.

She was confused.

She remembered that she'd been rushing because of the baby. She remembered Roman, incoherent for the first time since she'd met him, just shouting "Baby!" over the phone. She smiled slightly, and winced.

They'd had the baby.

She opened her eyes again, this time slowly, giving herself time to adjust. And she remembered other things. She remembered seeing that accident happen right in front of her at that dumb broken light, and she remembered screaming out loud, in her car, alone, because that van had run through the intersection and a tiny little compact had gotten t-boned, and all she could think about was the people who'd been hurt. She remembered thinking they were all in trouble. She remembered pulling over, her hand grabbing desperately for her phone to call 911, thinking she just had to do something. She remembered getting out of her car.

So why did *her* ribs hurt?

She blinked again, up at the flickering fluorescent lights and the ugly ceiling tiles. She looked to her left, and saw that an intravenous line ran from the bag dangling above her to her own arm.

Why was *she* in the hospital?

And then she looked to her right, and she remembered something else.

Ford.

He was sprawled in a visitor's chair that was too small for him, his casual suit rumpled, his stubble starting to come in. Sleeping, yet so…

She didn't know the word for it. He looked like he was fighting some battle, even when he was unconscious. It made her want to curl up beside him and rub his back.

And then she remembered something else.

Oh God, Ford.

She'd ended it. She'd done her best to end it for good, she'd said things…

She was in a haze of painkillers and pain, but nothing hurt quite like that memory. It was a particular kind of pain, mixed with embarrassment and shame, the kind of thing she felt whenever she knew she was on the wrong side of an argument, even if she couldn't remember what she'd been upset about in the first place. It meant that even though he was here with her now, at some point she'd get better, and then they'd be over. He'd be gone. *That* pain stayed with her while she watched him as she fell slowly back into unconsciousness.

***

When she woke up again, much more lucid this time, Ford was still there, in the same chair, practically in the same position. All that had changed was his shirt and the length of the stubble on his face. She had never seen him like this, and she was pretty sure nobody else had, either. Ford looking like he'd slept in a waiting room? Absurd.

He'd slept in the waiting room.

Wait, no. He'd slept right where he was. How did he do that? Hospitals didn't let people just do whatever they wanted. How…

He was here.

Whatever had happened, he was here. She had left him, tried to leave him, whatever. And he was here.

She knew why she'd done it, and the worst part was that no matter what she felt, she could still see the logic of it. She remembered more now, she remembered going to Charlie and Nicole's, seeing the state her brother had left his wife in, knowing where it would lead. She remembered how she'd fooled herself into thinking she could be any different. She remembered doing the hardest thing she'd ever done, just because she thought it was right.

And he was still here.

And like he knew she was watching him, he woke up.

She'd woken up slowly again; Ford was up instantly. He jumped out of that chair, his face as pale as she'd ever seen it, but his eyes…his eyes practically glowed. They were fierce. Determined.

He didn't say anything at first. Just came to her bed, sat down carefully, and held her hand.

Then he said, "Do you hurt?"

Adra shook her head. Obviously the answer was yes, but not in the way he meant it. Not in a call-the-nurse and morphine-drip kind of way. That sort of pain…whatever they had her on now was pretty amazing, actually. Highly recommended.

"You're crying," he said.

"Tearing up," she said. Her throat hurt for some reason. "There's a difference."

Ford cracked the most brilliant smile she'd ever seen, and his eyes shone. If she didn't know any better, she'd have thought he was about to cry.

"Cracking jokes," he said. "That means one thing."

"What?" she said.

Ford took her hand and raised it to his lips.

"I'm going to turn your ass bright red for this," he said.

Adra tried to laugh, and that *did* hurt—her ribs hated her. Then she remembered that this thing couldn't last, and that hurt more.

But she couldn't say it again. Looking at him, sitting there, right in front of her. She couldn't say it.

"For getting hurt?" she said, her voice weak. "Seems harsh."

"No," he said. "For getting out of your car at the scene of an accident to help someone else, getting thrown by another car in the resultant pile on, and *then* getting hurt."

Adra stared at him. "I got hit by a car?"

"You got hit by a goddamned car."

"How am I not dead?"

Ford frowned, his thumb rubbing the back of her hand. Then he leaned forward, brushed her cheek, and held himself high above her aching ribs while he kissed her.

"Because I'm the luckiest man alive, that's why," he said.

Adra swallowed. Her throat still hurt, and the seriousness of what happened, or what might have happened, and where she was, all of it started to seep in past the heavy fog of painkillers.

"Am I…?"

Ford smoothed her hair with his big hand, and shook his head. "They'll do neurological tests because you were knocked out," he said. "But they think you're probably fine. You have some banged-up ribs, bruising, contusions, but other than that you're ok. You're incredibly lucky. We're both incredibly lucky. It was a damn miracle."

"They told you all that?" Adra asked. She smiled a little, in spite of herself. "Isn't that, like, a massive violation of…something?"

She couldn't remember the word. Freaking painkillers.

Ford just shrugged.

"I didn't give the doctor much of a choice," he said. Then he smiled at her, and it lit her up from the inside. "I regret nothing."

She almost let it win. She almost let that joy he kindled inside her win out.

But she remembered. She remembered all that pain, she remembered Nicole's house. She remembered her family.

Don't cry.

"Nothing's changed, Ford," she said.

And that's when he stood up, one hundred percent fierce, implacable Dom.

"*Everything's* changed," he said.

That. Voice.

It was an order, or a declaration. An order to the universe, maybe. It was the voice he used when he wasn't fucking around.

"Adra, look at me," he said. He still held her hand, and he brushed her cheek again, gentle and light as a feather, but his face was firm. "Everything has changed. I'm going to take you home as soon as they clear you, and I'm going to take care of you. And then we'll talk about whatever you want to talk about. But this is non-negotiable. I can't *live* if you—"

The sudden silence felt heavy. The words he didn't say felt heaviest of all.

He put his hand on her cheek again, and angled her face up, pinning her eyes with his own.

"The only time my life needed fixing was when I thought something had happened to you," he said.

"I'm so sorry about what I said," she whispered. "But it doesn't change what I am."

"Can you tell me to go away?" he asked. "Can you do that?"

She couldn't look away if she'd wanted to.

"No," she said.

She'd never be that strong.

"Then I'm not going anywhere," he said. "I'm going to bring you home as soon as they let me."

He bent down to kiss her forehead again.

"But first, there's someone you have to meet," he said, and his smile came back.

It actually took Adra a second to figure it out. She blamed the painkillers still, but on the plus side, Lola actually got to see Adra's surprised face when Roman wheeled her into the room.

Well, Lola *and* the baby got to see Adra's surprised face, but probably only Lola appreciated it.

"Oh my God," Adra said.

"Right back at you," Lola said. She looked tired but happy, and had this tiny little pink bundle in her arms, and Adra just couldn't stop staring. "You know you're not allowed to jump out into traffic until Emma has gotten a chance to meet you, right?"

Adra tried to laugh, and winced. Screw it. "Emma?" she said.

"Emma," Roman said. The man was beaming like a lighthouse.

"She's actually never allowed to jump out into traffic," Ford said. "Again, anyway."

"Can I?" Adra asked.

There was that moment of hesitation, when Lola was reminding herself that babies didn't break, and Adra felt, for a second, kind of bad—she hadn't thought, she'd just spoken up. Painkillers again. But that baby…

"Of course," Lola said softly. She was smiling. She was beyond smiling. Adra had never seen anyone look as happy as Lola and Roman did, and it made her heart swell to the point of aching.

And then as Roman wheeled her up to the bed, Ford intercepted.

"I want to get in on that, too," he said.

Which was how Adra got to watch Ford for with the baby. She watched him pick her up, so carefully, in those huge hands, and then just…hold her. This giant man holding this tiny little life, his whole being focused on just that little light in his arms. And then he looked at Adra.

Adra tried to breathe. She couldn't. And not just because of her ribs.

She saw about a million things, there. She saw the life Ford almost had, the life he wanted. The life *she* wanted. She saw this person that Ford hadn't had a chance to be yet, this amazing father. She saw *promise*. And she wished, more than anything, that she was able to live up to it.

And then Ford tucked little Emma into her blanket just a little bit better, and gently, so gently, placed her in Adra's arms, and that was it.

Adra was in love.

"You're going to have to give her back eventually," Lola said.

"Hush," Adra said.

chapter 27

"I'm pretty sure I can walk, you know," Adra said.

Ford shook his head and wheeled her around a corner, toward the big bay doors of the hospital entrance where his car was waiting.

"Bull," he said. "I saw your face when you put weight on that leg."

"That doesn't mean I can't walk!"

"I can pop a wheelie for you," he said. "But that's the best I can do. You are not getting out of this chair until we get home. That's an order."

Adra tried to look over her shoulder, and Ford tried not to laugh at the expression on her face. Pretty much everything made him smile now that he knew she was ok. In comparison to those first few hours when he couldn't find her, and couldn't get any information? When he thought the worst was possible? Fucking *everything* made him happy now.

"Wheelchairs only have two wheels," she said accusingly.

He shrugged. "I didn't say it would be a good wheelie."

Man, he was glad to see her joking around, considering the circumstances.

Adra sighed and leaned back in the chair, content, for the moment, to let him wheel her around, but Ford could see the uneasiness building inside her. And he got it. This was weird. This was uncharted. Ford knew where he was, what he wanted, and what he was doing, but he knew she didn't have all that quite figured out yet.

He'd help.

In the meantime…

He'd do whatever he had to to make sure she was taken care of, including, but not limited to, carrying her to and from cars. When they got back to his house, he didn't even have to look to know her hand was already reaching for the door handle.

"Nope," he said.

"There's no chair! We left it at the hospital!"

"Sit," he said.

This was just a proxy argument. She was testing him, and testing herself, trying to figure out what it actually meant to let him take care of her while she was injured. Adra was ambulatory, even if it hurt, and she was a grown woman; she could take care of herself if she wanted. But she didn't want that. She wanted Ford, just as badly as he wanted her. She just didn't think she deserved it.

That, that more than anything else…

Jesus, when he'd seen that accident, the bottom of everything had fallen out. Like the earth below his feet had disintegrated and he'd fallen to his own special kind of hell. He barreled through that accident scene like a fucking mental patient, demanding to know where Adra was, who had taken her, whose blood that was on the ground. It was a minor miracle he hadn't been arrested, but the whole time, the whole damn time, he kept thinking: No. *No*. This was not right. This was not how things were supposed to end. This was not how he would *allow* things to end.

And then, speeding back to the hospital, he'd thought about how Adra's last words to him had been about how she wasn't good enough for him. How *she* wasn't good enough for *him*. He'd clenched his jaw so hard he'd nearly cracked his teeth, thinking he'd let her go even one damn second without showing her how wrong she was. He would never, ever forgive himself for that.

No more letting things play out. No more soft touch. Enough of that. That was done. He'd nearly lost the most precious thing in his life, the only thing that mattered, and he wasn't going to take any more chances. He would find a way to move the goddamn ocean to show her what she really was, if it came to that.

Besides, he had almost all his plans locked up already. He'd needed to do something while Lola was in labor and Adra was unconscious, and he'd had his cell phone and about a bunch of people who owed him favors. He'd put the time to good use.

Now? Now it was time to take care of the love of his life.

He walked around to her side of the car and locked eyes with her through the glass. She looked softer than she'd sounded, her eyes telling him more than her words at this point.

She was still scared. He was determined to fix that, too.

He opened the door.

There was a moment.

Then Adra gave him a crooked, uncertain smile. And then she said, archly, "Thank you, Jeeves."

"Man, you're gonna pay for that one, too," Ford said when he was done laughing.

"Hop to it, man," she said, raising an eyebrow.

"How do you make an English accent sound Australian?" he said as she wrapped her arms around his neck. Carefully, so carefully, he slipped his hand under her legs and began to lift. She was light as a feather, as always.

"Talent," she said.

He smiled. "This ok?" he asked. "Do you hurt anywhere?"

"I'm fine," she said.

He would be lying if he said he didn't like having another reason to hold her. And he'd be lying if he said he didn't enjoy taking care of her in this more mundane way. It actually had a lot in common with the way he controlled everything during a scene with her, only he didn't take his pleasure in taking her so much in taking care of her. Which he would do any day of the damn week if need be.

When he had her set up on giant mound of pillows and blankets, ice packs and painkillers at one hand, TV tray at the other, he finally took a moment.

Damn. Beautiful, as always.

"What are you looking at?" she said. "I'm a mess, right? I feel like a mess."

"You're so fucking gorgeous it hurts, actually," he said. "But I am gonna have to check on those bandages."

She smiled weakly up until that last thing.

"What? We just left the hospital."

Ford shrugged. Checking out of hospitals always took forever, and Adra had bad case of road rash on her arm and shoulder. "Tough," he said.

He was already at her feet, gingerly picking up the leg that had taken a beating. Her hip hadn't dislocated, but it would hurt for a while. She winced slightly.

"Still tender, huh," he said, smoothing his hand lightly over the skin.

"It's not a big deal," she said quietly.

He'd done his best to make sure she was comfortable coming out of the hospital. He'd brought her this travel makeup kit that was the size of a freaking suitcase that she referred to as her "portable battle station," and he'd carefully helped her into a simple wrap dress and heels before he'd put her in the wheelchair. Should have been easy, but damn, that moment was fraught.

It was a different kind of nakedness, helping someone after they'd been hurt. And, to be fair, after she'd ended things. She'd turned away slightly, instinctually, as he'd wrapped the dress around her, and then she'd caught herself, and looked him in the eye.

That right there was another moment to fall in love with her.

Anyway, he thought about that now, as he undid the ties on her wrap dress. Because this time it was different.

There was a charge in the air.

She didn't move to do it herself. Just let him undress her.

Fuck.

"Lean forward," he said, and helped pull her up, as gently as he could.

Silently, she obeyed. Ford managed to position her between his legs, in the middle of this ridiculous nest of pillows and blankets, and she leaned into him.

It would not be even remotely appropriate for his dick to get hard at this particular moment, and yet Ford knew that fucker had a mind of his own.

Concentrate.

Looking at her wounds made him feel crazy all over again. Thinking about how much they must hurt drove him even crazier. If he could take that pain on himself, he'd do it in a heartbeat.

"How's it feel?" he said, removing the dressing.

"Um…" She was breathing a little bit too hard. Damn. "Not…great. Not terrible, but not great."

"You're due for another painkiller, anyway," Ford said. "Take it."

"Yes, sir."

They both paused.

By the time he got the bandages changed, he couldn't tell what was going on anymore. She was in some degree of pain, and so was he, just watching her, but that didn't seem to matter. Whenever he touched her, he felt it, that charge.

So did she.

When he repositioned her next to him, he could see that she was on the verge of tears.

"Tell me what hurts," he said.

He knew it wasn't anything physical.

She laughed, and wiped away that first tear. "Ford, this isn't fair to you."

"Bullshit," he said. "I decide what's best for me."

She hit him with those big, wet doe eyes.

"And for me, too?" she asked.

Ford took her hand. "Only when you're being dumb."

Adra glared at him, genuinely pissed off. Which was good. It was honest; it was real. He liked that.

"You are dangerously close to calling me stupid," she said. "I might be injured, but I can still find a way to kick your ass if you deserve it."

"I didn't call you stupid, I said you were being dumb. And you are. And you know it."

She looked at him, mouth open, but speechless. Then she frowned in frustration and looked away.

That was it. There was no more time to waste. She needed to be pushed, and Ford needed to say it.

"You think you're going to end up like your brother," he said.

She didn't say anything.

"You think you're going to pull a Charlie and hurt people, and that's why you can't be happy," he went on. "You can't let anyone love you because of the Davis curse, or whatever the hell it is."

She turned on him, then, angry for the first time, eyes flashing.

"No, shut up and listen, Adra," Ford said. "That is what you believe. Only it is total, complete bullshit. If you don't want to be with me, that's one thing. But I'm not going to let you talk shit about yourself and then use it as an excuse to run away because you're scared. I am *not* going to let you believe those things about yourself. And when I'm done with that, then you can tell me to fuck off if you want."

"Stop cursing," she said.

"Stop screwing yourself over," he said back. "And while you're at it, stop worrying about me. I'm tough as fucking nails, Adra, and you know it. I don't care if you break my heart anymore; it's already yours to do with as you please, and I'm better off that way. You could break my heart tomorrow and every damn day with you would still be worth it. What you're really worried about is you, because you know you're wrong, and you know I'll prove it to you."

There was a silence. Adra stared at the hem of her wrap dress and picked at it with a little too much concentration, but the tension had gone out of her shoulders.

"You're kind of being a bully," she said finally. Softly. Smiling ruefully while she said it.

"Hell yeah I am. If you really want me to go and you can tell me to leave, you know I'll leave you alone," he said. "But you have to say it. And I know you can't."

Finally, she sighed.

And then she relaxed against him.

"I'm too tired to prove you wrong right now," she said.

"Uh-huh."

"That, and painkillers," she said.

"I know."

"You don't fight fair, you know that?"

Ford grinned. "I'm a *lawyer*."

Adra laughed, and then winced, her hand going to her side. "Don't make me laugh," she said, smiling.

Goddamn, he was so relieved to see her smile. He could barely bring himself to let go of her, but he had to.

"Spicy beef and a movie?" he said, lowering her back onto a pillow.

"Yes, please," she said. "*Die Hard* marathon this time. All these injuries make me feel like a badass."

"You are a badass," he agreed. Then, an order: "Don't ever do it again."

Adra tried to fight it, but she gave him a satisfied smile. He'd take it.

The rest of the night, they settled in, silently agreeing to just table the big stuff until later. Which left them with just time spent with each other, which was always better than anything else, anyway. It was the easiest thing in the world.

Until Adra started to drift off, tired from healing and the drugs, and it was time to go to bed.

He carried her, with less protests this time, to his bedroom. To his bed.

She didn't say anything, but he could feel the question.

When he put her down, he said, "I can sleep on the floor if you want, but I'm going to be here in case you need me."

"Ford, I'm not stealing your bed."

"Don't argue," he said. Then, realizing he couldn't leave, even if he'd wanted to, he said, "I saw blood on the ground, Adra."

There was a brief silence.

"What?" she said.

"I saw the crash site. I saw your car. There was blood on the ground."

Before she could say anything else, he silenced her, his hand going to her cheek.

"It's ok. No one was killed—it just looked bad."

"And you thought…"

They looked at each other.

"I'm not leaving," he finally said. "Besides, you know you'll do something dumb like try to hop to the kitchen in the middle of the night."

"Stop being right," she whispered.

They sat there for a moment, Adra propped up against the pillows, Ford sitting on the side of the bed, just looking at each other. Ford watched those emotions play across her face again. If he'd had it rough thinking the love of his life had just died, she had it worse—every so often, he could see the reality of the fact that she could have died flash across her face.

Finally she took his hand in her tiny one and said, "I'm tired."

Then she pulled him down beside her and let him hold her for the rest of the night.

chapter 28

He was *relentless*.

It was difficult to keep her thoughts straight in the face of this constant barrage of...she didn't even know what to call it. It was like every two minutes he did something to remind her how hopelessly in love she was.

It was dirty, dirty pool.

She had already been feeling slightly foolish, just because she always felt foolish when she made people worry, and because she really shouldn't have gotten out of her car. But mostly she'd been feeling foolish with Ford. Every time Adra thought back to that horrible, horrible phone call, she winced from embarrassment, because holy God was the whole thing dramatic and kind of...she didn't know what. Adolescent, maybe? She thought of the words that had actually come out of her mouth, and she cringed.

And yet she still felt that way. Maybe a little less. Ok, definitely less, now that she wasn't sitting in Nicole's guest room, with the wreckage of her brother's screw-ups right in front of her. But she'd lived with this feeling of dread for so long, with the idea that she simply would not be able to have love as an inviolable truth, that she couldn't just…shed it, all at once, just because Ford told her to. Especially when she wasn't convinced.

Right?

So yes, she was confused, and disoriented, and every time she thought she'd regained her balance, he'd turn around and do something else.

Royalty didn't get treated like this. And she never knew whether to be happy or guilty, to be joyful that she had this man in her life, or scared that she'd mess it up. She could feel herself getting pulled in different directions, and wondered when she'd reach the point of maximal tension, and just…pop.

So most of the time, she gave up, and just tried to heal. Anyway, that kind of explained why she'd forgotten about Ford's promise to "prove" that she was wrong.

Until he got that look.

"I've got something different today," Ford said.

"Good, I think?" Adra said. "Not that lying around watching movies isn't great, but I think I might be starting to actually meld into the cushions."

"How's it feel when you walk?"

It had only been a few days, but whatever Ford was doing was working.

"Ok, for a little while. Miles better than yesterday. I bet by next week it'll just be achy ribs."

"Think you can handle some crazy kids?" he asked, the picture of innocence.

Then he grinned.

"You didn't," Adra said.

"You have visitors," Ford said, checking his phone. "They're pulling up now." He looked up to see her face. "Don't move from where you are, either, because I bet you're about to get tackled."

She had no time at all to prepare.

All of a sudden Ford's house was overrun by three small boys, all of them yelling and running toward their aunt with gory enthusiasm.

"We heard you got hit by a car!"

"Did you break any bones?"

"Can we see the scars?"

Ford scooped up the smallest boy, Aaron, as he was about to climb into Adra's lap—and probably bang on those ribs—and threw him lightly into the air.

"Careful, she's not all healed up yet," Ford said.

And then came Nicole.

If Adra felt sheepish for her own dramatic emotional outburst, she had nothing on Nicole. It was weird, but seeing that expression on Nicole's face, Adra saw how out of place it was. Nicole had every reason to be upset, to freak out, and here she was, looking concerned instead.

Adra felt just a little bit more foolish.

"I'll take 'em outside," Ford said, looking between the two women. "You guys want to see the pool?"

And the gang of little boy-shaped tornadoes headed outside with Ford in tow, leaving Adra alone with her sister-in-law.

Carefully, Nicole sat down next to Adra.

"How are you feeling?" she asked.

If she were in a cartoon, Adra's head would have spun around a bunch of times before her eyeballs popped out of her head. "Me?" she said. "How are you feeling?"

Nicole considered this. "Like I haven't been hit by a car."

"Har, har," Adra said. "You guys know I'm miraculously ok. Otherwise you would have broken down my door ages ago."

Nicole smiled. "Ford called pretty much immediately and gave us the scoop."

"How did he even get your number?"

"He seems like a resourceful guy. And determined. Very determined."

"He is that," Adra said. She looked up at Nicole and steeled herself. "How are you, really? Is Charlie…?"

Nicole shook her head.

"I'm sad, I guess. I'm in crisis mode, though, so I don't really have time for sad yet. I'm taking care of my kids. But Adra, this wasn't…look. This is bad—I'm not going to lie to you. I would like my husband back. I would like him to sort through whatever the hell it is he needs to sort through so he can go back to living his life. But this isn't the first time we've had problems, and I've had a long time to prepare for…I don't know. Am I prepared? Can you be prepared for this? That sounds crazy, now that I say it out loud," Nicole said, shaking her head.

"It does and it doesn't," Adra said.

"I'll take crazy if it makes it easier," Nicole said, smiling. "You know what I think it is? He almost did this enough times that I thought about it a lot. I got used to the possibility. And so now I know that it won't break us. I mean, it will be harder than I can really think about, and eventually I'll have to deal with a broken heart, and…but it won't break us."

Adra started to cry. Damn it, she was the one crying.

"I know…" Nicole hesitated, then took Adra's hand and squeezed it fiercely. "I know with your mom it was different. Charlie told me what used to happen when your dad would leave, with the drinking, and… And I just want you to know that that isn't us. Ok? It will be hard, and I want him back, but even if…"

Nicole took a deep breath, not quite ready to say it. Then she went on, "We're still a family. I'm not broken; the boys won't be broken. We're still here. You're still our family."

"Why are you the one comforting me?" Adra asked.

"Because I've never done it before, and I thought you could use it," Nicole said. "You're always there for us, Adra. It's nice to return the favor."

"Shit," Adra said and put a hand to her side.

"You ok?"

"It hurts to cry," Adra said, laughing in frustration through tears. "Oh God, that might be the dumbest thing I've ever said. 'Pain hurts.'"

"Water's wet," Nicole smiled. "Film at eleven."

"Stop it," Adra said. "It hurts to laugh, too."

"Basically you aren't allowed to feel?"

"That would be preferable."

Nicole snorted, and looked out at Ford, who currently had three kids climbing him like he was a jungle gym.

"Yeah, good luck with that," Nicole said.

"Nicole," Adra said suddenly. "Thank you."

Adra didn't know what this would do. She didn't know if it changed any of the things she felt about herself, or about her future, but she knew it did one thing: it helped to quell that aching dread she felt whenever she thought about Charlie. She still had Charlie to worry about, and she always would, but that tightly coiled, poisoned core of dread that she carried around because she was always worried that Nicole and the boys would have to go through what she and Charlie went through…

It began to unfurl, and it began to let her go.

Adra felt like she could breathe for the first time in months. Even with the ribs.

"Thank you," she said again.

"Stop thanking me," Nicole said. "This is just what family does. So stop that."

"You guys are ok? I mean, are your parents still there? And what about money? Are you—"

"No, you don't get to worry about us until you're all healed up," Nicole said, shaking her head. "Besides, we're taken care of."

Adra gave her a suspicious look, but Nicole just smiled.

"My parents are sticking around, so I'm not trying to parent the horde solo, and yeah, that's all you're getting out of me for now," Nicole said, standing up. "And now we have a surprise scheduled for the boys, so I gotta get going."

"A surprise? For the boys? Spill."

"Actually I think it might be more for me, since the boys are a little young," Nicole said, her eyes glinting. "But Ford said he could get the guys from Savage Heart to give us a tour of Los Angeles while we're here, and I jumped all over that, I gotta tell you."

"They are sweethearts," Adra said. "Just ignore the whole rock star thing."

"Who said I wanted to ignore it? I'm having a crappy week. If I get a chance to stare at some rock star eye candy while my boys get to play guitar for the ten minutes before they get bored, I will freaking take it," Nicole said and went to go collect her kids.

Adra couldn't help but watch as she did so. She couldn't help but watch Ford with them, either. He was good with kids. Like legitimately good. Easy. And Adra knew Ford probably had some hand in helping Nicole out, but there was no way she was going to get answers any time soon.

He'd made his point, bringing Nicole here. And Adra had to thank him for it, because seeing Nicole and the boys, seeing that they were hurt but not down for the count—yeah, it helped. It did more than help. It felt like a black hole had been surgically removed from her chest. She hadn't realized how much that fear had been weighing her down until it was suddenly…gone.

Adra felt loopy enough to laugh to herself, and this time she didn't have any painkillers to blame.

"How you feeling?" Ford asked as he strode back into the room.

Goddamn, that man in low-slung jeans and an undershirt was sexier than…

Not a helpful thought, Adra.

"Better," Adra conceded. She eyed Ford somewhat suspiciously as he walked toward her. "But that was your point, right?"

Ford shook his head as he stood over her. "I haven't made my point yet," he said.

She stared at him for a split second too long. She couldn't help it. She was human, and he was standing there with those muscles bulging out of his crossed arms, his blue eyes shining down, his jaw just…

Damn.

"Don't leave me hanging, then," Adra said. "What's your point?"

He grinned at her.

Then he bent down with his arms leaning on either side of her, making great big depressions in the soft couch, pinning her exactly where she was. He let his eyes trail over her slowly, lazily, until he finally locked her eyes with his.

And he looked serious.

"Yeah, Nicole and the boys will be ok," he said. "And that's not nothing. But you know who was there for them? You. At the drop of a fucking hat, you showed up. You have never run out on anyone, Adra. That's what you do. You show up."

She was speechless.

She'd never thought of it that way. She didn't know what to think, much less what to say.

Adra tugged at the thin cotton material at his chest, unable to help herself, her breathing coming in short, ragged gasps. As the pain receded her body had woken up, and being anywhere near Ford was just...

Still, something in her mind forced her awake.

"I've never run out on anyone but you," she said.

Ford laughed. "Nah, you came back. And we're working on that. Besides, the spanking I'm gonna give you once you're healed up will make sure you won't forget it."

Adra sighed deeply, a warm ache spreading between her legs. This would be frustrating.

"This doesn't—"

"Quiet," he said. "No more heavy stuff. I'm putting a quota on that for each day."

"Each day?"

He only smiled.

***

The next day brought more heavy stuff, only this time it wasn't so much "heavy" as it was "profoundly embarrassing."

In fact, Adra didn't realize she would ever be uncomfortable with people telling her how wonderful she was. In theory, that actually sounded like an awesome way to spend an afternoon. Or at least now it did. When she was younger, Adra had realized that she had a problem accepting compliments, and so she'd worked on it until she could accept them without becoming a big ball of embarrassment, because in the cutthroat entertainment industry it had seemed like a necessity. Plus, the older and more sure of herself she got, the more she realized that sometimes she just deserved a freaking compliment.

But apparently an all day procession of people singing her praises still had the power to make her blush. Who knew?

"Ford, this is ridiculous," she said.

She was sitting in his living room again, legs up on the chaise lounge, almost entirely physically comfortable, so long as she didn't move much. That alone was an accomplishment. She was healing at basically a superhero pace, for which she credited Ford.

Of course she was feeling incredibly awkward. Ford was enjoying it way too much, lounging back in his own chair, getting up only to let in the next friend or acquaintance to tell Adra how awesome she was.

She moved to get up and Ford acted quickly.

"Sit down," he ordered. "I have the rest scheduled in fifteen-minute blocks."

Adra stared at him. "You're kidding."

"Am I?" Ford grinned.

"No, I mean it," she said. "This is like…this is weird. This is straight up weird. I mean, are there cameras? Is this a reality show? I have no idea how I'm supposed to react."

"I said sit down and I meant it."

"You know what, you only think you're getting away with this because I am essentially your captive," Adra said. "But the joke's on you, because I can totally walk now."

"If you were my captive, you'd know it," Ford said. "Don't make me tie you down."

Adra froze and stared at the man in front of her. Every word of that sentence had sent a small, singing shiver down her spine, and every word had reminded her that it had been far too long since they'd done a scene. If that was even something they were still supposed to do, which it wasn't, technically. She just kept telling herself that she was doing the right thing, even if it was starting to sound like nonsense, and even if she couldn't always stop herself from flirting back at him.

God, she was tired of thinking. Especially when she wanted him so badly.

"You know I'll do it," he said casually. "I will bind you and then make you suffer through every goddamn person I can find who has something nice to say about you, and I will dare you to safeword out. And if you give me any more lip, I'll make sure that bondage comes with something that vibrates."

Adra managed to speak on her second try.

"Oh my God, you would, wouldn't you?" she said.

Ford looked her over and smiled. "And you wouldn't be able to tell me no. What's that like, to know I can get you to do anything I want?"

Holy fuck, that's hot.

It was incredible—that's what it was like. Adra licked her lips.

"It's not so bad, most of the time," she said. She could barely breathe, and not just because of her ribs.

Ford checked his watch, and then looked back at Adra with a curious expression.

"You can usually take a compliment," he said finally. "Why's this different?"

Adra was having trouble thinking about anything other than being bound with something that vibrated, but she knew if she didn't pay attention she'd soon have occasion to think about that a whole lot more, only in front of a bunch of people she knew.

"Um, I don't... It's not the same," she said, trying not to stare at his mouth. "This is just...it's a freaking parade. No one is used to this much attention. And I feel...I don't know, naked, in a way. And I'm not a saint, Ford, I haven't saved a life or anything. I just like to help out my friends."

"I'm calling bullshit," he said, leaning back. "It's the cognitive dissonance. It's all these people telling you how you helped them find love or took care of them or whatever. All stuff you don't think you get to have. Either they're all wrong, or you're wrong, and it's making your brain explode. See how that works?"

"Can we stop before my brain actually explodes?"

Ford laughed. "And deny your friends the opportunity to make you blush? Hell no," he said. "Besides, Declan and Molly want to thank you for bugging them until they got together, and Soren and Cate, too. And Chance and Lena called from the new Volare location and sent their love. Now stop complaining, or I'm adding a bunch of strokes to that spanking."

Adra's mind dallied for a bit on that promised spanking before she caught that promising piece of information.

"They found a new location?"

Ford nodded. "New Orleans." He looked up again. "They'll be here in five minutes, sweetheart, settle down."

That was when Adra started to giggle. She was arguing with a man she loved who was trying to convince her that she was…what? Better? Deserving? And she was fighting him. It made her laugh, because it was stupid, and it made her want to cry, because…well, because. Because she couldn't just be different and get over it, not just yet. And it made her love him all the more.

"I'm sorry I'm like this," she said finally. "I wish I wasn't. I wish—"

"Shut up," he said gently. "You're perfect. Exactly as you are."

And so it went.

All the friends she'd helped set up at Club Volare over the years stopped by to thoroughly embarrass her, and after a while the barrage had a cumulative effect. As frustrating as Ford was, he was good. He had a point.

Her brain was exploding in little increments. And the only thing to survive all those tiny little explosions was how she felt about Ford.

Sleeping was going to be difficult, and not for the usual rib-related reasons.

They'd gotten a sort of system down. Adra would lie on her unaffected side with a flat pillow under her to even her out, Ford's arm underneath her, and his leg between hers, and he'd hold her as gently as possible, usually with his hand on her hip. It was very careful spooning. It actually wasn't the most comfortable position possible for her ribs, but it was for the rest of her, because lying flat on her back without Ford would have made it impossible to sleep at all.

This time, though, it was tough. Maybe it was the fact that her body was healing, or maybe she'd just learned to ignore the dull ache from her injuries, or maybe it was just…time. But Adra lay there, with Ford all around her, feeling him at her back, his leg between her legs, and oh God did she want him to move that leg. Or that hand. Or anything, really.

It would be so easy for him to take her like this.

She tried to just close her eyes and block it out, but it was no use. It wasn't just his physical presence, and it wasn't just that they hadn't had sex since before her accident. She craved closeness with him, too. She just wanted to be with him.

He'd won.

Adra opened her eyes and stared out into the dark, Ford's body wrapped delicately around her own while her heart hammered in her chest. It really came to her, just like that: he'd won.

That was kind of misnomer, though. They'd both won. She just…it didn't mean she wasn't still scared, because she was, and it didn't mean everything was perfect now, because it wasn't. But it was inevitable. In that moment, she recognized that it was inevitable. She'd been like one of those lunatics raving against the weather, thinking she could fight it. Thinking she could fight herself.

Ford had known.

He kept saying that she was the one who showed up when things got tough, that she was the one who was there. He deserved to have her show up to this, too. Only she wasn't sure how.

But she was sure of how she felt. And she was sure of what she wanted.

Carefully, wincing only slightly, she moved her arm until her hand rested on his, on top of her hip. She laced her fingers with his and felt him shift, even that little movement giving her a slight thrill, a slight pull toward that inevitability. She sighed, the sound loud in the darkness, and pulled his hand to her belly.

She felt him move, and this time it was because he'd begun to harden.

"Adra," he said, his voice muffled in her hair.

"Please," she said. Her voice was hoarse.

His hand expanded, the fingers spreading over the sensitive skin just above her sex, and she inhaled sharply.

"I don't want to hurt you," he said roughly.

Adra breathed heavily for a few seconds, in time with the pulsing pressure he'd started between her legs.

"It hurts every second you're not touching me," she said.

His fingers dug into her, and she moaned. She reached behind her, even though it forced her to twist, even though it hurt, just so she could grab him. Just so she could feel the full, heavy weight of his hardness in her hand.

There was a pause.

And then there was a rustling sound, her panties were being pulled to the side, and then he was pushing against her, his already big cock feeling even bigger with her legs in this position. She groaned as he pushed inside her, her fingers twisting in the sheets as her body stretched to accept him.

She was panting. Already, she was panting. It hurt, but she needed it so badly.

"Please," she said.

His hand moved down her stomach and slid inside her underwear until his fingers found her clit, one on either side of the sensitive bud. And then he began to move.

Barely, at first, just rocking inside her, but after so long, and with his hand moving in time, it was enough to push her to the edge. Just the fullness of him inside her felt like coming home, felt like right, and made her want to scream.

Soon she was screaming.

Oh God, did she scream. Her first orgasm came quickly and tore through her with unexpected ferocity, the pain blossoming with pleasure as her body tensed up and pulled on her injured ribs. It hurt, but it was wonderful at the same time, and she tried to twist her neck back, her hand grasping for his face as he leaned over, just needing to kiss him, to see him…

"I do love you," she said as he kissed her breathless. "I love you so much, I do…"

***

The next morning Adra woke up feeling...

Well, two things: sore, and certain.

Her ribs were pretty pissed off about her decision to have sex, but she could live with that. She was happy to live with that. It had been totally worth it.

And the rest of her knew that the rest of her life had started last night.

It was actually an incredibly calming, blissful feeling. She watched Ford get up, shower, and get dressed in this kind of haze of happiness. She was done fighting. She was still scared, and it might take a while for her to get over some of her hang ups, and some of them might never go away, but this man...

This man deserved everything she could give, and apparently he wouldn't accept any thing else. Apparently he believed in her. He believed in her so much that she'd started to believe in herself.

And dammit, she was going to tell him that.

Somehow.

The thing was, he'd basically dazzled her in the time she'd spent recovering with him. Like, truly dazzled. Maybe it was her competitive instinct, but Adra wanted to dazzle him back. It was just that Ford had such a head start on her.

She smiled, watching him. He had no idea.

"What are you smiling about?" he said, toothbrush in hand.

"Nothing," she said. She kept smiling.

"How are you feeling after last night?" Concern flashed across his face.

"If I told you I was sore, would that mean you wouldn't do it again?" she asked.

Ford frowned, and got that you'll-be-disciplined look. Adra wanted to see that more often.

"Are you sore?" he demanded. "Did it re-injure you?"

"It's a good kind of sore," she promised. "You're gonna crack a joke about making me sore, aren't you?"

Ford grinned. "I was thinking about it."

Adra could feel the weight of what she wanted to do, of what she wanted to say, bear down on her. How did he make it look so easy? Sweeping her off her feet the way he always did?

She took a deep breath.

"Ford…"

"Hold on," Ford said. "You've gotta get dressed."

She was embarrassingly relieved for the distraction.

"What for?"

"Company."

"Ford! Again? Seriously?"

"Move it or meet them in that get up," Ford said, eying her up and down again. "Which means you better move it, because I don't want anyone else looking at those legs."

They held each other's gaze, and Adra thought back to the times he'd told her that they belonged to each other. He'd been right, every single time.

And this time he was giving her space.

She had to take advantage of that.

"Yes, sir," she said, and resolved to figure out how to tell him she would be his forever.

Turns out it was actually harder than she thought. By the time Ford had some omelets whipped up and the front door bell rang, she had approximately nothing. Zilch. No words. Being romantic was hard.

"Damn it," she muttered.

"I got it!" Ford shouted.

"Ford," she said, walking into the living room in her bare feet and her comfortable jeans, "is there really—"

She stopped short. There was a man in the living room.

"You are not Ford," she said.

No, but he could be an alternate reality version of Ford. One with dark hair, so dark it had those almost blue highlights, and a five o'clock shadow at ten in the morning, and a general rakish kind of attitude, like he was always looking for some kind of angle. Other than that, he was the spitting image of Ford.

"Close," the man said. Then he grinned. "Gavin Colson."

"Colson?" Adra said, somewhat stupidly. "You're his—"

"Brother, yes, ma'am," Gavin said. "You must be Adra."

"Ford," Adra said absently. "Your brother is here."

Then she realized that Ford had been the one to answer the door, and that he was already back in the kitchen. Maybe she was still a little stunned.

She knew Ford had brothers. A bunch of them, in fact. But she was under the impression they were kind of far flung, each of them off doing something wild or crazy. She had no idea one of them was actually nearby. Just...dropping in for brunch.

Ford's brother.

"You're really that surprised?" Ford asked, coming up behind her. "You're about to go crazy, then."

"Wait, what?"

Gavin gave that grin again, something that apparently ran in the family, and nodded his head. "I came into town for the wrap party. I would have introduced myself, but I got distracted, and you seemed busy, and then, well, I got busy."

Adra's mind clicked into overdrive. She hadn't though about the wrap party itself much at all; she'd been so focused on Ford. But now she remembered that conversation with Olivia Cress, and Olivia's blush when she admitted, sort of, that she'd met someone new.

She smiled. "I bet I know what kind of busy," she said.

Gavin's face lit up. "You'd bet on it?"

"Don't," Ford interrupted. "He's a professional gambler."

"I used to be a professional gambler," Gavin said, mock offended. "Now I'm a venture capitalist."

"How's that different from professional gambling, again?" Ford asked.

"It's classier."

Adra looked between the two brothers and narrowed her eyes. "I'd still win," she said.

Gavin shook his head, smiling. "Well done, Ford."

"I know it."

"So you want me to show her what I found?"

Adra was suddenly less sure of herself. "Ford, what did you do? Why am I about to go crazy?"

Ford put his hands on her shoulders, and kissed her on the forehead. Then he turned to his brother.

"He's in the car?"

"The foyer."

"Jesus, bring him in."

Adra couldn't take her eyes away from Ford. She suddenly knew what was coming, but it seemed like too much. Like too much good. She couldn't take her eyes away from Ford, and she couldn't stop them from filling up with tears.

When he spoke, his voice was so sad, and hesitant, and so damn sorry, and she was just so glad to hear it.

"Adra?"

She turned around, and there he was. Charlie.

"Oh, goddamn you, Charlie," she said, wiping away the tears, and went to wrap her brother in as much of a hug as she could manage. "Why are you here? Why aren't you with—"

"Because Gavin told me I was screwing up your life, too, and we needed to stop here on the way down," Charlie said. "And Nicole agreed."

Gently he peeled Adra off of him, and she looked up at him. What she saw there both broke her heart and gave her hope at the same time.

He had that look she remembered so well from when they were kids. That determined look he got whenever he felt like he needed to get it together because their parents couldn't. Whenever he felt like she needed protecting. He had a beard and kind of a belly and he was a big, huge guy now, but inside…

He was her brother.

"I fucked up," Charlie said.

"You really, really did," she said. "You can't keep doing this."

"I won't."

"Charlie…"

"I was scared," Charlie said. "I panicked. But I'm going to do whatever I need to do to make it right. I just thought that Nic and the kids were better off without me—"

"Jesus, Charlie."

"I know I'm screwed up," he said. "I'm going to fix it."

"How?"

"Work at it, I guess."

"Your ass is going to therapy," Ford said from behind her.

Adra almost burst out laughing.

"Charlie," she said softly. "I wouldn't argue with him."

"Argue with the guy who had me delivered like a pizza?" Charlie said, looking over her shoulder at Ford. "Yeah, no thanks. I just wanted to say I was sorry, Adra. It's not an excuse, but after a while, you just start thinking…"

"You deserve it," she finished for him.

Charlie looked at her.

"I wish you hadn't been able to answer that."

She shrugged, and smiled up at her big brother. "I'm getting over it."

"I've gotta get back to Nic and the kids," Charlie said, smiling softly back at her. He knew he had a long road ahead of him, but at least he was on it now.

"You called them, right? They know—"

"I called them," Charlie said. "You don't have to worry anymore. I promise."

"Fat chance," Adra whispered.

She watched her brother walk away in another kind of daze. If she said goodbye—or thank you—to Gavin, she was totally unaware of it, though she bet she'd have time to fix that later. She just couldn't believe that he'd found her brother.

And she would have expected to start crying soon after that, except the opposite happened. Ford came around took her elbow, his touch light, careful, like he thought she might break down. And instead she turned to him and wrapped her arms around him with a ferocity she rarely let show.

"Hey, doesn't that hurt?" he asked her.

It did. It also didn't matter.

"I don't care," she said.

"Adra—"

"No," she said, pulling slightly away. "No, let me do it. Please, let me talk. I've been trying to figure out all morning how to say it, and then you go and get my brother, and I just... Don't talk Ford, ok?"

He had a slight smile on his face as he slipped his hand up her neck to cup her face, his thumb brushing against her cheek.

"Ok," he said.

Adra tried to find the words.

She thought about how Charlie had been just as scared as she had been, but how in Charlie, she could see it for what is was. Fear wasn't bad; it was just a signal, telling you to pay attention. Telling you that something was important, that it was worthwhile. That it was real.

"You showed me it's worth it," she said finally. She looked up. "If we broke each other's hearts into a million pieces tomorrow, today would still be worth it. That's why I'm scared. But I can be scared with you."

"I love you," he said simply.

"I know," she said. "And I was gonna say yes! Damn it, I'd been thinking about it all morning, how I was going to get the jump on you. And then you went and found my brother."

She laughed, and hopelessly banged her fist against his chest.

"Yeah, I would've done that anyway," Ford said, brushing a strand of hair away from her face.

"I know."

"I'll get you anything you need," he said.

"I know," she said again. "And I'll abuse that just enough to warrant some discipline."

Ford inhaled sharply. "You need to heal already."

"Working on it," she said. She put her head on his chest and just breathed him in for a few, blissful seconds. Then she said, "Ford?"

"Yeah?"

"I want to make you as happy as you deserve to be," she said quietly.

"Already done," he said.

epilogue

The christening was beautiful. Adra fought to hold back tears, and then, after a while, she just gave up. The tears came, and they started a kind of cascade effect, until she and Lola were both quietly crying, and Adra could have sworn that there was something in both Ford's and Roman's eyes.

Oh yeah. And they were Godparents.

She and Ford. Godparents. It felt...

All of it felt real.

And Adra was *happy*. So happy, in fact that she'd taken a little moment for herself, at the party Roman had thrown for his daughter at their hotel, just to take in the whole scene. She was looking at a huge hall full of people she loved, and her life was practically perfect. Seeing Roman and Lola and baby Emma, seeing how happy they were, seeing Ford and knowing he was hers, she felt like she was boiling over with this...energy. This happy knowledge of the potential all around her. She could barely contain her excitement. Which was maybe why she was sort of hiding in the corner, just a little bit, while watching from behind one of those huge floral displays.

She knew it was weird. She also *should* have known that Ford would find her no matter how weird she got or where she hid.

"I checked out all the other floral arrangements first," he said into her ear. "Third time's the charm."

Adra smiled, and sighed as he wrapped his arms around her.

"We only needed two tries," Adra said.

"Three."

"What?" Adra said, turning to look up at him. "I did not screw up twice."

"We should have taken a shot the first day we met," he said. "I thought I was being smart. Coworkers, and all."

"So we're even on screw ups?"

"Nice try," he said, squeezing her tight.

Adra's sigh turned to something a little more urgent sounding. Any time he touched her, she felt that need start to build. Not that she minded, but they weren't at Club Volare; they were at a very nice hotel.

Still, though.

"What about your brother," she said, desperate for a distraction.

"What about him?"

Adra had been spying on Gavin, too. Specifically, Gavin and Olivia. They always seemed to be very aware of each other's movements in a way that seemed very familiar to Adra. Any time the two of them came into each other's orbit, they seemed to…gravitate to each other. And now that they were talking? Adra doubted they were aware of anyone else in the room.

"Look at him with Olivia," she said.

"Yeah, he's got it bad," Ford said. "I actually haven't seen him like that before."

"She told me that her next movie is shooting in Louisiana," Adra said, and then stopped speaking, suddenly, when Ford's hand slid across her stomach.

"Hmm," he said.

"Something about tax credits and vampires," Adra said, breathless as Ford spun her around and against the wall.

Ford looked at her.

"Vampire accountants?" he said. "That sounds boring as hell."

"No, the vampires aren't…" Adra's eyes half closed as Ford pulled her hips toward his. "Oh God, shut up, the vampires aren't accountants, the film gets tax credits. What are you *doing*?"

"Shut up, huh?" he said, smiling.

He put his leg between hers.

"Ford…"

"Yeah?"

He swept her hair to the side, and let his fingers trail down her neck. Adra was about to lose her mind. She had one very pressing idea she needed to get out before that happened.

"Didn't you say the next club would be in New Orleans?"

"Yeah," he said.

He kissed the delicate skin just below her ear and her knees buckled, just a little bit.

"Oh dear God, just get your brother to go to New Orleans," she said, grabbing his lapels. "Don't you see?"

Ford pulled back slightly, and let his eyes rove over her body.

"I see that you're getting flushed," he said. "I see that your pupils are dilated. I see that your breathing is fast and shallow. Why the hell would I be looking at anything else?"

Adra stared up at him, willing him to touch her again, willing them to be suddenly very much in private.

"Am I supposed to be able to answer that?" she said.

"Don't worry about Gavin," Ford said. "Worry about what's going to happen to that dress."

"Not here," she said, barely able to breathe.

He grinned. "I could just give the order."

Oh God. Instantly wet.

"But we have the rest of our lives for public sex, and right now, I want to take my time," he said.

Adra put a hand on his chest and froze.

The rest of our lives…

She swallowed, and met his eyes. He would be the brave one again.

"I meant that," he said.

"I know," she whispered. "Me too. Only…"

"Only what?"

Her heart thudded in her chest like it was trying to escape, and that happy energy roiled inside of her, looking for a way out. She had to just say it. She *needed* to say it.

"Only I don't want to wait," she said.

Adra didn't think she'd ever see Ford look this close to stunned ever again. She tried to savor it, but the words, once she'd said them, didn't want to let her go.

"I don't want to waste anymore time. I don't want to wait to be married to you," she said. "I want it to be yesterday. I want it to have been always. I just…Ford, I want to be married to you."

He blinked at her.

Then he kissed her.

Then he took a step back, breathing hard, and looked at her again.

"You're sure?" he said.

"Yes," she said. "Please, yes. Whenever you want, whenever you think we're ready, I—"

"Stay *right* where you are," he said. "I mean it. Do not move. That is an order."

She knew what he was about to do. She grabbed his hand.

"*You're* sure?" she asked him. "You're sure of me? I mean, I'm the crazy pants who tried to break up with you, I—"

"I've known for a long time," Ford said. "Just tell me you're sure, and it's done."

"Yes," she said. "I've never been more sure of anything, if we're being honest."

And she was. It was possibly the only thing she'd ever been certain of in her entire life.

Ford smiled down at her, the happiest she'd ever seen him.

"Then I'm gonna marry you," he said. "Right now."

"This isn't too crazy?" she said, laughing.

"I don't care if it is," he said. "No more waiting."

He came in for another kiss, this one deeper, longer, the kind of promise that made Adra's mind shut down and her body spring to attention.

"I love you," Ford said, pulling away reluctantly. "Do *not* move."

As if she could walk after that, anyway.

She watched him with what she was sure was a stupid smile on her face. She watched him marshaling Gavin and Roman to do whatever needed doing, watched him whisper something to Lola, who tried not to scream, and instead just hugged him. Watched him work like a man who just couldn't wait any longer.

In less than thirty minutes, he'd tracked down Reverend Bob.

Reverend Bob himself seemed somewhat surprised to be at a famous hotel, and made it known that he usually did these kinds of things at his own church, because that's where his African gray parrot Murray was most comfortable. For special occasions, however, Murray would travel, as he had today. He was sitting somewhat impatiently on Reverend Bob's shoulder.

Truthfully, Adra was pretty transfixed by the parrot. Reverend Bob explained that Murray was what set him apart from the other same day, same hour marriage licensers and full service wedding providers in the state of California, and Adra believed him. The parrot, besides having several key lines of the traditional vows memorized, seemed to have an intense interest in her hair.

"This is really happening?" Adra said, dodging Murray. She couldn't stop smiling.

"Yeah," Ford said. He had his own big, goofy grin. "You can always divorce me later if you want. I won't tell Murray."

"Don't you want a prenup?" she said. "You know, lawyer-code, or whatever it is?"

"I don't do prenups," Reverend Bob said, frowning.

"Don't worry about it," Ford said, smiling. "She's got all of me anyway."

"Well, who are the witnesses?" Reverend Bob asked. "Let's get this show on the road."

They had five witnesses, though only two were necessary, and only four could sign anything, anyway. Olivia, who seemed almost as swept away by Volare as Adra was by Ford, and Gavin, who was grinning just like his brother, and then Roman and Lola, who were too happy to say "I told you so," and of course, little Emma, who was sleeping. Either Roman and Lola had hit the baby lottery, and that child slept better than any child in the history of children, or they were going to have a sleepless night. They didn't seem to care.

So much of the ceremony, such as it was, was a blur. Adra didn't really register much, except for the maybe overly amorous parrot, besides Ford. She just…couldn't tear her eyes away from Ford. Now that she had him, now that she'd woken up to what was right in front of her, she just didn't want to let go.

"You're getting a real wedding, if you want it," he said. "I mean big. The whole deal."

"I do," she said. "To all of it. I do, I do, I do. Let's be married."

"And I'll marry you every day for the rest of our lives," Ford said. "Just to prove it to you, I'm going to put this guy on retainer."

Reverend Bob perked up.

Adra laughed as she dodged Murray the parrot, who was trying to claw at her hair again.

"I'll end up with a bird living on my head if you do that."

Ford drew her close, away from parrots, from distractions, from the rest of the world.

"You are the love of my life, Adra," he said. "I want to spend every day I have on this earth showing you what that means."

"You already have," she said quietly. "Now kiss your wife, please."

He did.

THE END

A note from the author…

Hi! Thank you so much for reading *Submit and Surrender*. I hope you enjoyed Ford and Adra's story, and that it brought you a bit of happiness. If you liked it, I hope you'll share it with friends you think might like it, too.

And I'd love to hear your thoughts on *Submit and Surrender*. You can connect with me on Facebook or email me at chloecoxwrites@gmail.com, or leave a review on Amazon or on Goodreads. I sincerely appreciate every review—I think they help other readers out, and I learn something with every review, too.

'Till the next book!

Chloe